AFTER THE EVIL

CARY ALLEN STONE

FINE LINE BOOKS
*285 CENTENNIAL OLYMPIC PARK DRIVE
SUITE 1906, ATLANTA, GEORGIA 30313
404-522-9505*

Copyright © 2005 by Cary Allen Stone

All rights reserved. No part of this book may be reproduced in any form or by any electronic or mechanical means, including information storage and retrieval systems, without permission in writing from the author.

Fine Line Books, Inc.
285 Centennial Olympic Park Drive
Suite 1906, Atlanta, Georgia 30313

The characters and events in this book are fictitious. Any similarity to real persons, living or dead is coincidental and not intended by the author.

ISBN: 1-4208-5555-7 (sc)

Printed in the United States of America

*To all of you…
you know who you are.*

1

After she placed the duct tape over his mouth it became difficult to make out some of his words. "No" was muffled but reasonably understandable. "Don't" didn't sound quite right but she got the idea. She mimicked his muted pleas pretending to feel his fear and pain. It was the end of Father Anthony Moralli.

He began the day on an airliner. His destination was a resort-gambling oasis which coincidently included a well-stocked pond of young females. He was on what he liked to call a "personal pilgrimage." The expedition had nothing to do with religion. Anthony simply wanted to, no needed to get laid. To accomplish the task required leaving the confines of his parish in order to maintain the façade of his vocation.

Father Anthony loved the whole religion thing – the ceremonies, hearing confessions, and especially saving lost souls. He planned to start saving his soul right after unselfishly saving all of the others. But after years of religious studies and training he came to the conclusion that it was beyond his comprehension to truly understand God so he simply preached the commandments.

What Anthony really understood were the basic physical needs of a man. He struggled with his vow of celibacy finding it to be in direct conflict with his deep and firm conviction that sex was a gift from God. To abstain he believed was a slap to the Creator's face.

The "Love thy neighbor" commandment was his favorite and he took every opportunity to apply it to his life. Of course that did not include molesting boys like some of his classmates in the seminary.

He boarded the flight sans white collar and slumped into his assigned seat by the window in the emergency exit aisle.

A good-looking man with dark, wavy hair and olive complexion, Anthony would exhibit his best Elvis smile whenever women smiled at him. His deep-set, dark eyes suggested compassion mixed with forgiveness. They also hinted at a touch of mischievous intent. In airline terminology, it was easy for the good father to make his connection.

Certain that a power nap during the flight would pay benefits later that evening Anthony closed his eyes and quickly drifted off to sleep. While he napped curious female "parishioners" inside the Church of the Holy Aircraft Cabin were tempted by the handsome, incognito stranger.

The older women eventually relinquished the temptation and placed a gentle hand over their husbands'. But a few of the younger, more adventurous women on board felt up to the challenge.

Lori first noticed Anthony as he searched for a place for his Reebok carry-on bag in the overhead bin. She made her way around the other passengers and offered to help him. It was one of her duties as a flight attendant. Safety was her first concern. Passenger comfort was another.

She carefully choreographed every move. As her uniform dress rose up along with his bag to be stowed Anthony smiled. He was immediately taken by her compelling cyan-hued eyes, sensual lips and cascading California blond hair. Everything about her confirmed that the Creator was truly a master craftsman.

Drawing stares was commonplace for Lori. The women envied her stunning looks while the men undressed her with lust-filled eyes. They behaved like schoolboys whenever she was near. But it was manifested passenger Moralli, Anthony, who held her attention.

He seemed different than the others.

2

She playfully protested while he fondled her as if they were in the back seat of a '56 Chevy at a drive-in movie. Passengers in various stages of chronological maturity who stood near them stared with disgust. Any children present were oblivious to their sordid adult behavior. They were more distracted by all of the other goings-on associated with flying and airport security.

"I...don't...care. I want some Susan Johnson right now!" he insisted.

With feigned indignation she corrected him saying, "I believe that as recently as two days ago that changed to *Mrs. Nicholas Parker*!"

"Right," he said teasing. "I forgot!"

Susan's arms dropped to her sides and she frowned. She wasn't finding his brand of humor very funny. Cognizant of her distress he pressed two fingers to her lips as he pulled her close. Their verbal banter ended with an embrace and a passionate kiss. When their lips separated, he obsessed.

"Susan, I need you. I can't live without you, you know that!"

The embrace, the kiss and the words accomplished exactly what he wanted and she melted in his arms. Holding him tight she spoke softly into his ear.

"Nick, I love you so much! You are everything to me, you are my life!"

Holding his face with both of her hands she kissed him again. He stroked her shoulders and his hands slipped down to fondle her spandex-smooth behind. A worried look appeared in her brown eyes. "Be safe my love, and come back to me!" she begged.

He assured her with an "I promise." Nick was the consummate sincerity machine and had the uncanny ability to charm his female victims better than any of his contemporaries. The other travelers observing the two lovers rolled their eyes and groaned.

Finally the captain released his grasp on her and turned to reach into the back seat of his oversized Lincoln Navigator SUV. He gathered his flight and overnight bags and placed them curbside.

After a final caress Susan stepped back to take one last adoring look at him. She blew him a tender kiss goodbye. Although she would have liked to stay longer she was already late picking up her daughter from school. Nick pantomimed catching the flying kiss with his hand and pressed it to his lips.

She pivoted and after an awkward climb into the driver's seat cranked over the engine. The Bose CD player blasted out her favorite "rap" song. He hated rap music but tolerated it enough to appease and keep her. She gave him a doting smile this time and a brisk wave goodbye. Knowing full well how much he cherished his toys Susan concentrated on her driving.

With a pathetic pout on his face, he stood at the curb like a little boy being dropped off at camp. His fingers slowly and sequentially fluttered in the air to emphasize his displeasure at having to fly off without her. Nick watched her drive away.

As she made the turn at the end of the terminal to exit the airport grounds he quickly turned to look in the opposite direction. It wasn't too long before a Yellow Cab pulled up alongside him and parked. The back door sprang open.

A pair of firm, long and proportioned legs extended from out of the back seat of the taxi. Although she was petite, the heels made her at least four inches taller. The exposed stomach below the halter top was tightly compressed, which only served to accentuate her artificially-inflated breasts.

The plaid skirt was snug and scarcely enough cloth to cover her dignity. The complete package belonged to a barely above-legal-age woman Nick had met at a club when Susan was out of town visiting relatives.

"Hey, babe!" he shouted.

The other travelers who had witnessed his earlier carrying-on rolled their eyes knowing his new wife had just driven off moments ago. They became furious when he scrutinized the young woman from head to toe as if evaluating the purchase of a slave. Of course it went without saying that he fully intended for her to play that role later in the evening in order to satisfy just one more of his sexual perversions.

"Oh my Nicky, you look so hot in your uniform. I'm getting wet just looking at you!" she squealed delightfully.

Tricia knew how the game was played and was adept at using suggestive sexual innuendos having lost her innocence when she was a young girl. Nick was a successful airline pilot wanting to play. And she wanted out of her boring town.

She also desired to have his upper-level income spent lavishly on her. She knew that meant he was going to make her tug hard on his leash before she reaped the reward.

But putting out to get out was fine with her even if it meant humping a man twice her age. Besides age didn't matter any more to a generation that believed sex was solely for pleasure and no longer required a lifetime of commitment.

As Nick snuggled with Tricia he could sense that the men standing nearby were enjoying their own filthy fantasies. Nick devilishly grinned knowing their women were growing more nervous by the second. The performance reached a climax when the captain gathered his baggage on wheels and Trish held out her small overnight bag for him to take.

"I packed all of your favorite things!" she teased.

With a broad smile Nick added the undersized bag to his. He reached out to take her hand and they walked into the terminal together. Nick wasn't sure he could hold off until their destination. The fierce animal desires he had for her led him to consider improvising along the way. But he cherished sexual tension as an integral part of the chase so he decided to simmer rather than boil over.

The men standing curbside watched her provocative gait and sighed right up until the automatic doors closed behind the old guy and his juvenile date.

3

Soft fingertips lightly stroked his forehead. He blinked repeatedly trying to clear his vision. His head was throbbing. He could barely make out the shape of a face. He thought the facial features resembled a woman smiling at him with one of those after-great-sex smiles.

He struggled to remember who he was while trying to determine who she might be. He couldn't focus. The room appeared to be underwater as if the ship had overturned at sea. Nothing made sense. The last thing he remembered was becoming extremely drained and drifting off.

Where...how...who was...

There was something restricting the movement of his arms and legs.

...name is...name is...is...

The face with the smile that had floated past him before reappeared. Blaring in the background he heard the lyrics and hammering of heavy metal music.

> It's the way that you feel,
> It's the truth in your eye,
> Cause you're up against the world,
> And still you rise.

Holly? Jean? No, Lori! The flight...

But what was holding him? He passed out again until he heard the words that shocked him back into reality.

"Poor Father Anthony, that is it isn't it ? Father Anthony?" The effects of the drug had given Lori more than enough time to secure him and search through his wallet.

"Lori, what's going on?" he asked slurring the words. As he tugged against the ropes it hit him. "You know?"

With her head tilted she said, "I want to confess my sins, Father. Will you hear my confession? I want you to absolve my sins and forgive me!"

"What is wrong with you?" he asked as his head fell back onto the pillow. He tried to compose himself but he jerked back up again with anger and revulsion. "Are you insane!"

Her jagged reaction to his interrogatory outburst caused a quick reevaluation of his options. His head fell back again as his mind raced. There wasn't any way out of the tight spot he was in. He had to be repentant, and negotiate.

"Lori, what do you want from me?" There was a strained pause. "You want the truth? Okay it's true, I'm a priest. And I don't have any excuse for my actions except to say that I'm just a frail human like all men, and I sin, too!" He studied her face to see if he was getting through.

She bit at her lower lip while contemplating his answer. Then she smiled and slid her index finger from his forehead down to his lips where they rested for a moment. She pursed her lips.

I really enjoyed kissing you.

Her finger continued down and stopped at his genitals. She massaged him there softly. He glanced down at what she was doing and squirmed uncomfortably.

Maybe this is just some weird sexual game she plays.

He tried an end run this time with, "Did you like it? We could do it again, make love again!" After a slight pause, "All you have to do is untie me!"

Smiling she said deprecatingly, "Now Father we never did make love. And as far as untying you, you know I can't do that."

Indignantly he yelled, "Untie me goddamit!"

"Oh my, thou shall not take the name of the Lord thy God in vain!" she scolded him. "You're just like that little pope of yours and the archbishops and bishops ? the pious hierarchy ? so holy when you want to be and so arrogant with authority! You priests think you have all of the answers and can tell the rest of us how to live."

Anthony turned away ashamed. He shifted trying his best to distance himself from her.

This can't be happening!

"This is some kind of a joke, right?" he asked with a nervous laugh that did not conceal his fear.

"Father, I can assure you this is no joke." She looked off into the distance and asked, "Do you believe in life after death?"

Her eyebrows furrowed. Lori focused intensely on him trying hard to appear sincerely interested in his answer.

You are a handsome man!

"Of course I do!" he answered with a self-assured tone.

Her gaze left his as she looked down and watched her fingertips slowly dance around his manhood. She posed another theological question.

"If heaven is such a *heavenly* place why does everyone want to take an eternity to get there?"

He had to think about that one. He often thought that heaven must be a very small place out of necessity and hell quite enormous. After all there were far more damned than there were saved in the world.

"Is evil the same in every religion Father or is evil different from one religion to the next?" She stared at him. "Father Anthony, you are not a very good person!"

His sarcastic answer was, "Even Jesus wasn't loved by everyone!"

"You are not Jesus, Father Anthony." Bowing her head she declared, "I want to confess my sins now."

Reaching over to the nightstand she grasped the roll of duct tape. Tearing off a small piece she ceremoniously placed it over his mouth while his head thrashed violently from side to side. As hard as he possibly could he struggled to free himself.

Lori started confessing.

"Father, like yourself I have taken the Lord thy God's name in vain. I have not honored my mother or my father." There was a brief pause. "And I am about to break the commandment ? Thou shall not kill." She looked deeply into his wide, terrified eyes and said, "Bless me Father for I must sin again."

Anthony perspired profusely. His pounding chest heaved. Tears fell down the sacrificial lamb's face. With his eyes shut tight he hastily prayed for God's forgiveness of his sins.

When he opened them again he saw the raised, shimmering blade of the knife. He tensed and shook violently. He screamed from behind the tape sealing his lips.

The good father felt the first but because of the shock infiltrating his body not the rest of the repeated punctures to his torso. If

Anthony's God were truly merciful he may have been gifted on his deathbed with a few seconds of the painless "golden hour." Another heartbeat passed.

His eyes finally rolled back and disappeared. Had a heart monitor been attached to him it would have revealed a complete cessation of all cardiac function with flat brain wave tracing. It would have confirmed that Father Anthony Moralli was dead.

Then with the artistry of a gourmet chef she dragged the blade across and severed his genitals. A massive river of blood spilled from the wound between his legs. She held the organ up while more blood drained down from her hand to her bent elbow. It made a muted thud when she dropped it onto him.

To complete the act Lori stabbed him one last time directly into his heart and withdrew her hand. The knife stood erect like a tombstone protruding from his unmoving chest.

Father Anthony mouthed his last words behind the duct tape during the brief seconds he had left but she never heard them. She had no idea that he had forgiven her.

Slowly she walked to the foot of the bed where she sat down on a chair facing him. While staring at the corpse she became lost in an out-of-body experience that took her mind along for the ride. Her fingers roamed until she found the special place between her legs. The face of her dead husband appeared over Anthony's and spoke to her.

That's right baby, daddy loves you!

She asked him, "Did I do it right, daddy? Like you taught me, daddy?"

You're daddy's little girl!

Matching the rhythm of her hand she recited, "Daddy loves me, daddy loves me, daddy...loves...me!" But like every time before she could not reach a climax and the rapid motion of her hand ceased.

She pleaded, "Why daddy...daddy it hurts! Please stop, daddy, no more, daddy! Mommy, make him stop!"

Lori awoke from the dream and became mechanical. From the bathroom she retrieved a white washcloth. Returning to the bed she soaked a corner of the cloth into the puddle of blood between Anthony's thighs. She climbed over him to the headboard and wrote crimson letters on the wall.

She retrieved her things including the CD from the stereo. She was careful to leave the room clean with no way to connect her to the murder. Nobody knew she was with him. She took one more look before leaving quietly.

It was just before midnight when Lori returned to her layover hotel. She showered then climbed into bed and fell asleep. Her alarm clock went off minutes before daylight and within an hour she met with her crew in the hotel lobby.

Like an apparition she would completely disappear without a trace. The early flight departure gave her the distance that would prevent her capture. Like all of the other murders she had committed this one would absolutely confound and mystify investigators.

As her flight departed into the early-morning haze she contemplated what she needed to do when she got back home. She would stop by the food store for groceries. Renting a movie from Blockbuster was an option. She had to water the plants and there were bills to pay.

She also thought about the man who had beaten her and who sexually abused their young daughter on the pretext of love.

4

The odor drew the first witness to the gruesome crime scene. She reported the repugnant smell to the front desk. When the manager arrived he knocked heavily on the cottage door. Not receiving a response he announced "Manager" and went inside. After a few short steps he saw all that he needed to see and radioed the front office to call the police.

The girl with the halter top and tight shorts looking on from the doorway let out a terrifying, chilling scream. Her boyfriend ran to join her. Both stood frozen and gawked at the twisted carcass with the severely contorted expression.

While the three of them waited for the police they debated going back inside to see if the victim was still alive. Finally the brave manager told the two lovers to stand back while he checked for a pulse. Forcing himself to go back in he slowly made his way to the bed. Just as he was about to touch the discolored wrist the feel of a hand on his arm nearly sent him into cardiac arrest.

A Kevlar-vested female officer behaving in typical maximum-threat fashion quickly herded him and the other two witnesses away to safety. With her laser-sight illuminated she tightened her grip on the Berretta held out in front of her as she searched the premises.

Blues and reds flashed in rapid succession against the drizzle and overcast. The entire cottage was illuminated in white light as more emergency personnel arrived. Everyone was adrenaline-soaked as they performed their duties.

The discovery of the dead man was contagious. News trucks with painted station logos arrived and extended their antennas high into the night sky for satellite feeds. Reporters descended on the scene like vultures with their outstretched hideous wings. They went to work on the carcass using blood to sell valuable advertising space.

The first reporter on the scene desperately seeking network recognition spewed directly into the camera lens the earliest details as they were relayed by investigators.

> ...the victim, a Caucasian male, was stabbed repeatedly, and castrated. Although unconfirmed, this reporter has been told by sources close to the investigation, that the victim is a Catholic priest. Just moments ago, Bishop Archibald, from the Mother of Soul's parish here in Gulfport, has administered last rites...

It was riveting television. "Reality" death always held a captive audience. The news stations played the gruesome scene over and over, albeit with parental warnings.

Jurisdiction of the crime scene, a treasured pearl of law enforcement, passed from the Gulfport locals to Special Agent Mika Scott when she and her Evidence Response Team arrived from Quantico a few hours later.

5

After waiting for over an hour, I recline on the couch but shift into several uncomfortable positions. I can't sit still. I hate having to surrender my thoughts and my emotions to him. God forbid I say something that causes him to take me off the streets. I would leave except that department policy requires that all cops involved in a shooting have to see the shrink.

"I watched as the Molotov cocktail flew in an arc and crashed through the stained glass window. Jesus the Shepherd was at the center of that window only moments before."

I feel like I'm suffocating, cornered. The place and surroundings couldn't help but make you feel flawed as a human being.

"It rolled across the sacristy floor spitting yellow and orange flames. Heavy, coal-colored, swirling smoke billowed out. There was nothing I could do while the blaze burned the house of God to the ground." I take a break.

"Then the dark angel responsible as if receiving an order directly from Satan began the last barrage. The weapon discharged and my windshield exploded. Shards of glass and debris flew all around me. I dropped to the pavement and prayed."

After a long swallow from the glass of water on the end table the rest of my nightmare slips out.

Easy Jake, don't talk about anger in front of the man!

"One of the 'cop killers' found Sergeant Peterson a few yards away from me. I couldn't get to him. I was pinned down. Then I took a hit. I didn't feel it at first but then I felt the burn. I returned fire. My first round shattered the larynx and the perp's arms extended as if begging to be crucified."

"My second round tore open the chest. The black, fatigue-clad body danced beneath the yellowish glow of the fluorescent street lights." I cough before continuing.

"It stood like a statue before finally collapsing to the pavement. My bullet-riddled radiator hissed. Stepping through the blood I cautiously approached and kicked away the weapon. I took out my 'cuffs but the body appeared lifeless. My still hot Glock dropped to my side. It was over."

Trying to alleviate the pains and stress in my body I shift again. He sits quietly, hands clasped together and gives me time to get it all out.

"The paramedic removed the ski mask and her auburn hair limply cascaded down. Her face had a horrified look that said an angry God was already passing sentence. Her lips quivered and I thought she was trying to speak. I dropped down to hear but I only felt her last breath touch my face." I blink as the corners of my eyes begin to tear.

"Rapid cerebral replays of the shooting and heavy doses of guilt have dogged me since." I shrug and head wave at the same time. "She was just a kid!"

Abrams allows my words to hang in the air. His unnerving silence makes me squirm and twitch. Is he waiting for me to collapse? He asks a simple question with a calm voice.

"Can you go on or would you like to stop here?"

That really cranks me off so I blast back, "Hey, tell me what I'm supposed to do here, what I'm supposed to say! Tell me how I'm supposed to heal!"

With a compassionate tone Abrams calmly answers, "Jake, it doesn't work that way. You had physical trauma from the gunshot and the doctor prescribed a pill for the pain but what's in your head cannot be cured with a pill."

Dr. Thaddeus Abrams, mid-forties, is wearing his trademark heavy-rimmed, black eyeglasses. He is soft-spoken and polite. In addition to his own practice he is included in the department's payroll.

A shooter like me is supposed to attend therapy once a week. Those who work through their pain can regain their life and career. But if the scars are too deep sometimes recovery is impossible and then it will be just a matter of time before their prolonged misery ends in suicide. I'm not going to be counted among the lost.

"I can't erase what happened to you Jake, it will always be in your memory. All I can do is to try and help you find some closure and that's going to take time."

I know that I have to but I don't want to talk to him anymore. As I make my way toward the office door I turn to face the eminent psychiatrist. The words I thought would come out ? don't so I close the door behind me.

"Jake?"

The receptionist behind the glass window in the waiting room makes a gallant effort to corner me for another appointment. Faces look up from their magazines as I hurry my escape. I feel exposed. I can't reach for the doorknob fast enough but instead the door opens in my face.

An extraordinarily attractive woman enters. She holds everyone's attention as we stare at her as if she were a model strutting down the runway at a fashion show. She seems unaffected by the gawking. We make eye contact and she smiles but in my jammed up state of mind I can't smile back.

Along my journey down the long, empty corridor I think about her. Walking out of the building into the stabbing sunlight that temporarily blinds me, I think about her. As the freezer chill of the air-conditioned offices dissipates rapidly in the heat, I think about her.

When I open the door to my apartment I realize she is the only other thing that I have thought about in my bruised and crippled psyche since killing that girl.

6

There was no resemblance to the other hard-core patients in the office. After checking in with the receptionist she found an empty seat and sat straight up with her purse neatly placed on her lap. Her breathtaking eyes stared straight ahead and didn't acknowledge anyone in the waiting room. She didn't read any of the old and torn magazines.

Instead Lori replayed in her mind the entire visit she had made to the cemetery before her appointment to see Dr. Abrams. Whenever she returned from a flight she made sure that she went to see her daughter Emily.

In her daydream she saw herself walking past the many headstones along the manicured lawn. She arrived at the one that rested above her daughter's grave. Her fingers lightly stroked the name on the marble then cleared the grave of fallen leaves and debris. She replaced the bouquet in the holder with freshly cut wildflowers.

"Hi baby, mommy's here."

I missed you, mommy.

"I missed you too, honey."

Lori's head tilted to one side and was followed by a sigh. Soft tears trickled down her cheeks as the anguish of Emily's passing returned. Even after all of those years it hurt deeply. As all parents do when preceded in death by their children she mourned the loss with heartbreak, sadness and overwhelming guilt.

Where did you go, mommy?

Wiping away tears she tried to sound upbeat replying, "I had a flight to Gulfport baby, just an overnight. We got back early this morning. I unpacked and came right over to see you."

Did you have fun there, mommy?

"It was okay, it wasn't fun just okay." Lori quickly changed the subject. "Did you remember that yesterday was my birthday?"

Oh yes mommy, Happy Birthday to you!

The child's voice sang the birthday song. Lori's dire expression turned to a half-hearted smile as she touched her daughter's headstone after it had changed from a piece of granite to her young daughter's face.

I wish I could have celebrated it with you!

"I know baby, I know. You look so beautiful Emily, so beautiful."

I love you, mommy.

"I love you too, baby."

Mourners at a nearby grave site looked in her direction but she quickly turned away from their curious stares. Without looking up again she spread a small blanket on the lawn next to the grave. The recently mowed grass had a sweet scent.

She sat down and brought her legs up beneath her chin and wrapped her arms around them to hold them in. With her chin resting on her knees she stared at a small beetle making its way through the grass then she heard the other voice.

Don't be fooled into believing that luck got you this far and will take you the rest of the way. Many have stood before a magistrate because of such a flawed thought.

"I know, I know," she whispered like a scolded child.

Don't take that attitude with me!

The voice was demeaning and punishing. She hated the voice and would have done anything to make it stop.

You listen to me! No one cares about you but me!

"I won't disappoint you," she said apologetically having heard the lectures before.

You've got to follow the rules!

Lori's head nodded twice and she said, "Yes I know, no records; don't leave anything behind; don't attract attention; know the geography and alcohol is a truth serum - I got it."

Well if it's all so clear then what did you think you were doing in Gulfport?

"He was an authority figure just like the rest and ?" Lori wanted to argue but knew it was useless.

Murder is as empowering as it is compelling!

After that Lori didn't hear the voices. The other mourners had all gone and she was sitting alone in the cemetery shading her eyes from the bright, unrelenting sun. Before she left she took one more look at her daughter's name on the headstone. Then another voice, an unfamiliar voice interrupted her daydream.

"Ms. Powers, the doctor will see you now."

7

Terrorism had hit home and was on everyone's mind. Outside the terminal airport traffic officers ordered the towing of unattended cars that were no longer permitted to park curbside. As Captain Parker walked briskly out of the terminal and into the noonday sun the last thing on his mind was terrorism.

Nick was much more concerned about unintentionally revealing any evidence that the sweet, young Tricia had left behind. She had kissed him goodbye only minutes before with a heavy smear of lipstick and then headed out the opposite side of the terminal.

He wasn't sure he had gotten it all off. He rapidly surveyed the roadway to his left and right searching for the new Mrs. Parker but she wasn't in sight.

Trish had a wonderful two days in Los Angeles. Nick bought her expensive gifts and took her to dinner at an exclusive restaurant. She screwed his brains out in return and that made them even she figured. The next time he called though she planned to tell him to drop dead unless there was nothing else or no one else to do in town.

Seeing his new bride Nick waved as if she was the only woman on earth. She pulled up in the macho SUV and stopped at his feet. He liked it when women deferred to him. He expected them to treat him like God. After all that's who pilots thought they were.

Mrs. Parker leapt out of the car and rushed toward him enthusiastically throwing her entire perfect body into him causing the air to burst out of his lungs.

"Oh baby, I've missed you so much!" She enunciated every word.

"It feels like a millennium since I've been able to hold you," Nick said knowing exactly what to say to get what he wanted. "I've got to have you right now, Susan!"

It fascinated Nick how easily women fell for his smooth talk and lies. They were willing to do just about anything to have someone to call their own. They would clean, cook, iron and even squeeze out babies for love!

What was even more amazing he thought was that they couldn't see it, didn't get it. To him love was a fabricated concept created simply for a man to justify the fulfillment of a biological need to release millions of microscopic, aggressive sperm. And a woman was nothing more or nothing less than a late-night depository.

"Where's Tabitha?" Parker asked knowing that Susan's young daughter was an object of his degenerate affection.

Susan made up a story because she knew Tabitha detested him but she could never figure out why. He would constantly spoil Tabitha with lavish gifts that often made Susan jealous. But she found his constant concern about Tabitha's well-being reassuring and believed that Nick was the perfect father figure for her.

"Home, she had homework to finish." Smiling she added, "You know how kids are."

With contrived concern he asked, "Is everything all right with her?" He had to know if he had anything to worry about. She was jailbait after all.

"Yeah, she's fine just a young girl trying to figure out the big world. It's not easy you know," Susan answered with a shrug attached.

Seeing Parker in uniform a traffic officer approached and reprimanded him saying, "Captain you need to move it along, sir. The rules apply to everyone."

"Sorry officer, you're absolutely right and we're moving it." Nick answered apologetically.

He detested it when those he considered his inferiors, the lower rung, told him what to do. He didn't take direction, he gave it.

Nick quickly opened the passenger door for Susan and she slid her long legs inside slowly so that he got a good look. He grinned and closed her door.

Tossing his flight and overnight bags in the back he gave a small wave to the impertinent officer. He thought about berating the man but decided he was too exhausted after the weekend with Tricia.

I owe you one officer!

The Navigator cranked over and Captain Nick Parker drove home with the woman he presumably loved to the step-daughter he wanted to love later.

8

The magnificent mansion he shared with Mrs. Abrams made up for having to tolerate her incessant whining. An expansive estate it was far more than two people needed to exist. A brand new Bentley was parked in the curved driveway. The thought of having children was not even a consideration because of the great imposition it would place on their own spoiled lives.

Thaddeus Abrams loved his career and all of the perks that came with it. He especially loved when clients such as the troubled but stunning Lori Powers stared helplessly into his eyes seeking compassion, comfort and understanding. Life was good for the good doctor and nothing was going to interfere with his happiness.

"So how are you doing, Lori?"

Abrams had a knack for sounding concerned which was why he was so successful in his line of work. He was a master at giving the impression that he cared about your miserable life. With Lori he found his career to be particularly rewarding.

"It hasn't been a very good week," she said sadly.

"Let me see according to my notes we were discussing your family history during your last visit. Why don't you pick it up from there?" He looked over the tops of his glasses at her.

She closed her eyes and thought. The moment she felt prepared and comfortable, organized, she began. Abrams gave a slight nod.

"I remember the very first time he slithered into my bed. He wanted me. And I was too young, too trusting to protest, to say no." Her mood turned sullen.

He missed most everything she said after that. He really just wanted to get her talking so that he could look into her captivating eyes and listen to her smoky voice.

Whenever she turned away he would sneak a peek at her breasts and legs. Her very first statement sent him drifting off into another fantasy daydream about her.

She stood in the garden below in the black French-cut bikini that for good reason was his favorite. He called to her and she looked up adoringly at him standing on the balcony.

"Daddy was like a…"

He heard only the first four words of that sentence.

She lit candles inside the darkened room and extinguished the match with a soft, sensual whisper. Romantic melodies filled the background as she nudged him onto his back on the bed. With a naughty, teasing expression she took her hair up and let it fall wildly over her soft shoulders. Her bikini fell to the floor.

"Mother didn't have the courage to say no to him. When I turned to her, she turned away from me."

He caught just a piece of that statement.

She straddled him provocatively and playfully traced his naked body with her fingertips. Kissing his face and neck she reached down between his legs and…

"Dr. Abrams?" Lori asked. She had the impression that Abrams had missed the last few pages of her life story.

He jerked back into reality and recovered smoothly by asking, "Who was he?"

"Who was who?"

"Go back to the part about 'I was too trusting.' Were you referring to your father?"

"I was referring to my ex-husband, doctor."

Abrams took a moment to think while he wrote notes on his legal pad. She appeared to be confused about episodes between her father and her ex-husband. The husband was missing, wasn't he? Perhaps the trauma of her daughter's suicide was affecting her memory. He couldn't quite put a finger on it.

"I'm sorry Lori, please continue," he prodded.

Although relieved that he had escaped detection Abrams knew that he had missed something important. He had to listen closer and get to the bottom of it. As she pulled a tissue from the box on the table next to her chair the doctor leaned forward in his chair. Certain that he was listening this time Lori continued with the rest of her story.

"I remember a night. It was raining very hard - thunder, lightning. We were parked on a hilltop surrounded by dense woods. The leaves on the trees partially obscured the moon and stars. I had an overbearing feeling or sense that something evil was present." She dabbed the tissue in the corner of each eye.

"Lying back on the upholstery, sweating, frightened with my legs spread, he entered me. I wanted to scream but he wouldn't let me. Finally he finished." She squeezed the tissue tight in her clenched fist. "Then his hand raised and came down swiftly!" Lori shook.

Abrams flinched and was surprised by his own reaction.

"Too young to comprehend the purpose of being struck my baby cried as she sucked in her first seconds of life. She was so beautiful, my Emily!" Lori looked away as if seeing her daughter in the room. "I was just fourteen."

Abrams still couldn't put it all together and it bothered him. But before he could ask another question Lori started again.

"I have a recurring dream." She looked deep inside of him. "I'm alone and there is no one else left in the world except me."

Then Abrams made the elusive connection between the father and the missing ex-husband, the daughter's suicide, the beatings and the sexual abuse. He had heard similar references from other clients that he had treated over the years.

He scribbled quickly on his notepad and tore off the page then reached forward holding the page between the two of them. Lori took it and read what he had written. It was an address.

"Unfortunately Lori, our time is up and as you know I have a few more patients waiting outside. But I think we have made some real progress here today, in fact, so much so that I need for you to continue this session later this evening...at my home." He pointed at the page. "That's the address."

"I don't understand, Dr. Abrams."

He moved closer to her and exuded compassion. "I believe we've made a major breakthrough today and it is imperative that we discuss this further before you leave on another flight."

Lori considered the option Abrams presented but wasn't quite sure how that meshed with her revelations. But as patients do she trusted her medical practitioner. Taking the address he gave her she stored it in her purse and nodded silently.

He desperately tried to appear reserved and controlled while she stood and walked out of the office. Inside he was churning.

She was perfect!

9

After the shooting and subsequent investigation by Internal Affairs I was exhausted and crashed into one of those comatose-like sleeps. But since then I just lay in bed for hours staring at the ceiling. Abrams said the depression is a normal reaction to what happened and that it would eventually subside.

My apartment isn't far from the precinct. The neighborhood is nondescript, middle-class and what I could afford on my salary. There aren't any gated communities here. The nearest one would be "lock-up" inside the precinct.

The place is small, crowded with worn furniture and has the comfortable ambiance of a bachelor pad. Being the dedicated cop that I am I never used to spend much time here. Now it's the cave I hide inside.

On the porch newspapers are piled up from the newsboy who could care less. The mailman curses every time he has to jam more mail into my overflowing mailbox. The priest from Saint Dominic's stops by but I give him an appreciative "no thanks." I don't feel holy.

Over the years I have seen stabbings, domestic violence, abuse cases, gunshot wounds – you name it. But none of that damaged my head as bad as shooting that girl. The doctor prescribed Hydrocodone for the hole in my arm. I have taken much more than needed to stop the pain.

In days past I used to take better care of myself considering the line of work I'm in. I ate right, worked out in the gym, got plenty of sunshine and lived a relatively healthy lifestyle. My fellow law enforcement officers joked about it all the time but found my efforts to be admirable. Now that's all gone and it's just me and my pills.

Abrams isn't much help. Psychiatrists are a waste of time anyway as far as I'm concerned. There was a time when I thought...hoped God would jump in and send a guardian angel to save me. But then I figured out that He knew I was going straight to hell anyway so why waste a perfectly good angel. I'm just going to have to deal with the bad juju single-handedly.

"JAKE! HEY JAKE, OPEN THE DOOR!"

The banging stops when I open the door. Harmon Blackwell, homicide detective and partner, bends down and picks up the morning's paper out of all the others which he nonchalantly kicks off to the side of the porch. He storms in throwing the newspaper at me. It falls to the floor as I turn toward the bedroom. My arm hurts.

Where did I put that prescription bottle with the child-resistant cover?

Finding it I shake out another pill. A sip of Jack Daniels helps the little bomber go down easier. "If you're here for some talk-therapy ? I'm all talked out!"

"No, I can see that you're too screwed up for that," he says. "And stop taking those damn pills, man! What's the matter with you?" He doesn't approve of my helpers.

Harmon can kick my butt without breaking a sweat. He really likes to kick butt. You should have seen him on the street. "What did you say? What? Come here! I'm talking to you!" That's Harmon. He lightened up a little when he got his detective shield. Homicide hasn't been the same since.

There has been a Gary Larson calendar on the wall next to the refrigerator every year since he started publishing them. It isn't up to date because I haven't kept up with it and of course he hasn't either – early retirement. They used to make me laugh but I don't laugh much these days. Harmon grabs my arm, the one attached to the bottle of pills.

"Jesus, Harmon!"

I flinch because he squeezes hard. Whenever Harmon is near I take the name of the Savior in vain. His mom taught him not to disrespect Jesus or the church. He knows from several years on the street together that I have serious theological issues. He religiously corrects me about it.

"The old man wants you back at work, let's go!" He presses harder on my sore arm and I forcefully push him away.

"I'm on medical leave! That means you and he, have to leave me alone!"

My butt falls into my Lazy Boy. With my eyes closed, I kick back and slip into a dark hole. For some strange reason probably because I had blasphemed I think about the nuns back in the orphanage who raised me from the crib. They're probably the reason why I'm so dedicated. I remember they taught me that I could accomplish anything if I just tried.

"Get your sorry white butt up and let's go!" Harmon is becoming more threatening than before but he is going to have to improve in the tact category before he ever has a chance at moving up the crime fighter career ladder. While he speaks, I think about the girl until that is replaced by whether or not I think I could handle my job professionally ever again.

"Roberts, are you listening to me?" He takes another look at me in the dim light and says, "Man, you look like hell!"

"Thank you for your support," I answer trying to be as gracious as possible about the intent of his criticism.

"Those pills are going to screw you up good!" He shakes his head to emphasize his very strong feelings about it.

"Don't you mean screw me up bad? And it's *red* butt how many times must I tell you? How long have we been partners?"

"Red, white, I really don't care, Jake! Fairchild told me to bring you back pronto Tonto, so let's go!"

"Screw him!"

"Screw him?" Harmon's reaction, the mocking laugh and the "say what?" face, is classic.

"Yeah, screw him! It's just another example of the white man and the black man keeping the red man down!" I have no idea where that came from.

"Hey Geronimo, you need to give it a rest. Why don't you dig deep down into your inner man and get back to respectable?"

"You know Har, I've been in this place..." I say looking around at the dreary walls of my apartment, "...feeling like I'm already six feet down, just waiting for someone to throw the dirt on top, and here you are with a shovelful!"

I lean back, close my eyes again and think.

She was just a kid!

The next thing I know, I shout it out loud. "SHE WAS JUST A KID!"

"That kid put a hole in your arm. A few more inches and she would have put you in a hole." Harmon isn't taking prisoners.

"She would have done me a favor!" I fight back. I need sympathy and I have no one else to get it from. I'm counting on Harmon to pull me up. The others talk about how lucky I was but I'm not so sure.

Harmon softens his tone for a moment and asks a curious question. "Did you cry?"

Tough guy Harmon never asked me that before. He obviously wants to know how it feel in case it ever happens to him. I can't answer. We just look at each other while the second hand freezes.

Finally to break the awkward silence I comment that scientists believe the universe is permeated with dark matter. It's a thing Harmon and I do when things get confused. We read science articles constantly, it helps.

"Are you talking from my neighborhood?" He laughs and then adds, "The string theory says that tension strands fill the entire universe and vibrate. The resonating creates life. It could be part of the dark matter."

"The entropy theory says that there is a degree of disorder in all systems," I reply and shrug. "Second Law of Thermodynamics, everything tends toward a greater disorder."

"Yeah, that's where we come in as professional lawmen." he says followed closely by, "Hey man, we got to go or the old man's going to have my butt!" Harmon is done playing but I still need to play.

"Aristotle, flat universe with the earth at the center; Copernicus, 1514, the sun is at the center of the very same universe; Christensen, 1676, light travels at a constant speed; Hubble, 1929, the galaxy is moving away; Hawking, the universe is here for us."

"Fairchild, today, get Roberts back to work!" Harmon says grinning.

"I can't."

"Yes, you can."

"She was just a kid, man!"

"Are you coming, Crazy Horse?" He quotes the great warrior. "It is a good day to fight; it is a good day to die!"

"I'm not ready..."

I love Harmon Blackwell. He is there for me with no limits or barriers. As he stands he blocks whatever sunlight is shining through the shaded front windows. He looks interesting backlit like that. He squeezes out through the front door knowing it is better to leave me alone for now and is gone before I can finish my sentence.

"...to fight."

After the door closes I see my Glock lying beside me on the table.

How easy it would be to end the pain.

10

Her instincts told her to stay alert. She had an uneasy feeling in the pit of her stomach as she rang the bell and waited for someone to answer the door. Behind her an incredibly intense, one-of-a-kind sunset silently faded from the horizon.

A smiling and anxious Thaddeus Abrams briskly opened one of the carved-glass, double doors. His greeting was warmhearted. She returned a shy hello and he invited her in. As she stepped inside the smell of freshly cut flowers and burning scented candles filled the foyer.

Admiring the incredible craftsmanship that went into the construction of his home Lori thought it was obvious that a woman had designed and decorated the detailed interior of the residence. A man however had strongly influenced the exterior of the mansion with its manicured lawn, stone and wrought iron work and the steeply pitched roof. A visitor was given the overpowering impression of success and power.

Still Lori felt uncomfortable and suspicious. Men she had learned time and time again could not be trusted. She hoped that it wasn't the case with Dr. Abrams because he was the best at what he did and she desperately needed his help.

It just seemed odd that he needed to address her issues under less than clinical conditions. When he took her hands and held them for too long the red flags went up in her mind. When her hands were free Lori said, "Maybe, this isn't the right time."

Speaking in the professional tone that he was so good at he said, "No, Lori, this is exactly the time. There are no distractions or time constraints like at the office. I often see patients here. I just need to find my notes." Leading her into the den he pointed to a leather sofa. "Please."

Insistent on standing she asked, "Where is Mrs. Abrams?" The familiar sensual, sultry tone of Lori's voice was missing.

"Mrs. Abrams...is out." He paged through his found notes. "She does a great deal of charity work for the American Cancer Society as Vice-Chairperson, very devoted."

"I'm not sure I want to do this, not here," Lori said with a nervous undertone.

Hearing that she wanted to bail out Abrams knew he had to make it clear why she had to stay. His next statement was more direct and to the point. He looked directly into her eyes.

"I know Lori. I've been in the psychiatry business a very long time and have heard more than my share of the dark sides of people to know that there's a very, very dark side to you!"

Startled by the remark her eyebrows crushed in tight and she felt a tremor in her hands.

How could he know? And if he knew, what did he want?

Maybe she thought he didn't really know jack and just wanted to frighten her into bed.

Swirling the expensive scotch in his glass he waited to hear her denial but it didn't come. Turning away he spoke while he searched for a book on the shelf.

"Your choice of words, your expressions, history - all suggests murderer to someone who watches and listens to them for a living." He forced a smile.

"I'm supposed to cure them but you know and I know there is no cure, right Lori? No once that line has been crossed and in spite of some well-intentioned statements of regret and remorse a murderer always looks forward to killing again." He shrugged.

"It's the control, domination and the godlike decision-making that make it so enticing - so addicting. Wouldn't you agree, Lori?" he asked condescendingly. She didn't reply.

"And who is to say what's right and wrong? Who is to judge? Murder is often seen as a means of accomplishing the goals of a shared societal belief system whether it's war, abortion, euthanasia... I think you get my point."

After paging through the book that he had retrieved from the bookshelf he tossed it onto his rosewood desk. His glass was near empty so he headed back to the bar. Lori knew she had to say something and tried to do so as firmly and confidently as she could.

"So Dr. Abrams, what do you want?"

"A cold, calculated admission by default!" he said pausing before he hammered at her. "Let's see the direct approach, okay how's this? You were sexually abused as a child and went along because it was a family member that you trusted and believed in. It was hard to justify that your own father could hurt you in such a way."

Seeing the fire in her eyes he said, "Now that hit home!" He fired another round. "Why did you let it continue? Why didn't you tell someone? Why didn't you tell your mother?"

I knew what was happening to Emily!

The painful memories shot through her thoughts but none of it was as Abrams was saying. Her father was a good man she knew and had nothing at all to do with her traumas. It was her own transposition of what her ex-husband did to Emily that was the root cause. Lori was furious but held back biting hard on her lower lip.

Abrams, you're a fool!

"You didn't tell anyone and all of the subsequent guilt, emotional scars and mental anguish gave you countless reasons and excuses to kill!"

"You could never understand and I'm not going to debate my life with you." In a businesslike tone she asked again, "So what do you want, to get laid – some kind of perverted sex act?"

A broad smile filled his face. "Now Lori I fully admit that in my office while you poured your heart out I had some of my most memorable fantasies. I thought about doing you on my desk. In fact, I want you right now but first things first."

He walked to the sofa and nonchalantly sat down then motioned for her to sit in the chair across from him. She obediently took a seat as directed not wanting to show any sign of aggressiveness. Instead she wanted him to think she was completely vulnerable and at his mercy.

"Aren't you afraid to be alone with me?" she asked with a quiver in her voice.

"Well, let's think about that." He looked off and calmly remarked, "No, in fact the thought of being alone with you actually excites me. It probably has something to do with my mundane and boring life as a psychiatrist."

He sipped at the scotch. "I'm even quite certain that while you have been listening to me you have considered at least five different ways to kill me!" Believing he was in control of another dangerous murderer he rambled on and speculated.

"All that needs to be resolved in your mind is would anybody know? Who else knew that you were coming here, Mrs. Abrams? Is there a surveillance system inside this enormous house? Did you leave fingerprints on the glass, the door? There's a lot to think about and you haven't had time to think it all through – my murder that is."

"You still haven't told me what you want. What am I supposed to do, drop to my knees while you're aroused with unsubstantiated suspicion?"

"Is sex all that flight attendants think about?" he teased. The smirk disappeared from his face and he stared at her with a piercing, burning look. As clearly and coldly as he could he said, "I want you to kill Mrs. Abrams."

It was finally out in the open. The unmistakable words came out of the respected, successful and talented Dr. Thaddeus Abrams ? a trusted pillar of society. How very disappointing, she thought.

He's insane!

To Abrams Lori seemed confused and lost about his last statement.

Maybe she's more unstable than I thought.

At the moment he wasn't sure what to do if she didn't go along with his plan. He tensed until she spoke.

"If you're right about me and I'm capable of such dreadful behavior what makes you think that I would do such a thing to your wife for you?"

Abrams smiled relieved to hear the question and mischievously leaned closer to her. "Because Lori, she's the only thing that stands between me and you. You take her out...and all of this is yours." His hand waved around the room.

"In return for doing away with the annoying, predatory and domineering Mrs. Abrams ? you will enjoy a lifetime of me, untold wealth, security and free consultations!"

She wanted to laugh in his face. Abrams wanted her to kill his wife and then be his mistress.

Curtly she said, "You can't walk the walk so you want me to do it for you." She pulled at her lower lip with an index finger. "And in return for my cooperation you're going to let me share in the wealth?"

Once again she was completely convinced that men were nothing more than testosterone-loaded, perverted animals that would say and do whatever necessary to get what they wanted. The others had paid dearly for that arrogance. One thing was clear in her mind - another male control freak was going to have to die.

Abrams felt somewhat relieved that she was at least considering his diabolical plan. He needed to push her to close the deal. And he wanted to make it perfectly clear that he was in charge.

"Well not exactly share the wealth more like use the wealth. And you are correct ? I can't walk the walk!" he said almost apologetically. "But then I don't have to because I have you. Now talking the talk I can do…right down at police headquarters!"

He gave her time to consider his proposal as she paced the spacious room with its ornate, expensive décor. She pretended to give his scheme her undivided attention while the clock ticked down in her head.

What would it be like to live in a place like this. All I have to do is off her and hump him.

As she studied the various displayed artifacts a more familiar voice spoke to her.

They're all the same! He's just one more shining example of how disgusting men really are! You know what to do! You have my blessing and my permission!

Until then she felt cornered, trapped and caged. But now that she had permission it would be easy. Men were so predictable. A simple mood swing was all she needed. He was a better-than-average-looking man with beautiful eyes so she knew she would actually enjoy playing him. Mentally she prepared to be absolutely convincing.

"You would want me, do you mean that?" she asked demurely.

How many times do I have to play this game?

"I offer you my heart and my soul!" he said with a bite of sarcasm. "After all we're going to burn in hell together!" He waited patiently.

"You don't even know me, nothing about my life except..." She played her role perfectly.

"I knew all about Mrs. Abrams, the social register, family history, moods and sexual needs. We've been married for many years. Feeling and love had nothing to do with it, I married her for the money. I'll be filthy rich when the insurance company pays off."

Abrams held out his empty glass for her to refill. Deferring to him she took it and approached the bar while he continued. "I'm not looking for love. I'm in it purely for the money and the pleasure it brings."

She decided to take the chance that no one knew she was there. It didn't make sense that he would have announced her appointment to anyone or be crazy enough to record their conversation. Abrams was still blustering when she dropped the pill into his glass. He took the replenished, tainted drink from her as she queried him.

"What assurances do I have that after the fact I will actually be sharing all of this opulence with you?" She thumbed through his CD collection while waiting for his answer and was astonished to find her favorite, The Cult – Beyond Good and Evil.

Bocelli had long since ended and she replaced his music with her selection. She pressed number three and play.
Thaddeus believed that he had convinced her to kill his wife. He

was feeling safe, secure...and light-headed.

"You don't get assurances. You simply have to trust me." He slurred the last two words.

As he finished his drink Lori watched his small head take control. Slowly she walked over to him and knelt down at his feet. With perfection she played the role of seductress.

"After the evil...I feel release, freedom. It feels good, better than sex!" She paused to let his imagination run wild. "Daddy taught me. He taught me how to be a very bad little girl. Do you want to see? Just thinking about it makes me so hot!"

He felt invincible as he watched her stroke his thighs. He controlled her and she was going to give him everything he ever dreamed of.

Then the room spun around once, twice and finally out of control. He blacked out, returned in a haze and blacked out again. When he briefly came to he tried pushing her away but the push was limp and struggling was pointless. His arms flailed in random directions but it was too late.

The special evening Dr. Abrams had planned with Lori was over. His last breath included a gurgling sound. The red letters had been painted above the headboard and the room was cleaned. They found him lying in a pool of his own blood on satin sheets tied to the bedposts, his severed manhood lying beneath the bloody blade protruding from his heart.

Lori had to kill "daddy" again. She succeeded but still she didn't climax.

* * *

The call was made to 9-1-1 immediately after she found him. A shocked and horrified Mrs. Anna Abrams barely heard the sirens or noticed the police officers rushing in.

It would be awhile until she was not considered the prime suspect but it was less than an hour since Lori had gone. Ironically it would be much later when Anna would collect a substantial sum from the insurance company.

His eyes fixed and open Dr. Abrams became the star of the macabre crime scene. Newton was right. A body at rest tended to stay at rest. The phrase was uttered by at least one of the investigators sometime during the evening, it always was.

Most of the personnel present at the investigation knew the doctor but not one understood why he of all people would be the victim of a homicide. At 11:42 P.M., the Medical Examiner pronounced Thaddeus Abrams officially dead.

Edward Fairchild surveyed the crime scene. His only question was, "Where is he?"

"Still out on medical leave, Ed," Harmon answered.

"I don't care, call him in!" he ordered. It wasn't that Fairchild was a heartless man. He simply needed the best investigator the department had.

Harmon walked off to a less chaotic area and pretended to make the call on his cell phone. He pretended because he knew Jake wouldn't pick up anyway.

Jurisdiction once again passed from local to federal when Agent Mika Scott arrived. The fact that "Daddy" was painted in blood over the headboard was the reason. To the FBI agents assigned to the case the murderer had become known as the "Who's Your Daddy" killer.

11

My torn bath robe open, unshaved, hunched over and drooping like Cro-Magnon Man, I'm pathetic in my current state of existence. Nudged by some unknown force I reach down and pick up the morning paper. Flicking it open I see what I had missed while comatose. Rubbing my eyes harder doesn't help to clear them. The effects of the sleeping pills are still lingering.

Newspapers have always been full of bad news. The big world outside was constantly coming apart. There is enough on my plate with my own little world crumbling that I can do without reading the paper but a particular sensational headline starts to clear my cloudy eyes.

Local Psychiatrist Murdered

The article below it spews the grisly details.

Dr. Thaddeus Abrams, prominent
local psychiatrist, was found
murdered late last night by his
wife Anna...

Ouch! I didn't like Abrams much as a person or a shrink but he was all I had.

Special Agent Mika Scott with the
Federal Bureau of Investigation
was quoted as saying...

My hand slaps my forehead. In my first flashback she had just arrived at the precinct as a new officer with a ton of spirit, fearlessness and attitude. She wanted desperately to make the world right. She was never at a loss for words when defending her beliefs.

My second flashback was of an incredible intimate moment that we shared. Mika was completely unafraid to expose her sensuality and passion. She cherished romance, loving and being a woman. I fell deeply in love with her. Unfortunately I was afraid to take the next step and it cost me.

12

Mika hadn't seen her previous boss since she left for Quantico and a career with the FBI. His hair since then had thinned and turned completely white. His familiar political smile still blinded. And his mesmerizing cobalt-blue eyes still mesmerized her.

Fifty but built like a burly, young Turk, Ed acknowledged his protégé inside CID - the Criminal Investigation Division with a warm hug. "You look wonderful, Special Agent Scott!"

Fairchild's reputation for fairness was legendary on the force. As long as you paid attention to your safety and well-being on the street and followed Fairchild's rules everything was fine.

If you tripped up, made a mistake and admitted it, he would back you up all the way. If you didn't confess your sin Ed made you the example. It was rare anyone repeated the same mistake.

He took Mika under his wing when she arrived fresh out of the academy. It was his intention to protect her from the wolves.

She was as attractive as the day she first arrived for duty in a wholesome, didn't-need-makeup kind of way. Most of her contemporaries found her to be a hardened, clawed feline until they got to know her. Ed just thought she was determined and feisty.

She mouthed a humble "thank you" and then was caught off guard by the change in his demeanor and tone.

"And just what the hell do you think you were doing pulling jurisdiction over my people! My guys are more than capable of solving this case!" Ed insisted. "Besides why so much interest in a local murder from the FBI?"

She tried to ease the blow but wasn't about to be steamrolled either.

"Ed, have you been following this on CNN? The M.O. is the same in every case. The victims are prominent, powerful, authoritative men from congressmen to Catholic priests and now a psychiatrist. Our killer is off and running. The murders are coming closer together. I have a string of murders that crosses state lines. That's why the FBI is involved!"

Harmon, carrying a case file, interrupted their meeting when he saw her. He affectionately raised Mika in a big bear hug. After placing her back on the earth he looked her up and down. She was Jake's partner before he was.

He was a big man. With a single hand he could crush the skull of a human being. He liked to say that he had a Rice Krispie punch – Snap, the head goes back; Crackle – the facial bones crack; and Pop – down they go never to come back.

"Mika, you're looking good momma! What are you doing here? Come back to steal my boy away!"

The three former compatriots laughed out loud each reliving cherished memories in their own thoughts. After the laughter ceased an uneasy silence grew among them.

"How is he?" she asked.

Blackwell and Fairchild exchanged quick looks. It didn't require great intelligence to know that something wasn't right. Harmon did his best to answer her question.

"Good…yeah good…well maybe not good but – okay. I mean, well maybe not okay, I mean…" He saw the concern grow in her face. "He took a hard fall recently. It's not been pretty but you know Jake, he'll pull through."

Fairchild interrupted Harmon. "Did you call him like I told you to?"

"No answer. But I'm going there right after this. I'll give it my personal, face-to-face sir, and report back with all due haste. In fact I'm out of here!"

He rapidly rotated in the opposite direction but didn't leave until he gave Mika another squeeze. "Later, baby!"

Fairchild watched Mika watch Harmon head down the corridor. When she turned back toward him he just shrugged.

"Come on, Mika I've got a lot of work to do if I have to baby sit the FBI."

As she glanced back down the corridor Mika replied, "Right, there's a lot to do."

13

The medical examiner, a gremlin of a man in his early sixties, was anxious to explain the special nuances of performing an autopsy to his newest assistant. The enthusiastic young student hung on every syllable as if his career depended on it. It did.

"You can hear what they're saying if you know how to listen," the gremlin said and added, "A forensic pathologist is a physician trained in criminal investigation. Are you writing this down?"

Few of the other medical professionals there paid any attention to the gremlin anymore. He craved the spotlight so they let him break in the new ones.

The clinical and dire setting of the morgue caused Dr. Moss to do his best to keep it as upbeat as could be to take the edge off. The tiled room was ice-cold and very bright inside. The two of them wore Plexiglas visors. The chemical smell, the discoloration of the human skin and the fact that a man had been murdered was just some of the gruesome details they had to deal with.

As he spoke into the microphone hanging over the cold, dead man lying on the even colder stainless steel examination table a recording of his findings was made. For some stupid reason the man would mimic a Gestapo voice and then he would lean over the cadaver's mouth as if the dead could answer.

"How are you feeling today, a little achy, muscles stiff - got a little gas?" He alone thought he was hilarious.

With scalpel in hand Moss proceeded with the "Y" incision. He recited the exact location of the incision he was making.

"Left shoulder, drag, split the nips, raise, and right shoulder," he said sounding more like a workout video or dance instructor.

Moss glanced at his new assistant to see if he was picking up on the cadence and to see if he was still standing. Most observers fainted and dropped to the floor at that point.

From the right shoulder he started another deep incision that continued straight down toward the genitals. In this case the genitals were missing from their original location and lying in a plastic bag at the end of the table.

The assistant followed closely with his nose noting that the escaping gas from the body cavity wasn't as strong as it should have been. When queried about it Moss explained that the open wound had allowed most of the gases to escape at the crime scene.

While Moss also explained the difference between a slash and stab knife attack the student simply looked on and didn't seem fazed at all. Moss figured he'd surely get to him when he reached in with both hands and popped the victim's brain out later. If the "Y" incision didn't get them that usually did.

Moss waited for a laugh when he said he might take the man's larger organ home to surprise his wife that night. None came. Dr. Moss could only hope that his next assistant had a sense of humor. The job was tough enough without one.

"What do you think God would say about what we're doing?" his assistant asked.

Dr. Moss was not prepared to be quizzed. He stopped, held the scalpel straight up and considered the question. Then he let loose.

"There is no God," he said letting his cold statement hover. "I couldn't do what I do if I believed there was. People do horrible things to each other all of the time and nothing stops them. If there was a loving, all-knowing, merciful God why would He allow that?"

The student considered Moss's answer and wisely let it go without a reply or argument.

Their visors met and the new assistant said, "You're right, doctor – there is no God." The future pathologist nodded toward the forensic pathologist who wasn't quite sure if the assistant was for real or just sucking up.

But it didn't matter really and it was time to finish up the gruesome task he had started. A murderer was running loose on the outside and couldn't be apprehended until Moss finished the autopsy.

After the "Y" incision Moss began sectioning the organs. Tissue color and stomach contents were next. A ladle was used to scoop out the contents of the stomach. Plain brown paper bags wrapped around both hands were removed. The CST's had bagged them to preserve fingerprints and any other evidence present beneath the fingernails.

Identification in this particular case was not in question. Dr. Moss knew Thaddeus Abrams personally. Moss agreed that dental x-rays for identification would be overkill but he still planned to have the forensic odontologist make an impression. He thought that statement was hysterical so he laughed out loud.

Well into his first autopsy Moss's assistant mentally prepared himself for what was coming next. He had heard it was dreadful but it would not compare to what he witnessed. Moss moved to the head of the table.

A body was a body but a face was different. Less than twenty-four hours earlier words had come out of his mouth and thoughts had roamed in the dead man's head. The smile on his face distinguished the man from others.

After making an incision along the curvature of Abrams' hairline Moss folded back the face. With the electric saw elevated he buzzed through the skull. A fine white dust filtered up into the surrounding airspace.

Archaic as it seemed he chiseled away the skull cap. It made a popping sound and almost flew up and off. Out came Abrams' brain and Moss held it up to the light as if a child had been delivered.

The student felt like retching but needed the job and remained standing. He also wondered if there were any last thoughts trapped inside the exposed brain.

Completing the autopsy Moss and the new guy labeled the blood, saliva and semen samples. DNA would be sent away for analysis. All Thomas Moss had to do was write the report which would cross the desk of his impatient and easily annoyed boss.

The demands of the position made the coroner a man who wouldn't hesitate for a second to impale anyone who approached him at the wrong time with shoddy work.

14

The cacophony outside Ed's office door included scratching computer printers, humming computer terminals, ringing telephones and fax machines. The "homeless" were there too, homicide detectives with no home lives who scurried from desk to desk while conspiring to stop the bad guys. The third-floor residence of the homicide division was chaotic. It always was.

And Ed loved everything about it. He was the Elmer's glue that held it all together.

Framed over his desk were the words "Myth of Full Enforcement." They were in bold red letters. It was a constant reminder to him that not all of the law was applied equally to everybody and in spite of all of the efforts of the good guys, some of the bad guys would get away. It was ugly and dirty out there on the street but he did his best to make it all work.

"People," he shouted from his office door. Heads rose and it got quiet real fast.

"I want you to go out of the box on this one, beyond solid, basic police work. Above all keep your heads. Do not, I repeat, do not jeopardize this investigation in any way. This is part of a federal investigation and I don't want this department to look incompetent!' He paused.

"Also, most of us knew Dr. Abrams. He's been a friend of this department for years. He has been there for many of us when we needed him. For that and for the sake of his wife Anna I want this perpetrator found and brought to justice. Now you all have work to do. I want all detectives in briefing room A, that's alpha, in ten minutes!"

They scattered like ants with their heads down racing around performing multiple tasks. All detectives within earshot of Fairchild's command hustled to the briefing room. Special Agent Mika Scott stood outside room A's doorway and Ed joined her there.

Fairchild marveled to her with, "The place has filled up since you left with energetic, aggressive females proving they can do the same job as a man."

"Do you have a problem with that?" she asked.

"Should I?" He thought about it a moment and then shrugged. "The complaining is the same."

Beneath the bright, buzzing, fluorescent ceiling lights Fairchild asked her if she thought it was quite a climb to the third floor. He was referring to the floor they were on and the elevator that the architect neglected to add because the city refused to pay for it.

"It's a tougher climb into a man's world," she tossed back not at all interested in the elevator.

"Get anything out of the National Crime Database?" he asked.

"I checked right before I came up. Nothing we didn't already have," she answered.

"You can start without me. I've got some calls to make." Ed watched his subordinates file past and then disappeared into his office.

Mika walked confidently into the briefing room. Another FBI agent followed her in and quickly took a seat after closing the door behind him. The male detectives in attendance noted Mika's striking features and strut.

One whispered to another, "Monumental pair of credentials."

"And an amazing pair of qualifications," the other replied.
The rest surmised she was sharp, intelligent and prepared. Taking the hint from the second agent everyone sat down and stopped talking.

"Good morning." She did not smile. "My name is Mika Scott. I'm a special agent and profiler with the FBI." She allowed a moment for that to sink in as she worked the crowd. "I even worked right here for Captain Fairchild at one time." She added a stern warning.

"If any of you harbor any 'misogyny' keep it to yourselves. For those of you with a limited vocabulary that means a hatred of women as a group. We have something far more important to deal with than gender squabbles." She looked at each of them to reinforce her point, "Like stopping a serial killer."

Both female detectives present gave a thumbs-up.

"Our most conservative estimates state that murder is on the rise across the nation. Serial killing in particular is becoming a national pastime. Humans are natural predators. Up until recently that predatory nature has been controlled and kept in check by law, religion and television. But our over-entertained society seems bored with simulated death. Now there are calls for televised, "reality" executions." She paged through her notes.

"Background-wise you should know that serial killers come from all walks of life. You would suspect they are psychotic or deranged and some are but mostly they are your everyday variety with a significantly low score in the feelings and compassion categories. Some of them actually believe what they are doing is normal and justified." She stopped. "I see a hand."

A male detective commented, "You seem highly emotional about this case, Agent Scott."

"Yes, I am. I've been with the families of the victims – all of them. They want closure. Our killer is increasing his activity. Physical evidence at the various crime scenes I've tracked suggests sadistic tendencies with sexual overtones. I want this one stopped and put away."

Another agent slipped into the room and stood off to the side deferring to Mika. He was holding some papers. She briefly smiled at him and then studied the detective's faces for reactions.

"Statistically, eighty-five percent are male; eighty-two percent Caucasian; fifteen percent are African-American; a mere two-point-five Hispanic and the remainder is Native American or Asian. They're normally between the ages of twenty-two and fifty years old. Eighty-seven percent are loners. It is rare to find one that is McNaughten Rule insane...."

* * *

Ed spots me as he leaves the briefing room and makes his way toward his office. I just entered through the double doors at the end of the corridor. He waves me over. Along the way I say hello to several of my peers before reaching his doorway.

The grip of his handshake is firm but brief. Some guys feel the need to turn it up hard to establish control early on but not Ed.

His eyes are those of a professional hunter and warrior ? eyes that see *you* in a crowded stadium. They are eyes that noted every characteristic, scar and tattoo. Standing before him you could almost see the mental notes he was writing in perfect penmanship.

"Roberts, you're abusing the payroll!"

"Stealing is a necessary form of survival!" I half-smirk and add, "Steal a little, all of the time; steal a lot and do the time."

"You're a lawman for chrissake!"

He isn't quiet during all of this. Most of the department is listening in on our private talk. Using well-chosen words from his body-language dictionary Fairchild sits on the edge of his desk and towers over me. There is no doubt that he is in command. I take it all in -- the sights, the sounds and the smoke from his cigar.

"Got your act together yet?"

It is clear to me that my tactic of blatant disrespect isn't working and wearing him down like I thought it would. I'm no longer too proud to try for sympathy so I go for the man's heart.

"I can't seem to shake the nightmares, feel like I'm on my seventh, eighth and maybe even my ninth wind." My head drops. "She was a kid, Ed!"

He puffs and the smoke rises to the fluorescent lights.

"So were the kids from Columbine, what did they have - semiautomatics and Uzis?"

Fairchild's been around. I'm not going to get anywhere with him. His nonchalant reply is second only to his determination. He gets off the edge of his desk and does an end run back to his high-backed leather chair where he parks his behind. He leans forward and looks fiercely at me.

"I want you on this case. I need a problem-solver with initiative."

"What you're asking of me is hard."

"Yes it is, but it's the hard that matters the most." He stares me down. "You'll be working with Mika."

"That's impossible, we still have issues." I sound weak as if I don't have any fight left in me.

"Get over it," he says.

I think about her, us. I always felt at peace when I was with her.

She knows all of my secrets, weaknesses. She understands my inner, whining child. Mika somehow knows how to heal me. She is calm water to someone battling raging seas. I need her more than ever.

Fairchild interrupts my thoughts. "Don't you have something more important to do besides harass an old man?" He starts shuffling papers on his desk.

"Where is she?" I ask as I meekly get up and head for the door.

"Briefing room A, remember where it is?" He looks up and adds, "Glad to have you back, Jake. You're one of the best ? I need you, son."

Whatever small amount of pride I have left at this point begins ever so slightly to grow. I leave without saying another word.

15

Without signaling I cut into an open lane in the hallway's rush hour traffic. Taking the off ramp to the briefing room I feel as if I had been gone more than just a few days.

As the door to the briefing room opens everybody looks to see who is brainless enough to show up late. I half-smile while taking a seat in the back. After my butt is in the chair Mika restarts the briefing. I can only hope she notices the sentimental look in my eyes.

"Our serial killer is geographically transient like a Theodore Bundy or Henry Lee Lucas. He is intelligent and has kept us guessing. He's done his homework and is apparently familiar with our methods and tactics. The crime scenes are very clean, antiseptic actually.

There are only two things that tie them all together. One, the word 'Daddy' is written above the headboard in blood. And two, the victim's genitalia is castrated."

A hand rose in the front row.

"Castrated?" a detective blurted out. He made a notation on his legal pad as he spoke. New to homicide he decided that it was the perfect time to establish position and a rapport with his male contemporaries. Besides, Mika was a good-looking woman and he wanted to hear her say more about the victim's genitals.

"Can you expand on that, Agent Scott?"

Having spent a great deal of her career among the lower animals of the species and well aware of how juvenile they become whenever sex was the subject, Mika answered unnerved.

"Removed, detective, cut off, sliced ? severed." She waited knowing his motive for asking.

"Thank you, Agent Scott. Would it be true then that our perp is not only a murderer but a homosexual as well?"

"Very possible, detective," she replied. "Do you have any special insight to offer us about such tendencies?"

She was clearly the top seed in the match. The paralyzed detective was left without a witty retort. The rest of the group proceeded to harass him with conjecture, catcalls and whistles. After they settled down Mika drove home the more gruesome details for our digestion.

"Our perpetrator appears to be motivated by anger, hate and a desire to dominate. It is likely he experienced physical or sexual abuse early on in his life and is seeking revenge for it. Usually serial killers are control freaks, just like most of you."

That one did not go over well but she wasn't at all interested in their affection as much as their respect. She softened the blow by adding, "Well, like all of us."

Their startled faces slowly smoothed out.

"The murders are savage, brutal and violent. He inflicts multiple physical and psychological punishments if you will. The victim struggles and our boy apparently gets off on it." She scanned the room, "Any more questions?"

I know better but it's like a joke that rumbles around inside of you and has to be let out. I raise my hand. She has no choice but to call on me. "Yes detective?"

"Did they teach you all of that in *Quantico*?" I ask with a perfect touch of sarcasm.

She gives me the cold stare. Fortunately for me Fairchild walks in and interrupts with his usual philosophical speech regarding incarceration.

"And none of them ever finds Jesus or has a change of heart until they are in the slammer and somebody's wife!"

After a round of applause he added, "You have a copy of all the current data in those files in front of you. Make me proud!"

16

She floated with her eyes closed. Her toes protruded from the calm water like two miniature periscopes. Her outstretched arms waved ever so slightly. There was no one else around. The water was warm and soothing.

All she wanted was to float on her back down that stream forever. She was completely relaxed, more relaxed than she had been for quite some time. But the feel of the water wasn't right. It felt more like syrup.

She opened her eyes to look at it and saw she was floating in a sea of blood. Startled she awoke from her deep sleep and quickly looked at the red digital numbers of the alarm clock on the nightstand. They said that it was 3:23 A.M.

Where am I?

The room was dark except for some light coming from the street through the crack in the curtains.

Think.

It was a common occurrence for someone who traveled as much as a flight attendant. Often a crew member would find himself or herself momentarily lost in space and time. Cities and hotels, dates and time zones would become blurs.

Oh yeah, Philadelphia.

Lori thought about the dream of floating in blood. She knew the psychological ramifications of it. It was amazing how the subconscious worked. Knowing it would be difficult to fall back to sleep again until her 5:00 A.M. wake-up call she decided to read. The only thing available was a magazine she had found that was left behind by a passenger on her flight.

The magazine, MAXIM, had an article about bizarre murders. Lori used the article as a source of reference or comparison to see how far she had gone over the edge.

> Erzebet Bathory, Hungarian countess,
> killed 600 girls, bathed in their blood,
> and then had her servants lick her clean.

She had read that right before nodding off to sleep.

> Gilles de Rais, French protector of
> Joan of Arc, killed 800 boys and then
> performed necrophilia acts on their bodies.

Roman rulers she read had wild animals ravage humans while the empress Messalina would masturbate. From previous research she learned that "ritual killing" was performed in order to consume the better human "qualities" of the victim. What wasn't clear was whether the bad qualities were swallowed along with the good.

She laughed aloud when she read about the "revenge murder." The husband had put his wife in the oven and baked her. When the police arrived he was found laughing hysterically.

She thought about her abusive ex-husband.

17

The look on her face told me I was in deep trouble. The pointed toe and lean on the hip punctuated by the crossed arms – yeah I was going to get it good. I was going on trial right there in the hallway in front of my peers.

Legal counsel would not be provided. Contrite sounded like a good approach right now, a good suggestion.

How do you plead, Roberts?

"Good to see you, Mika," squeezes past my lips. "Har told me you were here."

It as if I'm ten years old again. Inside my cranium I watch the stream of words forming into sentences then slide toward my mouth. Each of them is carefully scrutinized by some kind of verbal-quality-assurance mini-Jake. Then the motion picture of one particular night we shared begins. The opening credits warn me about the rating.

Her thrusts made the wind spill from my lungs. Her contractions were powerful.

Establishing some common ground by rebuilding on our past relationship might have helped but she sensed it coming and her eyes said not to go there. What I should do is fall to the hallway floor on my knees and beg her for forgiveness. I decide to drop the personal and go with the practical.

"Look, I believe we can still work together, we're professionals. And, I think we're still friends." I take my shot.

Shifting her weight she rotates to a more controlling stance. Her raised eyebrows scrunches down and rests over a serious face. She looks stunning in her business suit.

Stop it, Jake!

"Did you have to belittle me in front of them?"

The level of anger in her voice is deafening but the words are a forced whisper through grit teeth. A strong retort would help but the basic male grunt comes out.

"Huh?"

"I have a job to do, and it doesn't help one damn bit for you to walk in late and make wiseass remarks!"

The best thing would be to take the high road and apologize. The worst is to disregard my inner sensitive female and let my testosterone speak for me.

"Why did you leave, Mika?" I say rejecting the high road.

It is a tactic I learned long ago probably as long ago as in a classroom with the nuns. If asked a difficult question buy time by asking a question back. I also want to hear her answer, again.

Mika's eyebrows crunch and she gives me an "I gave you a chance" expression. She answers with that annoying, rising inflection used by teenage girls. "Because Jake, you had a significant issue with commitment."

It worked, it always did with Fairchild. And it always worked on the street during investigations. My briefing room behavior is now the furthest thing from her mind.

Mika continues with, "And don't try that ask-a-question nonsense with me - I know you!"

On the outside I simply raise both eyes. On the inside the bells and whistles look like an arcade.

Keep moving, Jake!

"Well what do you expect from a poor Native American boy from a poverty-stricken reservation?" I plead.

"Please!"

Turn it up, Jake.

"I guess it started in the orphanage - the commitment thing." My smile disappears as my head droops. "When you start out alone you don't think anyone really cares."

Slowly now look up at her, Jake.

"I cared, my parents cared - you just couldn't see it."

Her tone is less caustic this time. As a detective I detect a shift toward sympathetic understanding. I push the envelope.

"You were lucky to have parents, someone to teach you about commitment."

Mika considers that for a moment. Her head twists a little to the side and her eyes glance down at her 9-Wests. Guilt has its good points. A look away enhances the moment.

"My parents have always been there for me," she said almost apologetically. She glances from face to face as strangers pass us in the corridor until her eyes lock on mine.

I lightly brush her hand. "Life has a way of punishing us for our mistakes. For the past few years I've been punished by being without you. It's been just me, and me."

I feel bad about making her feel guilty, I didn't mean for the conversation to take this turn. I just went into survival mode because I'm swinging in the wind.

Mika's voice is gentle and low when she speaks. "Har told me about the girl." She takes my hand. "You did what you had to but just the same, I'm sorry. If there's anything I can, well…"

The moment hangs over us. Swallowing hard I sheepishly add, "Listen, I was way out of line in there and I apologize. It really is good to see you again!" The words I should have used earlier finally spill out.

"Truth is Jake, I've missed you, too." Silence, thought, a look and a dramatic pause pass by. "But you must understand that I've been chasing this guy and I'm obsessed with caging him." A second break and she adds, "Maybe after he's caught…"

Maybe?

18

Mika never exaggerates. What she says is exactly what she means. She also has that uncanny, womanly way of seeing even microscopic details like picking out a flaw in a diamond.

Guys can't do that and miss the details. A man is only cognizant of the big picture after the billboard falls on him. I'm not good at much but I know details better than most and I really am good at my job. At least Fairchild thinks so.

"His simplicity clouds his complexity," she says.

My curiosity compels me to ask, "How do you know the killer's a male?"

I need to start at the beginning so I can get a grip on what we are dealing with. For me I need to place things in a logical order or equation so that I could solve the problem. It's why Harmon and I fool with science. Cold, hard facts fill in the empty spaces in the equations and timelines.

"A woman couldn't do this," Mika says looking at the people, places and cars going by but focusing on some metaphysical nothingness beyond them.

"P-M-S?" I ask.

Mika smirks without looking at me and said, "That's how you men see us, don't you?"

Levity takes the pressure off for me. One minute I'm analyzing blood and guts, and the next I'm doing one-liners on the corpse. It was the same when I'm in a hospital or a funeral parlor. The gravity of death brings out a nervous anxiety that I have. Abrams probably knows the reason but he is in no condition to say.

What I do know is that you can only wallow in human suffering for so long before you became cynical, sarcastic and a comedian. Unless…you killed a girl whose entire life was ahead of her.

We walk past the activity at the front desk where officers move in random directions in search of truth and justice. We push through the main doors of the house and head toward the parking garage. Along the way Mika describes the details of the "Who's Your Daddy" case.

I hang on every word deciphering and sifting through her suppositions and intuitions about the killer. I guess she did learn a lot in Quantico. She is the expert now. I can learn a lot from her if I don't let my ego get in the way. The screeching tires of his unmarked car announces the arrival of Harmon who coincidently severs our path.

"I'm driving, get in," he commands.

Without hesitation we both grab a door handle and climb in as directed. Mika's briefing goes uninterrupted and I pretend not to hear Harmon's rants.

"I hate when he drives!" Harmon blisters. "Man can't see a stop sign or a pedestrian. I can't tell you how close we've come to running over everybody in this city at one time or another!"

Detective Blackwell is large in size and even larger in his opinions but he is my partner. His abrupt arrival is replaced by a very conservative drive through the crime-breathing back streets.

He knows a shortcut as we head toward Abrams' mansion. Some of the graffiti on the buildings is quite artistic and some of it is actually funny. I recognize some of the tags from my days chasing gangs.

I just saw Abrams two days ago.

"We should have gone the other way. This 'hood has never even heard the word 'po-lees' because the police won't come in here," he enunciated. Harmon was maladjusted to our current location but he had a reason to be. He knew these streets better than any other cop because grew up here.

While Harmon is concerned I know he likes to check the working girls in their tight, short skirts and five-inch heels. "Oh momma, would you look at that?" His head swings like a gate in the wind. "How delicious!"

Mika could care less about the streetwalkers. Ignoring Harmon she sounds frustrated. "He's one step ahead of us all the time!"

"Why do you say that?" I ask.

"Each of the crimes scenes, all ten - eleven now, are spotless. Not one single fingerprint has been found except for those that should have been at the scene. There has not been a drop of saliva, semen or DNA. There are never any witnesses.

All that's ever left behind is that hideous scrawl of 'Daddy' above the victim. It creeps me out whenever I see it! Burglary and robbery are never a factor. All jewels except for the family jewels are where they should be." Mika starts pointing out directions for Harmon and I start thinking more about the case.

Why Abrams? Was there a connection - the Internet, a personal ad for lonely hearts, was he kinky, perverted, something none of us picked up on over the years?

He seemed normal for a psychiatrist.

As we drive up and into the driveway I can see that he lived well. The residence looks more like a posh hotel. Every house looks huge to a man who lives in a one-bedroom apartment. We aren't even in the suburbs. Apparently Abrams liked to live among the natives and relatively close to the precinct.

She said a congressman, a union leader and a priest were some of the characters on the killer's victim list. There did not seem to be a common thread except for the authority thing. This is going to be interesting and a challenge.

"Did we get anything helpful back from the 'eternal care unit'?" I inquire.

"I think Moss is still digging - get it, morgue, digging, undertaker?" Harmon waits laughter that doesn't come. "The report isn't due out until later today."

No one is home now. Anna Abrams can't bear to sleep there. The crime scene has been deserted since the night of the crime. I missed the initial investigation. The only things that are left are the insects, the rancid smell, the bloodstains and the revulsion.

I take out my cassette recorder and start making entries. I hate using a notepad mostly because my handwriting is poor to doctor-type unreadable. Besides my arm still has a bullet hole through it and hurts to write.

The only difference between this scene and the others is the fact that the victim was discovered early on. Mrs. Abrams arrived home from her charity function within an hour of his death. Because the time of death is relatively easy to determine in this case there isn't any need for an entomologist to "bug" the corpse.

Insects typically discovered the body before anyone else did. Depending on whether lice, mosquitoes or maggots got there first they deposited their eggs in the eyes. The larvae, depending on their state of maturation, can give a pretty exact time of death.

Sometimes we get lucky if the mosquitoes get there first and are still in the area. It's possible to snare them. Often times they carry the DNA of both the victim and killer after the bites. This murder happened inside so there is little chance of that.

Mika is right, "antiseptic" is a good word for it. The disheveled, trashed, disorganized mess you usually expect to find isn't here.

The sheet on the bed is bloodstained and the splatters are from Abrams. No doors were jimmied and no windows had been broken. I have to believe that the victim knew his assailant.

Fingerprint dust covers everything. No trace evidence such as fragments, filaments or fibers was found by the techs. This guy is knowledgeable and talented in the techniques of slaughter. The photos are back at the precinct.

Of course the area is already contaminated. The uniforms, EMS, investigators and even Mrs. Abrams have trampled through here. I wish I had gotten out here sooner.

I hope Fairchild doesn't expect a miracle.

Mika stands in one corner and takes in the panoramic view. She has been here before for second and third looks. Sometimes what you just don't see the first time became painfully obvious the next.

"Looks empty without a body," Harmon adds. "I'm going to walk around outside and work my way in. There might be something between here and there, you never know." He walks out into the hallway.

"Who had access?" The words are meant for my recorder but Mika who is pacing out the room for some reason answers.

"The wife, there aren't any children. Closest relative is in Bloomington." She thinks she sees something but it turns out to be nothing. "The doctor wasn't particularly friendly with the neighbors. He and Mrs. A traveled mostly outside of the immediate neighborhood and its inhabitants. There weren't any fights or arguments, just no contact."

"Clean, huh?" I shrug.

"Not much to work with, maybe Harmon will find something."

Any evidence however minute helps. Evidence doesn't have the ability to lie, be confused or not remember exactly. It's just there. The problem with it is it can be misleading if your interpretation of what it is trying to tell you is wrong.

This case is definitely going to take all of my stamina because of the lack of leads. It's going to demand any street smarts and intuition that I have accumulated over the years. I speak into my cassette recorder.

"Look not for what's there but look for what should be there." I make another entry. "Look in the garbage."

The sound of heavy footsteps signals Harmon's return. He glances first at me then at Mika. "I didn't see a thing."

"Did you check the garbage?" I ask.

"First place I looked, nothing."

"What a surprise!" The sarcasm in Mika's voice betrays her normally cool exterior. "You want to run through it?"

Harmon and I join in an affirmative nod followed by one "Sure" and one "Uh-huh." Mika runs through it all hoping that some minute detail has been overlooked.

"Abrams, Thaddeus, psychiatrist, age forty-six, Caucasian male, married to Anna. Case number: CR 897-4453. Address is here, six foot even, one hundred ninety pounds, brown hair, green eyes and small scar on right elbow. Victim found by spouse who has been eliminated as a suspect. Head facing northwest, face up, feet to the south and southwest, hands and feet secured as previous victims."

Harmon rolls his dark eyes and scrunches his face when she says the part about the castration. I can feel a phantom wound between my legs as well.

The first forty-eight hours are critical to a homicide investigation. I'm standing here at the forty-ninth.

19

It has been three days since Abrams' murder. As an insider and a man considered one of their own, Abrams is talked about in the precinct with affection and honor. There are outpourings of sympathy for Anna. How could anyone know his soul was thrashing and burning in the flames of hell at this very moment?

My two partners drop me off at my apartment just after our visit to the mansion. It's late and I'm exhausted. My troublesome nightmare, return to duty and seeing Mika again all in one day has drained me. I can't decide what beat me up worse.

The pain in my arm is still there but not as bad. My little helpers are easily accessible and a cold beer helps.

Sometimes when you are alone it can be too quiet. As I recline on my Lazy Boy I think about getting my television repaired. But most of the shows suck anyway. I never shop from home, never cared about the Middle East or the fabricated lives of movie stars, and I definitely don't care about over-paid ballplayers.

There are always the depressing news channels but I deal with real life and that's all of the entertainment that I need.

On the end table beneath my Glock is a vacation brochure.

>A small, rural town in Central Florida,
>Cassadaga attracts thousands of visitors
>each year for one unique reason. It's a
>camp and winter retreat for spiritualists…

>Current activities in the camp include
>psychic applications of: palmistry, Tarot
>reading, astrology, and numerology, past

        **life regression, dream analysis, spiritual
counseling and soul healing.**

No doubt about it, Cassadaga's for me!

As I toss the brochure it is obvious to me that I need to do something to stop the impending nightmare that will punish me soon. But the room is fading and my eyes struggle to stay open. The nightmare once again takes center stage.

The auburn-haired girl with the swastika carved in her forehead stares at me as she does every night. She asks me the same question every night, "Who gave you the right to kill me!" I never answer.

20

The steamy hot water felt good as it caressed her naked body along its path to the drain. With her eyes closed she thought about how rugged and handsome he was with his deep, masculine voice. She was always taken by his boyish, sentimental eyes above the character creases in his face. Jake was a classic lover-protector.

Maybe they...

Her head beneath the soothing, falling water she thought about the last time they had made love.

His two fingers lay across my lips and stopped me in mid-sentence. I felt comfort and safety ? pleasure in his arms. His eyes communicated his desires. I kissed his neck, his strong shoulders and his chest. He straddled me. His intimate thrusts became more aggressive and intense until we clenched and remained locked pleading for the moment to last into eternity.

Mika had suppressed those thoughts but now they were back again and very much alive. She wasn't sure whether to welcome them back or force them into their hiding place.

There was a job to do. She couldn't let her emotions blind her now. A serial killer was roaming, searching ? hunting for more victims. With all of the Bureau's resources behind her she still hadn't apprehended him.

How am I going to stop him?

The steam floated and formed a cumulous cloud in the bathroom as Mika stepped out of the shower. All she saw in the fogged mirror was a faint apparition.

I still love him.

Reaching for a towel she patted off the droplets. The case was taking an obvious toll on her. The aches and pains were relentless. The mental strain threatened to crush her.

The telephone rang and she moved quickly toward the nightstand covering up with the towel along the way. Midway through the third ring she picked it up.

"Scott."

"Mika, the medical examiner's report just came in."

"Anything that was helpful?"

"Just the usual disgusting medical verbiage with no major revelations. I can have a copy run over if you like. Sorry to bother you this late just thought you'd like to know."

"Not a problem, Ed. I would like to see it though. I can be there in…"

"Don't be ridiculous it's on its way. And don't stay up studying too long. You need to get some sleep. You never know when he's going to climb up out of the coffin and strike again."

"Thanks dad." She could almost hear him laughing on the other end. "I mean that in a good way Ed, you've always been…you've always looked after me and I want you to know how much that means to me. I've been so preoccupied that I haven't said 'thank you' like I should."

"Good night, Mika."

The phone disconnected. She held it for a moment before replacing it on the cradle.

Jake Roberts and her love life would have to wait.

21

There were only five small minutes left in the day when she placed the key in the lock. She bent down to retrieve the last two days of newspapers then stepped in to the foyer. She dragged her wheeled travel bag behind. Lori was traveled out.

It had been a particularly demanding flight because of difficult passengers, an unfriendly crew and overall tiresome jet lag. She needed sleep badly. And she had an early morning appointment with her Emily. There was a lot to talk about.

The train whistle from her alarm clock caused Lori's eyes to snap open. It wasn't an easy transition back from her fatigue-induced sleep. She sat up in bed but that was as far as she got on the first try. She went down again convinced that she was no more ready for the world than the world was ready for her. It was an hour and thirty-eight minutes later when she finally awoke for good.

She shuffled off to the bathroom for a brief visit then went into the kitchen to make a pot of coffee. While waiting for the water to boil she retrieved the latest newspaper to see what had gone on since she was away. As she paged through it the headline on page three caught her eye.

No Suspects in Murder of Local Psychiatrist

They were clueless as always and she was still rocking. If they found out anything it would have to be by accident and Lori didn't allow accidents. She was far too careful, organized and intelligent.

> FBI Agent Mika Scott was quoted late
> last night as saying that no further
> information is available regarding the
> Abrams murder case at this time. If
> anyone has information, please contact…

The caffeine was just what she needed and the whole grain wheat toast helped to absorb the acidic feeling in her stomach.

She briefly revisited the bathroom to apply makeup and brush her hair. After that she bolted into the walk-in closet where her flowered sun dress hung. It was Emily's favorite and the one she would wear for the visit.

I've got to get a move on, my baby's waiting!

Just as Lori reached for the front door handle a knock startled her. No one except for the postman, knew she lived there. She never invited anyone to her private sanctuary.

I'm not expecting anyone or anything.

Swinging open the front door she hoped to sign quickly for whatever it was and be on her way. A tall man with a muscular build stood at the door wearing a striped tie and a blue button-down shirt over gray slacks. He had a slight smile but looked as if he was on a mission.

22

She was stunning in the early morning just as she was in Abrams' office. I was excited about being assigned to interview her for the case.

"Lori Powers?"

"Yes."

"Detective Jake Roberts, Homicide, I'm sorry to bother you." I held up my wallet with my department identification and shield. "I just need a moment to ask you a few questions regarding Dr. Thaddeus Abrams. You were a patient of his, correct?"

"Homicide?" she asked as she nervously studied my identification. "Yes, I am, I mean, was. How awful! I just this minute read about it." She looks at the newspaper and shakes as if a chill has risen up her spine over the tragic news.

"I'm afraid I missed..." She saw I wasn't following.

"I'm a flight attendant and have been away for the past few days. I, I can't believe it!" She looks a little closer at me. "Didn't I see you there?"

"That's quite a memory you have!"

Beautiful and smart!

"Not really. I deal with people all day long on airplanes. With all of the terrorist things going on we have to pay closer attention now. I probably pay more attention than most people because the whole thing frightens me to death!" she says as she shudders.

Her beauty and charm are disarming.

Pay attention, Jake!

"You're right. I was just leaving when you walked into his office. Anyway I got your name and address from his client list. Again I'm sorry to bother you. Do you have a minute?"

She doesn't hesitate and says, "Sure, I was on my way out but for Dr. Abrams sure if I can be of help in any way." She pivots as if working an aircraft cabin and invites me into her home. As she walks in front of me her perfume inspires more than questions about Abrams.

We stop in her living room and she says, "He was a very good man, well-respected. I hadn't been a patient of his for very long though."

"You were one of the last patients that he saw that day, he was murdered later that evening. I thought maybe something might stand out, something unusual while you were with him."

"Unusual? How do you mean?"

"Did he receive any distressing phone calls or interruptions? It appears that he might have known his assailant. Did he show any signs of stress?"

I like the dress.

"No, did he show any before you left?"

That one jams me up. I didn't expect the question but she has a valid point because I was pretty much there right before she was. "Ah no, he appeared fine to me."

Now I feel clumsy, off balance and stupid for asking. It isn't easy with her. I'm supposed to be doing the intimidating. I can't stop looking at her.

"Can I ask you another question, Detective Roberts?"

There is a smile on my face as I state, "Normally, I get to ask all of the questions but under the circumstances of both of us being his patients I guess it would be fair. I didn't get a chance to cram last night so please don't make it too hard."

"Why were you seeing Dr. Abrams?"

With a simple question she makes me feel self-conscious and uncomfortable. My emotional state is fragile and I'm trying to keep it under some kind of control but for some reason I feel I can unravel in front of her without any penalties. The hurt floats to the surface but I push it back under.

"That Miss Powers…" A deep sigh suppresses my uneasiness. "…is a subject I really don't want to discuss."

"I'm sorry, I not trying to pry, just curious."

Detective Roberts you are a handsome man.

For some reason I can't help but feel at ease around her. She is warm and friendly, her smile is enticing and personal. I have the impression it is only there for me. It is probably one of the reasons why she was hired as a flight attendant. A great smile is one way to distract someone with a fear-of-flying.

Because Abrams isn't going to be any help I don't see any reason why I shouldn't let it out. Sometimes it's better to confide in a stranger.

"I was involved in a shooting recently - a militia group. A young girl was killed." I look down and away. "The department requires a shrink after that." It feel like I'm in a confessional.

"I remember reading about the kid with the Molotov cocktail and an assault rifle!" She doesn't back away and takes me straight on. "You were the officer that shot her? You were wounded too, weren't you?"

"Yes to both."

"Well I want you to know Detective Roberts that what you did was a courageous thing. You did something to try and make a difference in this world. You performed your duty and protected the rest of us and for that I thank you!"

Amazingly I feel redeemed and absolved. The back of my hand drags across each eye and I pinch my nose. "Thank you, I haven't been doing well with it."

With a sympathetic tone she says, "It must be very difficult for you. Was Dr. Abrams able to help?"

You have beautiful, honest eyes.

"It is…and he tried. We really didn't have much time to get anywhere."

She reaches forward and gently pats the back of my hand. I'm in the middle of a murder investigation and she is standing there with her reassuring smile making me feel good again. A lot is going through my mind.

She says softly, "I don't have a degree in psychiatry God knows I was a patient of his too but if you ever need someone to talk to, someone to listen, well you know where to find me." She points at her address and phone number on my notepad.

"Thanks" is followed by an exhalation. I don't know what else to say. It's weird but I don't know what to do with my hands either. "What about you, if you don't mind me asking?"

She looks at me with little girl eyes and says, "After what you just told me detective my story seems trivial by comparison."

"I'd like to know…please."

"Well." She becomes sullen and starts to pace. "My daughter a few years ago decided that this world wasn't a fit place to live in."

She started to straighten things along the way that she thought were out of place. Tears welled up in her eyes. "She had just turned sixteen when…" She looks off somewhere past me while she uses a tissue. "I never got to say goodbye."

"Is there a Mr. Powers, someone to help you through it?"

I try to make the question sound as if it is coming from a professional level rather than an obvious invasion of privacy for personal gain. She looks at me with more sadness and anger.

"Mr. Powers deserted us years ago. He wasn't much in the first place but he really wasn't much in the last place. The truth is I wish he had left sooner."

She looks away again during her recollection of how events of the past had hurt her. "You know sometimes we protect our relationships as weak as they may be for some strange reason."

Personally I'm glad to hear that Mr. Powers is history. She never mentioned a boyfriend so that door is open. Strangely enough Abrams' untimely departure may just have brought two of his patients together for no other reason than to console one another.

"The same offer goes to you, Mrs. Powers. If you ever need someone to listen, I'm here." I hand her my business card.

"Lori," she says looking up at me. She reaches out and offers a long, slender hand.

Maybe he is the one.

I take her hand and hold it. "Jake," I say smiling for the first time in a long time.

"Very nice to meet you, Jake."

We both sense that something unique has just happened but are uncertain about what the next move is. The possibilities are endless. The moment lingers while we consider them.

"Was there anything else, Jake?" she inquires.

While smiling like a little boy I ask, "Will you be flying off soon?"

"Actually I just got back and I'm leaving to visit my daughter. I make it a point to see her as often as I can." Her mood drops a few levels again. "I miss her a great deal."

I wonder what the militia girl's parents think of me.

"Well, I have everything I need. I still have two more of his patients to see so I better go."

Lori offered an invitation with, "I'll be back in the house about four if you need anything else." There's that irresistible smile again.

For so long I have protected my castle and yet she easily breached its walls and captured it. I'm puzzled by how much I want to let the floodgates burst open. I go with a simple "Okay."

As her door closes behind me I get back to reality.

What would she want with a broken-down cop anyway?

Lori watches me leave.

I have a good feeling about him. Maybe he's the one.

23

It was an exceptionally beautiful morning. The birds seemed energized and the air smelled clean. White-topped and gray-bottomed clouds floated indiscernibly by. There were breaks between the clouds that allowed shafts of sunlight to fall to the earth.

Before she left for the cemetery Lori stopped by the florist's shop and purchased a bouquet of daises and carnations. They were on Emily's list of favorite flowers.

Rejoicing at the warmth of the sun Lori made her usual trek through the miniature monuments with names and departure dates until she arrived at Emily's.

"Hi baby, mommy's here. I missed you terribly," she said standing with her arms full of flowers.

There was no reply. Lori tried again.

"Emily, mommy's here."

Silence, not hearing her daughter's usual greeting was a painful blow.

"Baby?"

No answer. Lori became stressed and listened closer but still nothing. Standing with her eyes closed Lori remembered Emily's suicide note.

> You should have stopped him!
> Why didn't you stop him?
> I hate you! I will hate you forever!

Finally, a very subdued child's voice spoke.

I'm here, mommy.

Lori looked rapidly left and right "Where are you, Emily?" She became anxious, possessed. Her baby was near. She didn't care if anyone saw her. "Baby, where are you?"

I'm in the dirt, mommy.

Lori quickly gathered the flowers that she had brought. She fell down on her knees and placed one hand on the grave. The other slid along the smooth headstone.

"Baby, what's wrong? I came as fast as I could. Please, don't be angry with me."

Who is he?

"Who, baby?"

That man mommy, who was that man you were talking to?

"You mean the detective, Detective Roberts, baby? The man who came to see me? Oh he's nobody just wanted to ask me some questions."

A groundskeeper, a black man with a rake, stopped to watch Lori. He stared at her and she glared back until he finally moved on.

He's bad mommy, a bad man!

"Oh no Emily, he's no such thing. He was just asking about Dr. Abrams," she said but her voice trailed off.

You mean the dead Dr. Abrams? Maybe he'd like to ask about the dead Father Moralli or maybe the dead Senator Whitman?

Lori looked down not knowing how to answer. Instead, she started to pull twigs and weeds from the grass and tossed them to the side. She never liked it when Emily was in a bad mood.

"Emily…"

Leave her be! She's only concerned! Jake Roberts is a problem!

Lori quickly surveyed the cemetery for other mourners and said, "I like him. He's not like the others." She waited but no one answered. Lori drifted off into the nightmare.

Daddy was on top of her. Emily gripped the sheets while he sexually assaulted her. It hurt so badly but she was afraid to tell on him because…she loved him. And she did not want to be the cause of any more problems between her fighting parents. When she tried to tell it was as if mommy did not want to hear. Just before he finished with her Lori returned to reality.

Then the image of Jake Roberts replaced the horror of the dream. A smile appeared on her face. Life did not have to be full of heartache.

Could he be the one?

Inside her heart danced with a renewed sense of optimism for a meaningful relationship. Lori felt hopeful again. It had been a long time since she had any feelings.

24

It's my job to be analytical and know the geography. There is an intense debate going on inside of my head as I think about Lori. I want to feel her passion, to share every minute, to listen to her words and be touched by her. I want to watch her breathe. My cell phone rings as I drive away from Lori's residence.

"Are you up for some lunch?" Mika asks.

Imagine that, a call from Mika in the middle of my debate about falling in love with Lori.

Divine intervention?

"I'm close to Hennigan's, got anything?"

"As a matter of fact I'm starving and Hennigan's sounds good!" I wisecrack the next. "I think it's a tumor."

"That's not funny - I'd miss you!" After the scolding she says, "See you there."

Because I'm just a few blocks away from Hennigan's I see no need to race there. Mika probably isn't even close herself. I hate waiting like a lapdog, tongue hanging out and tail wagging. The extra time gives me a chance to come up with an excuse as to why I was given three interviews to do and only finished one. Maybe Harmon has something so dial his number.

"I'd miss you?"

As I wait for him to pick up Mika pulls up alongside my car looking cranky. As I climb out of my car I watch her do the same.

Like the pant suit!

"Everything, okay?" I ask sensing incoming trauma.

She shrugs and heads for the front door of the restaurant without saying a word. I hate when women do that. And I hate the guessing game that always follows. I open the door for her.

It was the restaurant management's hope that you would somehow confuse the place for a popular restaurant with a similar name. Actually the food was good and no one cared about the name anyway. Mika told the waitress that there were two and possibly three of us.

The young hostess marches us to a corner booth. After she takes our drink orders she goes about retrieving them. Mika is still looking off to some far horizon but finally speaks.

"I want this guy! I've been through each case a thousand times and nothing but nothing plus more nothing! All I know for sure is that I have multiple deceased males. That is the sum total of what I have!"

Without anything to follow that with I ask, "Did Harmon stumble onto anything?"

"He would have called if he had."

Her answer is abrupt but I press on anyway. "Was there any more out of the M.E.?"

"Moss didn't have anything earthshaking just basic autopsy stuff." She says it while scrutinizing the other patrons. "The perp could be in here right now having lunch and I wouldn't know it."

"Easy, we're not in the Waterfront Tavern!" My reference is to the infamous bar where several prolific serial killers had once tossed down a cold brew together.

The county morgue is not my kind of place, in fact, I detest it. Although I make my living as a homicide investigator and required to go there I always thought it was full of creepy people who enjoyed a little too much what they did for a living. I often thought that they should be investigated. Fortunately my ex-girlfriend turned FBI profiler is in command so I do not have to go. I can just read the report.

Lori Powers. Her face keeps popping up in the upcoming events marquee in my mind. Mika on the other hand has a different look about her today. Until Lori Powers Mika was where I had hoped my luck in love would lead.

"Did you do something different with your hair?"

She looks at me as if trying to decide whether or not I deserve an answer. "No Jake, same hair, why? What's on your mind, something you want to talk about?" she asks as she pulls out a file three actual and not man inches thick. Press-a-plys are stuck everywhere.

"How did your interview with…" she looks over her notes, "…a Lori Powers go?"

Being a detail person she notes the change in my expression and watches my head turn away when she says the name. I'm not fast enough with an answer for her.

"Jake?"

"Let me give Harmon a call he might want to meet up with us," I need to buy some time and quickly press speed-dial. It's only a second when Harmon answers.

"Hey big man, where you at?"

"Passing Fifth and Sycamore, why?"

"Hennigan's, thought you might like to join us. Got anything?" I nod in Mika's direction to show that I'm on the case.

"On my way be there in fifteen at the most." Harmon whispers into the phone as if Mika might hear his next sentence. "Is she wearing the short red skirt?"

"Watch for those pedestrians!" I sign off and wink at Mika. "He's on his way. Hope the FBI is paying for lunch. A man Harmon's size can't be fed on what I make."

Mika is lost in thought. I'm afraid to ask what is going through her head. I think I'm out of the line of fire and assume it is about the "Who's Your Daddy" killer.

That was some shower!

She smiles and then asks, "When you were a kid what did you want to be when you grew up?"

Maybe I don't get the question or why she asked it but I go along with it.

"In my neighborhood you only had three choices ? a cop, a fireman or a priest. Because I don't like fire, fireman was out. The priesthood was out because I like women although some of the padres do very well with the parishioners."

"Stop it!" Mika says protesting.

"That left only one option."

"Organized crime?" she asks.

"Actually that ad said only Sicilian's need apply but I filled out the application anyway." I answer with a sneer.

Mika starts to laugh. It's the first time I have seen her laugh since our pitiful reunion. It wasn't your normal belly laugh, more like an adult giggle.

Could we fall in love again?

It's funny how distracted I have become from the trauma of the shooting because of Lori and Mika. I must be healing. I can still smell the scent of Lori's perfume on my hand. And Mika's eyes are more alluring than ever. I drift until Mika brings me back home again.

"What did they have to say?" she asks.

"What did who have to say?"

"The Powers woman and the others I asked you to question?" She keeps staring at me making me feel uncomfortable. "Jake, tell me you did what I asked you to do!"

"I only got to Ms. Powers. I didn't get to the others by the time you called to meet here."

I shuffle the silverware and salt shaker. Because the case means so much to her she is obviously disappointed that I didn't finish my assignment.

"What did she have to say?" she asks with a heavy sigh.

"Just that everything was normal, nothing out of the ordinary. There were no interruptions, phone calls or any distressing events during her session." I sound a bit too defensive.

"What was she wearing?" she asks with a heavy dose of cynicism.

25

Flying at thirty-three thousand feet and looking down at the blue-green earth you could see concrete cities, majestic mountains, snaking rivers, and green fields. As the world rotated beneath your feet you had the sensation that you weren't moving. You were also given the impression that the world was right and full of peace.

What you couldn't see were the people or the crimes they were committing.

The terrorist attacks on the World Trade Center pushed the airline industry into complete disarray. The Federal Aviation Administration had mandated new security procedures that ran the gamut from the simple-minded to overkill.

While some concepts improved safety and security, others had to be trashed. Anyone observing a newborn or the elderly being "wanded" at a security checkpoint had a difficult time accepting the changes.

In flight the rules had also changed particularly with an increase in the use of Federal Air Marshals riding on board flights. Flight attendants were receiving self-defense training. And passengers were offering their assistance to crews if needed them to overpower terrorists.

Captain Nicholas Parker was old school. Even before the attacks he was fearless when it came to defending his ship. "Pilot-in-command" to Parker meant that he was in total command. He only trusted the man flying the plane - and *he* was that man. The down side to his courage and authoritarian attitude was that he used it to abuse crew members.

The new reinforced cockpit doors were pure nonsense to Parker.

As far as he was concerned the door was only another barrier preventing him access to the female flight attendants. A "profiler" in a perverse way he profiled the female members of his crew that could fulfill his sexual needs.

His requirements included most assuredly young women, and the younger the better. Those in their late twenties were okay as long as they had young girl features. Pretty was acceptable to him but drop dead gorgeous was prized. Fortunately for Parker that's what the air carriers sought out as well – young and hot for the discriminating business traveler.

Megan fit the Parker profile. She had just turned twenty-one and was new to the airline. Although she wasn't on the drop dead gorgeous side of the scale she turned heads.

The road kill neighborhood that she had grown up in taught her early that life could be devastatingly harsh. And while she came from the wrong side of the tracks and her future looked bleak nevertheless she was determined to get out any way she could.

Megan's parents couldn't afford to help her out of the misery. The schools failed her as well. But she knew it was only a matter of time before she would rise up and out. She worked hard and managed to get hired as a flight attendant. She believed that all it would take to complete her story was that one pilot who would sweep her off her feet.

She considered sleeping her way into a secure financial future but believed she could get by with teasing. Keeping her eyes and ears wide open she too profiled targets. Upon being introduced to the captain she recognized his potential and waited for her moment. All she had to do was hook up and play the game. In the end she thought she would find the happiness she longed for.

"You've got the airplane, I'm going to the back," Parker told his first officer.

After being introduced to Megan before the flight he had locked his sights on her. Undoing his harness and seat belt Parker got out of the left seat and swung a leg over the center pedestal. Standing in the tight cockpit he looked in the mirror on the bulkhead wall to check his best captain smile. The first officer had flown with him many times before and actually admired the old man for his virility.

"Good hunting!" the pilot said encouragingly as he reached for his oxygen mask which was required by the regulations when one flight officer left the cockpit.

Parker grabbed the front of his pants and pretended to squeeze signaling his concurrence with the junior officer's remark. His sneer said it all. Turning one hundred and eighty degrees Parker exited the cockpit locking the door behind him. It was only a short distance and a brief moment, and there she was.

The bustling commotion inside the galley area seemed disjointed to unseasoned passengers but was actually part of a well-played third act. Alcohol was served to frequent and first-time flyers with the intention of settling their nerves by keeping them well sedated. After all though it wasn't advertised anything could go wrong at any time while they were held captive inside a man-made machine that screamed through the sky.

"Everything okay back here?" he asked Megan.

Parker turned up the concern and charm. Megan was the only flight attendant in the galley. The others were serving passengers from the cart. He glanced down the aisle appearing to survey the situation but was really looking to see if any of the other flight attendants would interfere with his next move. They had already noted his presence and were very much aware of his reputation.

In a sweet, elevated and innocent tone Megan replied, "Yes sir, everything is under control. Is there anything I can get for you, captain?" she added with a few playful looks.

"Some orange juice please, if it's no trouble," he replied.

He loved her deference to his authority. Is there anything I can get for you, Captain Parker, why yes! His eyes never left hers.

Seizing on the opportunity he asked, "Megan have you got any plans for the layover?"

"No sir, I'm still on reserve, the pay isn't much." She pouted. "I plan to stay in my hotel room and watch some television or read a book." She strategically turned away to fill another drink order.

Parker pressed on. "Well I was planning to go out to a nice restaurant. There is a particular one in town that I like, kind of exclusive. No one else in the crew wants to go. You're welcome to go along. It would be my treat."

Food he knew all too well worked for all junior flight attendants. They made so little money the first few years that they had to sacrifice meals. She flashed her bright eyes at him. Her excited, enthusiastic reply bounced off the galley walls.

"I'd love to go!" As she finished preparing drinks she stopped and looked at him fluttering her long eyelashes and adding a tilt of her head. "That's very kind of you for asking captain, thank you!"

He whispered back, "Nick. There's no need for the captain thing unless we're flying." Of course that only applied until he got into her pants. After that he would be Captain Parker again and she would have to understand the difference.

"Okay Nick!" she cooed back as she hunched her shoulders and played the game. "What should I wear?"

"Well how about something that will show off the beautiful woman that you truly are!" he said with maximum charm.

She knew the just-in-case miniskirt she carried was perfect and well worth the money she paid for it. If she could ensnare him she was certain that she could recoup the cost.

"You know I just might have something that will do!"

"Great, we'll have a wonderful time, I promise!" he said affectionately. He couldn't stand the pressure building inside his pants so he smiled, excused himself and returned to the cockpit.

After he left Megan glanced down the aisle to see if anyone had picked up on the captain's hit. One of the male flight attendants pantomimed a hysterical laugh back at her but she wasn't at all affected by it.

She knew that if her plan came to fruition she'd be out next to Parker's pool enjoying the noonday sun while the catty flight attendant in mid-cabin sucked in the thin air at altitude.

Back inside the confined cockpit, appropriately named he thought, Parker watched the first officer remove his oxygen mask. After placing himself back in command the captain looked at the first officer and commented, "Signed, sealed and delivered! All that's left is the crying."

The copilot gave his best compensatory laugh and a thumbs-up. He asked the captain, "How old do you think she is?"

"What difference does it make?" was Parker's cynical reply. "Old enough."

The junior officer actually felt a tinge of sympathy for Megan. He knew that she like all of the others had come into the airlines with stars in her eyes seemingly unaware that piranha like Parker swam around them. But Megan for some reason seemed extra young, extra innocent and naïve to him.

What a shame!

26

A menacing eclipse appeared over our table. As I look up I see Harmon slide his big frame in next to Mika. He is doing it just to irritate me. He also knows that he and I won't fit on one side of the booth. I smile.

"Who you cheesin' fo'?" he asks.

He normally spoke in perfect English but every now and again he went ghetto on me. He was good at it especially when the bad guys were around. Sometimes he did it just to put a grin on my face.

"Yo, sup? Peace out! Word to the mutha!" I abuse the colloquialisms and commit a crime against linguistics. My inner African should stay silent.

Mika just watches us hoping the nonsense will be over soon. Her fingers separate her flowing raven hair into strands. Her Asian features from her mother's side complement her father's European complexion.

"We need another flood," she says ever so seriously.

"A what?" We ask the question in unison.

"Another flood like the first one - Noah, the Ark, two of each species? Except this time we need to leave the males behind." She effectively takes both of us down without breaking a sweat. Glaring at Harmon, Mika drops her chin and raises her eyebrows.

"Do you have anything for me, anything the least bit encouraging?"

"You think it's that easy, don't you? You come down here from the F-B-I with all of your high-tech gear and gadgets and straight away you want results. Well in case you ain't noticed this here ain't no F-B-I! We's just poor police fokes try n' to do ourin' bes'!" Harmon opens his eyes as wide as he could to play the part.

Head shaking Mika blows him off with, "No wonder I'm jammed up!" She points at the two of us. "I'm working with Amos 'n' Andy!" Then she queries the room. "Pardon me, ah excuse me, can anyone find me a real cop please?"

"Hey, that's not nice! Besides you have the precinct's best and second best sitting right here!" I insist.

Harmon deadpans at me, "Which one is you?"

"You're absolutely correct!" She continues with the head bobs. "I have to say that you two are the biggest dicks in here!"

"Did you say the two biggest *dicks*? Now baby you know which one is which in that category, right?" While he pats my shoulder Harmon adds, "How you doing, man?"

Harmon has saved my life on the street on more than one occasion and my butt with Fairchild many more. I watch Mika who is laughing now and I flash back to another time.

Her hair fell to her shoulders after she loosened the braid. Her eyes radiated with confidence and pierced deep inside mine. Her face was soft as I stroked it. Her scent was inviting me. I leaned forward, took her in my arms, and kissed her.

"I found a clue," Harmon says and pulls me back from my dream.

"Harmon Blackwell," Mika shouts her head snapping in his direction.

Unfazed he snickers. "Well it's not really a clue in the *clue* sense."

She waves her fist at him and follows with a threat. "So help me I'm going to smack the daylights out of you. Come on, what have you got?"

Reluctantly and with a shrug he says, "Mr. and Mrs. Thaddeus Abrams were not a very happily married couple. She said as much in so many words you know kind of on the side like she forgot to protect him and play the good wife. She was distracted for a moment and let it out. It's got to mean something don't you think?"

"A struggling marriage," Mika asks and considers how that has any bearing. "That could be why she spends so much time at charitable functions. Do we have any proof he fooled around?" She pauses. "It might support that he knew his assailant."

That cranks me up a notch. "Knew his assailant? I should say so. He was naked and tied to the bedposts! I think it's safe to assume that he wasn't on the clock giving good therapy. More likely he was receiving some.

It's Harmon's turn. "Did we check his e-mails or regular mail, maybe there's something there. Maybe that's the connection – someone soliciting sex over the Internet? Maybe that ties all of these gentlemen together!"

Mika looks off into the distance while our orders are placed on the table. Mika is famished and starts eating. With a big smile the waitress turns to take Harmon's order. He asks for an appetizer and a cherry Coke.

The young, black woman brushes against my partner leaving him the impression that she finds him irresistible. He gives her one of those brother-type smiles. After she leaves he turns to me.

"Did you see that? Did you see that? I could get into some kind of trouble with that one I can feel it! What do you think?" He was glowing, red hot.

I shrug and continue trying to figure out what it is that I have been served. It doesn't look like the picture in the menu. Not sure what it is I just play with it. Pouting I add, "And I thought nothing would ever come between us Harmon, I'm really hurt."

Mika's eyes dart between the two of us. "I'll check the phone records of our victims to see if anything matches. I'm leaving now so that the two of you can have a moment." With her purse in hand she stands over us.

"I'm so glad I work alone." The pause is brief but properly timed. "Thanks for lunch Jake, I'm going back to the house and frolic through the files some more. Har, Har, over here, hey she'll be back – you're burning a hole in her behind!"

"She's fine, she's so fine!" His eyes have not left the waitress.

I slide my butt out of the booth. "Wait I'll walk out with you." Motioning in Harmon's direction I add, "That leaves him with the bill, I thought the Feds were paying for lunch."

Harmon turns in my direction and asks, "You going to be all right? Want to get together later and watch the Sopranos?" His concern is real and appreciated. He is sitting down so I pat him on the shoulder.

"No man but thanks, I'm looking forward to a quiet night of introspection and self-doubt."

As we walk out Mika has a funny look in her eyes. I'm not sure I want to know why.

"Lori Powers?" she inquires.

How did she do that?

It seems like another good time for a delaying question so I go with, "How come you never ask how I'm doing?"

She has that look. "Because I know you Jake and I know that if you've got something on your mind that you want to talk to me about, you will. I know when your inner child wants to speak," she says self-assuredly.

"I have been there and done that, remember?" Her arms fly up to punctuate. "And I know that you just dodged my question again!"

I look back at her with one of those stupid male looks feigning that I have been violated.

"So Jake, what's up with this Powers woman? Did you interview her or are you in love again?"

In love again?

I know what my desires are with Lori Powers but I'm getting some weird signals from the planet Mika. I don't know what to say. I wasn't expecting any emotional conflict over lunch.

"It got personal, didn't it Jake? And now you're headed back to do a follow-up with her, right?" She purses her lips and looks down at the pavement.

"Well Detective Roberts..." her tone is harsh, "...with that kind of dedication I'm sure you'll crack this case wide open ? so to speak." She waits but I have nothing to say.

"Well I've got to get back to the house. I told Fairchild I'd touch base with him, keep him up to date." She focuses on the horizon. "There's a killer loose out there. Just help me find him that's all I ask."

It would have been the perfect time to say something meaningful, intelligent but instead I watch her walk away. Disappearing into her car she backs up and drives off. I hear Harmon come up behind me.

"She still loves you, man."

"Where you headed now?"

"I thought I'd hang with you, you know and do the partner thing. You see, we..." He motions between the two of us. "...are supposed to spend time together that's what they mean when they say 'partners', get it?"

I smile back but my thoughts are about Mika, and Lori.

"Not this time but I promise we will. Did you get anywhere with the waitress?"

"I was doing real good right up until she found out I was the heat. Some people just can't seem to take the heat, you know what I mean?"

27

He was considered a visionary by those close to him but somewhat off-center by the normal population. His enemies despised him and were deeply envious of his success. Hardball was definitely his game, he had the balls. His shouting could be heard all the way down the corridor. He scowled at those attending the meeting.

"My head is pounding with all of the science! This is all too much to *download,* I believe that's the official term?" He shifted to his left and swiveled away from them brooding and annoyed.

Scientists, what a pain in the ass!

Rotating back to face them with a disgruntled look he calmly asked, "All right, what you're saying Dr. Caldwell, if I understand this properly, is that we have gone from Tesla theory to Tesla reality?"

"Correct sir," Caldwell curtly replied.

Dr. Patricia Caldwell, mid-thirties, was giving a presentation on weapons of the future to her CEO. Her hair was pulled up tight in a bun. It was her nature to hide behind the walls of science and research to prevent emotional contact.

"In 1886 an obscure scientist named Nikola Tesla, coincidentally the inventor of alternating current, also developed the principle of 'resonance' whereby objects can be altered by vibrating them. He said and I quote:

> It is possible to transmit electrical energy
> without wires to produce destructive
> effects at a distance and apply it for
> innumerable purposes including physical

degradation and even death.

A brilliant man in his own right and CEO of one of the largest defense contractors in the US, Robert Scott considered the possibilities. He knew that conventional weaponry had to be replaced some day so he was willing to keep an open mind.

"Physical degradation?" He spun around in his expensive leather chair to face out the scenic penthouse picture windows. "Attila," as he was known to his subordinates, contemplated the potential revenue boost.

A mid-level corporate executive made an observation that he could no longer keep to himself. He directed his questions to Caldwell.

"This is high-tech war isn't it? Like the crossbow was to the agrarians? The wave of the future is high energy radio frequencies and transient electromagnetic devices used as weapons?" He started beaming with excitement.

The CEO slowly rotated his chair and got back into the conversation. As he was about to speak his executive secretary who had been with him since the entire corporation was housed inside of a trailer entered the conference room.

In her mid-fifties but still a striking woman Maggie felt confident enough to stride in and interrupt the conversation. She knew all too well his strange habits and idiosyncrasies. She also knew important details about his offspring which included birth dates, anniversaries and the grandchildren's names. More importantly she knew how to handle all of the ex-wives.

In her hand was a small piece of paper with a message from a visitor who was in the outer office who had requested an audience with him.

"She's outside?"

Maggie could not conceal her smile.

"Meeting's adjourned, take a recess class!" His anxious face looked back at Maggie. "Send her in!"

Maggie shuffled across the floor in her tight pinstriped skirt, silk white blouse and the five inch heels she was legendary for. She stopped at the door and waved at the visitor who appeared a moment later. The next thing Robert saw was a timid wave from his daughter's hand.

"Hi, daddy" Mika said with an attached little girl smile intended to melt his heart.

"Mika, where have you been? Wait, have you got a pen and some paper? Quick, write this down."

Taking out her notepad she looked back at him with a quizzical look.

"1-8-0-0-5 ?"

After the first five numbers she stopped writing. A guilty look followed. "Okay, okay, I get it! But you have got to understand that I'm a very busy girl and I've got responsibilities!"

"You know you give me an ice pick headache and forget about the broken hearts!" he said clutching his chest.

"I would have thought the pain would be much lower." Grinning she knew she had just successfully one-upped him.

"Come here, it's time for the big hug scene!" Robert said with his arms held wide open.

They embraced like family members do after realizing they let life get in the way of their relationships. She was a sight for his tired eyes. To Mika he was still her knight in shining armor. To Robert she was still his little girl. She was just like him.

"What brings you to see old dad who has been in the same town with the same address and telephone number for forty years now? Need some cash?" He reached into his pocket but she waved him off.

"Those days are over dad but thanks for the offer." She grasped his hand.

"The Justice Department didn't send you here about those…" A wide grin was followed by a chuckle.

"Justice could never catch up with you, Robert Scott!"

Mika thought about how much time had passed since her last visit. Dad was getting older.

I need to spend more time with him.

She also thought about the fact that while she wasn't there for the cash she was there for his help and guidance. Like all fathers he sensed that she had a brought along a problem.

"What's the matter, honey?" He grasped her shoulders and confidently added, "I can fix whatever's wrong."

"Not this time I'm afraid. Have you been following the news about the 'Who's Your Daddy' murders?"

"Are you on that case?"

She nodded. "I'm afraid so."

"Is that the one where the young woman into Satan worship chopped up her friend with a meat clever, bashed her head with a hammer and then carved a pentagram into her chest? He displayed a squeamish, repulsed and agonized look on his face.

"Hmm, this is going to take longer than I thought," Mika answered.

"Good that'll give us time to have lunch. Where…"

"Dad stop, I can't go to lunch. What I need is some real good fatherly advice. I'm at a dead end. I've got this case and there are no clues, there's little to go on and people are dying! And I can't seem to find the answer." Her distress elicited his compassion.

His hand raised and scratched at an eyebrow. He paced. "I'm really not a criminal investigator honey but have you tried a bribe?"

"A bribe?"

"Yeah, a reward for information? Pay a 'snitch' I think you call them? Money usually produces results. I remember for five hundred you could send a guy to the hospital. For a thousand he wouldn't remember his name. And for five thousand he'd be floating face down…guess that wouldn't work for an FBI agent!" The joking ended and he became philosophical.

"That's some job you do always dealing with the bottom of the food chain, slimy bastards - just like old dad!" He paused. "Hey, you should work for me! You could have a nice office, be a vice-president, you could take long lunches *and* you could still deal with the bottom of the food chain!"

Mika laughed and the weight on her shoulders appeared to lift. "Actually dad you have no idea how good that sounds right now!" She let the offer float around in her thoughts for a while, savoring it.

"But I can't, I like catching bad guys. I love locking them up. I just can't find this bad guy." She grabbed his arm and tugged. "I thought you might have some fatherly wisdom gathered over the centuries that could help me!"

"Centuries, I look that old huh?" He plopped back down in his chair. "I need to start working out." He pretended to take his pulse.

"Anyway I don't really know what to tell you except that if anyone's going to find that screwball – it'll be you. You're relentless always have been ever since your were this high." He held his hand out parallel about four feet off of the floor for emphasis. "That guy doesn't stand a chance. Hell, they should have you chasing bin Laden!"

"I'm working with Jake on this." Mika's eyes locked on to her father's.

"Jake?" He couldn't hide his enthusiasm. "I always liked that one. You two were a good, no a great match! How's he doing?"

"He seems okay now but he had a rough one a few weeks ago ? shot and killed a teenage girl. She had it coming but he took it real hard. He doesn't want to show it but he's still struggling. Then on top of that the department's therapist, the one Jake was required to see because of the shooting, turns up as my perp's eleventh victim."

A head popped in at the conference room door and asked, "Are you ready for us yet, sir?" The eyebrows were high and the smile half-hearted. Robert glared back. The door closed again.

"its fatherly advice you want okay here it is. Keep your chin up and your head down. I don't know what to tell you about the murders but I do suggest you get out of crime fighting and get a life. You and Jake would still make a great team. You know when you two were together you were happy, happier than ever – than now. That's the best I got, babe."

As she kissed his cheek his words ping-ponged inside of her head. Deep down she knew that she still had strong feelings for Jake but the job had to come first.

"Thanks dad, I love you so much!"

28

I was never good at relationships. It probably had something to do with being abandoned as a child. It also had something to do with being a male. Men either try too hard or not hard enough. In our defense no one ever taught us how to behave in a loving relationship. And by the time we figure it all out it's too late.

"Lori?"

"Jake, I'm glad you called!" is her surprising reply.

She recognized my voice. If she did nothing else but talk to me with her sweet, sensual voice I could listen for a lifetime.

"How was your day?"

It is important that I don't scare her off, cops have a way of making people feel nervous enough, although I want desperately to tell her that I think about her all the time.

Don't screw this up, Jake.

"Oh, it's been a beautiful day. There is a special feeling in the air that I just can't explain. And to think it's not over yet!" Lori hoped that I was picking up what she was putting down. "Did you still want to get together?"

"I'm still at the office but I'm officially off duty." The tight fist pull-down was only part of my celebration.

Be cool, Jake.

"It looks stormy outside and I hate to drive in the rain. Any chance I can get you to pick me up?" she asks.

"Sure, what time is good for you? I need to stop at home and clean up first."

A date with Lori Powers!

"Seven, I'll be ready by seven if that works for you?"

I try not to sound over anxious. "Seven's perfect."

"All I need to know now Jake is what you have planned for the evening."

"I was thinking about a place that is rather unique and different!" I tease.

"Unique and different, sounds like I should dress to kill!"

29

"It's Quantico on line two, an Agent Wellington from B-S-U, Agent Scott," the operator said as Mika reached the short distance to the black phone on her temporary desk at Fairchild's headquarters.

"Thanks, Beck."

Not familiar with "B-S-U" Fairchild shrugged at Mika and whispered, "Bullshit University?"

She grinned and whispered back, "Behavioral Science Unit." She got a smile and a nod back.

"What have you got for me Wellington, it had better be good. I'm drowning in the dead sea of clues here!" She snapped on the speaker phone.

"Agent Scott, we added all of the new data including our latest gentleman to the stew and the C-I-A-P matrix has formulated a few answers," Wellington said trying to sound highly technical and official.

Ed, looking lost asked, "What the hell is the C-I-A-P matrix?"

She waved it off as unimportant and said deeply into the phone, "Give it to me!"

Agent Wellington had harbored that very thought on many occasions. He and Mika were new hire classmates and he had a serious crush on her ever since. Although he never expressed his deep feelings he was always the first to volunteer if she needed help.

Mika, aware of his puppy love, took every opportunity to use double-entendres and suggestive phrases to tease him to death. He loved it and she knew that he didn't have a chance in hell of getting into her pants. In her mind she classified it as legitimate-sexual-harassment-role-reversal. Wellington took a breath and passed on his findings.

"Our victims are all powerful men – a politician, priest…well you know the list. The only other authority figure that has not been targeted so far would be a law enforcement officer. There doesn't seem to be any other connections between the victims, no other overt connections anyway."

Mika replied, "I'd categorize him as organized. The fact that he leaves nothing behind supports that."

"Very definitely, he doesn't appear to have any other agenda except for the authority angle. He's not motivated by thrill or lust, fame, social change or religion. There is no robbery or blackmail. He is as you said very good at it and definitely organized. I checked the phone records, no matches there. Only one thing is for sure - he definitely knows who he wants dead."

The frustrated Wellington pictured the two of them alone on an island. He would be Kirk Douglas and she would be what's-her-name the actress. Snapping back to reality Wellington continued. He kept talking only to prolong contact with Mika.

"This one, while out of control so to speak, is definitely a control freak. Our killer wants to punish. Maybe it was something those guys had done to him personally or what they represented. I don't believe it has to do with his sexual orientation. Whatever it is the guy is highly intelligent, very careful and extremely detailed."

"Agreed."

Fairchild yelled a question at Wellington from across the desk. "What about timing? Is there anything in your computer that makes the timing stand out ? dates, time of day, holidays, things of that nature?"

"I'm sorry, who is speaking?" Wellington asked sounding annoyed. He thought they were having a private conversation. Someone was in his space with Mika.

Firmly Mika responded with, "That would be Captain Edward P. Fairchild, Chief of Detectives, Homicide. He's on our side, Wellington." She emphasized "our" to make him feel as if they actually shared some special connection. She loved harassing the man.

"Sorry Captain Fairchild, I'm just being careful, it's my job you know."

Ed could care less about Wellington's feelings and his tone clearly conveyed impatience with Wellington's arrogance.

"And the answer is?"

"The exact hours varied but all of the murders occurred late in the day. The methods were the same. The victims were drugged, bound, sliced and diced with the male genitalia left behind as either a statement or a warning. There wasn't any sexual intimacy during or after each attack."

Mika wondered if Wellington was getting turned on using explicit sexual references. In the back of her mind she always believed it was possible that had he not been in the Bureau he may very well have been on the most wanted list for sexual predators. Then again he could rise to the top spot in the Bureau like J. Edgar Hoover did.

"He's smarter than most," Wellington said in Ed's direction. "That's not to say Einstein. He's street smart, worldly. He's probably read a few basic psychology books in addition to knowing the law."

The agent was on a roll and started to predict, hypothesize. "I'd say that it's just a matter of time before he makes a mistake or loses it all together. The rational mind will come back and be devastated by what he's done."

"Are you reading from the Wellington crime-fighting manual now?" Fairchild asked harshly. Since he began in law enforcement he had serious issues with and a disdain for the Federal Bureau of Investigation. To him they were overrated, bumbling primadonnas. He only dropped his dislike temporarily since his protégé arrived.

Mika, interested only in solving the crimes, noted the male testosterone building and interrupted both of them.

"Do you have anything else for me, Agent Wellington?"

Wellington inquired as to when she would be returning to Quantico adding that she was missed by everyone. He really wanted to say that he missed her. He didn't care much for their long-distance relationship.

"Probably not for awhile although I don't have a specific time on that. Our perpetrator pretty much will decide when I'll return if your theory is correct. In any case I've got a lot of work to do here."

Knowing her answer was a setback for Wellington she left him with a well-placed, optimistic tease. "When I do get back we'll have to compare notes."

"I'm going to hold you to that, Agent Scott!"

I'd like to hold you to it!

"Later." Mika clicked off the speaker and the line disconnected. She looked at Fairchild for a reaction.

"Are all male FBI agents as horny as he is?"

"Sit Wellington, now beg Wellington!" she answered. They both laughed. It felt good to laugh again even if it was at Wellington's expense.

"You really enjoy this forensic profiling, don't you? You like digging into people's heads and trying to figure out why they do it? Me, I don't really care why I just want to know who so they can be locked up and off the streets."

Mika watched as Ed walked around and sat on the edge of the desk. Fairchild was definitely old school. He was certain that was the way of things worked, how it was done. Mika shifted and leaned back in her chair.

"I don't know, I like it ? love it actually. But at the same time it frightens me. Sometimes I think it will overpower me. It wouldn't take much to fall into its clutches by default. One minute I'm stopping crime and the next falling over the edge with it! Do you think that's weird, Ed?"

His eyebrows slid together over the creases in his face.

"Serious?"

She smiled. "Ed, profiling is just another way to get to the same conclusion. You use facts to see how. I use them to see why. In the end, we just want the bad guy!"

Ed looked deep into her lovely eyes and said, "I'm going to be watching you closer now. Not because you're a beautiful woman which is why I watched you closely all these years. Now I'm going to watch so you don't go over the edge!"

She stood and pointed an accusing finger at him. "And I always thought you were like a father to me. To think that you're a pervert like the rest of the boys. There goes my last hope for mankind!"

Fairchild mimicked Groucho Marx. "And the secret word is "pervert"!"

She looped her arm through his and they walked out of the office smiling.

"God, I miss this place!"

"Come back!" he answered without hesitation.

30

As I hurtle the last two steps of her front porch a pleasant tingle of apprehension runs up my spine. It fades when she opens the front door. I feel light-headed, dizzy and almost giddy. Lori is stunning.

Always detecting I make mental notes of her every feature – hair, makeup, breasts exposed by a drooping blouse, a platinum necklace and a golden, silk Oriental skirt. Her cerulean eyes sparkle and her smile invites. I wonder what it would be like to kiss her. I give her my best Jake Roberts smile.

"Well, I'm impressed, an on-time arrival!" she says. When she notices I don't get it she adds, "Industry talk, sorry. Hello Jake, it's wonderful to see you again!"

I feel awkward me the hard-nosed cop who had seen it all. She has some kind of mystical power over me. She is like my kryptonite. At that moment I can barely remember Mika, Harmon, my job or the girl. I just want Lori Powers to like me. She controls everything including my heartbeat.

"You look great, really great!"

The entire opening scene of our date is going by at light speed. Lori helps me to keep up when she asks, "So where is this 'unique and different' place we're going to?"

"I thought we'd give magic a try - the world of deception!" That brings a bewildered look to her face that suggests I need to sell her on my idea.

"There's a theater downtown where they perform magic shows. My favorite restaurant is across the street. I've always wanted to go to one of the shows but I thought I'd save it for when I met someone special." Her expression changed immediately to excitement. I had scored a point.

"What a fantastic idea! I've never seen a real magic show. Oh this is going to be fun!" Her reassurance opens my pressure valve.

"There's only one problem." My head drops and I solicit her pity. "I don't have a car you know like a real car. I just have my department-issued, unmarked cop car." I point at it out in the street with a look of hopelessness.

Glancing at my car she says, "Umm, that's a police car all right." She contemplates for a moment and then says, "I have an idea. We can go in my car but you'll have to drive." She digs into her purse and holds out the key.

"It's in the garage." Attached to the key ring is a dangling Lexus logo.

She drives my dream car!

I dream about owning a Lexus but on department pay there is no way I can afford it unless I start taking bribes.
Only with great self-control do I keep from jumping off the porch and running to the garage. While she locks up the house I pull up hard on the garage door. A moment of silence takes place as I take it all in.

Dragging my fingers across the smooth and silky silver finish I make my way to the driver side door. As I open it the rich smell of the leather interior permeates my nostrils. I breath in deep as my butt slides into the seat. For a moment, just a millisecond, I almost forget that the most beautiful woman in the world is waiting for me.

Trying to impress her that I appreciate the extraordinary and exquisite things of life I back out carefully. I also want Lori to know that I can care for something, or someone special.

I stop backing up when she is at the passenger door and hustle around the other side to open the door for her. As she is seated she looks up at me and smiles. I'm in fantasyland. In the driver's seat I press the automatic door locks and try to be funny.

"I don't want you to escape!" I laugh certain that she gets my joke but she has a strange and curious look again.

The theater itself is impressive. The interior is elegant with deep, rich wooden pillars that elevate the ceiling toward heaven. Balconies surround the main floor which is covered in thick, plush carpeting. The walls are adorned in tapestries and carved mirror. The crimson curtains drawn together on the stage are highlighted by spotlights. Classical music plays.

I'd never would have guessed that there was so much interest in magic shows. The place is sold out.

I watch every man in the room watch Lori as we find our seats. It is obvious that they are as captivated by her as I am. Each of them knows that if she suggested an encounter they would fall to their knees. As Lori stares up at the stage with anticipation she takes my hand and squeezes it tight. The curtains rise among other things.

31

Megan was to meet the captain in the lobby an hour after the crew had checked into the layover hotel. They would steal away to an elegant, expensive restaurant and dine the night away. Aware of his weakness for younger women Megan planned to keep baiting him to keep him coming back for more. As she strengthened her position over time she would convince him to leave his wife and marry her.

As she finished with her hair and makeup at the mirror she stepped back to take one last look. She checked for lipstick on her teeth. The print top that accented her breasts and the short black skirt over black heels was perfect. She felt tempting.

Her plan went even better than she imagined. The conversation at dinner was some of the best she had ever articulated. She laughed at all of his jokes and sympathized with him for the failing marriage he said he was forced to endure.

After the bill had been paid they left the restaurant and decided to walk back to the hotel. It was a night she would never forget. The moon was glorious, the stars brilliant and the temperature perfect.

At her hotel room door Megan maneuvered her computer-encoded room key in and out of the lock. Nick asked politely if he could come in as she gently nudged the door open. She stepped forward lightly touching the collar of his shirt.

Whispering she said, "Nick, I don't think that would be a good idea. The other crew members are on this floor. Don't you think we should wait until ?"

In an instant and without warning she felt his hand contact her chest pushing her back into the room. She caught herself before falling to the floor. She watched as he closed the door behind him. Right before her eyes, Nick Parker changed from a charming, respectful gentleman into a malevolent beast.

The smile on his face was gone. As he walked toward her she stepped back until she felt the bed against the back of her knees. He shoved her again and she fell back onto the bed. Startled and afraid she asked, "What are you doing?"

Determined Nick commanded, "Take off your clothes."

The shock of what was happening paralyzed her. She could not get her arms or feet to move. She didn't have the courage to fight him. She could never have imagined that the he would behave in such a barbaric way.

As he removed his shirt he insisted, "I'm not going to say it again take off your clothes!" He raised a backhand and she ducked to avoid the impact. Although he did not deliver the blow she got the message.

Paralyzed by what was happening she could only stare at him. She thought to distract him long enough to get to the hallway or to the phone to call for help but instead she did as she was told. The scene passed by her in slow motion. After having believed she was stronger Megan now trembled uncontrollably.

He maneuvered out of the rest of his clothes. "Resisting will only excite me!" he said with scorn. Then almost casually he said, "If you do anything other than submit, I'll see to it that you're fired. You know that whatever story you tell won't hold up against the word of a captain! I have a lot of friends at the airline."

Trying to sound like he cared he added, "Don't worry, nobody will ever know about our dirty little secret."

The rate and depth of her breathing made her lightheaded. She couldn't remember how he forced himself into her. She regretted drinking the champagne. She felt foolish for thinking she could control him and closed her eyes tight while he unmercifully ravaged her. Frightened by her belief of his purported power over her, she did not resist. And then it was over.

He huffed as he got off of her. Megan lay on the bed motionless with her eyes still closed. She prayed that she would not remember the nightmare. She felt dirty, abused – violated. The thought that he might attack her again gave her a chill but he dressed at the foot of the bed while he watched her.

She waited for him to speak, to apologize, to say something that would convince her that he wasn't an animal. She wanted to hear believable words of remorse but the only words she heard included blame.

"You asked for this ? it's your fault!" He continued to berate her while he tucked his shirt into his trousers.

"You're no different than the other crafty, conniving little harlots looking to hook up with a financial portfolio. You use your bodies to tease…" he said as he looked down adoringly at his manhood, "…and then pretend you're surprised when you get this!"

As he slipped his loafers on he said, "By the way you play the fearful young prey part very well, I liked it!"

Megan was revolted and quietly cursed him inside. She wanted him to be afraid of her. She wanted him punished. As he leaned into her face she tried to hit him with an open hand. He caught it in midair. They stared at one another with looks that could kill until he released her hand. He ratcheted her neck and held it tight. Megan started choking.

"That's not going to work little girl, it's too late for that!" He released his grip on her throat.

Megan's shaking hands covered her face. She did not see him walk toward the door. Before Parker left her to the solitude of her hotel room he left Megan something else to think about.

"Remember, keep your mouth shut." He let a second pass. "By the way we'll do this again, soon. Maybe next time you'll really persuade me that I want to keep you!" He left with a contemptuous smile confident that she would not break.

It was awhile before Megan got up and walked into the bathroom. She removed her clothes and entered the shower where she washed over and over again. When she believed that she had cleansed away his dirt she dried herself.

As if sleepwalking she returned to the bed and abruptly tore away the sheets letting them fall to the floor. She curled up on the exposed mattress in the fetal position and cried. She stared at the clock until it was time to leave.

She knew that he would be in the van with the rest of the crew when they left for the airport. Normally talkative Megan sat quietly and did not engage any of the other crew members in conversation. She was sure they knew what had happened. Parker she thought probably bragged about it.

Although she did not acknowledge him she could feel his stare during the brief drive to the airfield. She felt sick.

32

"I got something!" The confident excitement in Harmon's voice was unmistakable. He was dancing as if he had just finished six months on the road with James Brown. Mika launched herself at him grabbing at his strong forearms.

"What, what've you got? Don't you screw with me, Harmon Blackwell, not in my present state of mind!"

Mika had been on edge waiting for something, anything to move the investigation forward. She had searched files and crime scenes hundreds of times. She shook Harmon hard. It felt as if the San Andreas Fault was quaking.

Harmon acted out boxing with her bobbing and weaving just to instigate. He added some irritating needling that caused Mika to go ballistic.

"Come on little woman, bring it on!"

He stopped dancing and took a casual look around the room. He saw that most of his co-workers were snickering behind hand-hidden smiles. As far as he could determine, he had to surrender.

"Okay Wonder Woman, you win!"

Fairchild was on the perimeter grinning. Mika stood in Harmon's face with her hands pressed against her hips.

"Give it up!"

"I talked to a guy out by Abrams' place, a guy we missed the first time around, a neighbor. The guy's been out of town visiting somebody, relatives. He just got back. He said he saw…" Harmon read from his notepad, "...a silver foreign car leaving Abrams' driveway as he was driving away that night."

Mika's gaze went through him. Fairchild's eyebrow arched. Everyone waited while she contemplated this development. Finally she said, "That's it, all of it?"

"Uh-huh." Harmon's proud smile slowly washed away and he no longer expected a victory hug from Mika.

"Okay, a late-model, silver foreign car," she repeated while turning away. "Okay, it's something, something is better than nothing." She thought for a moment and then in a flurry started shouting orders.

"I want to know who owns a late model, silver foreign car in a radius of fifty miles people!"

No one moved instead they deferred to Fairchild for guidance. He didn't have to say a word because a simple gesture would have been enough but he said it anyway.

"You heard the agent, get moving!"

The hustle began. Mika looked at him and mouthed the words "thank you".

Ed simply returned a smile.

33

It feels like we have known each other forever and that I have been born again. A lot fell out onto the table during dinner. The world looks pretty much the same to us. She hears what I'm saying.

As we walk to her car we pass beneath a halogen streetlight that illuminates the parking lot. She reaches to take my arm but that brings a grimace to my face.

"Jake, I'm sorry!"

"It's okay, just a little sore."

"I forgot, I'm really sorry," she says with great concern.

"Really, I'm fine." I cradle my arm. "You looked like you wanted to say something just before." I watch as my little *do jet d'art* shyly looks back at me.

"You'll probably think it's silly."

In all of my years on the job silly wasn't something I had found anything to be. I want her to feel at ease and comfortable.

"There is no silly, now stupid, I know stupid but not silly."

She hides a smile behind her hand. I watch her eyes come up to meet mine. She hesitates, studies and then decides to go ahead.

"I was wondering."

"About?"

"I was wondering what a Jake Roberts kiss would be like." Her eyes widened.

A Jake Roberts kiss? She wants to know what a Jake Robert's kiss is like?

All I have been thinking about is what a Lori Powers kiss would be like. The only thing I wasn't sure of was whether or not I should chance it. We were both at a time in our lives when we needed someone to make us whole, someone to love.

As my arms surround her Lori's hands slip around my waist and up my back. Our embrace intensifies as we anticipate riding on some kind of emotional wave. We hold on tight. Her lips press against mine and instantly I spiral up into another galaxy.

I forgot what passion was like and I had given up on love believing that I had been sentenced to the isolation of my cave long ago. But right now at this moment I'm not alone. Lori feels it too.

After the kiss she rests her head on my shoulder and whispers into my ear. "I liked that." Her head tilts back as she looks at me. "It's been a long time since I've felt this way, Jake."

If only women knew how sentimental and romantic men want to be, how much we want that special someone to come along and make us feel the way she made me feel.

We lock in another passionate embrace and kiss. The few moments it lasts causes all sorts of feelings to surface inside of me. The most important was feeling like a man again. The kiss ends and I can feel her trembling a little.

Softly she says, "Jake, I have never been kissed like that before." She smiles another incredible Lori Powers smile. "Have you been saving that just for me?"

A boyish grin appears on my face. No one ever said that to me before either. I wish I had something clever to say. For some stupid reason I'm thinking about how I learned to take down a suspect in the academy. It probably has something to do with the fact that I want to make love with her right now.

I just don't want to scare her off. It also has been a long time for me. Besides I don't want just a take-down. I want her for a lifetime.

"Command center to Roberts!" she says in an elevated tone as the sensual expression on her face is replaced with a smile.

"I was just thinking."

"About what?" she inquires.

My hand waves toward the billions of stars over our heads. "About how gigantic the universe is and how it keeps expanding, and about how one day it's going to implode and then all this will be gone." My eyes came back down from the stars and lock onto hers. "And I was thinking about what it would be like to spend all of that time with you."

"Do you mean that?" she asks assessing my sincerity.

"Yes, I do."

Lori looks up at the night sky. "I've dreamt about finding someone who feels like I do, who understands, someone who means what they say, someone with a heart."

We kiss surrounded in the silence of the night.

Not much else is said on the drive home. The open moon roof allows the fresh night air in. The radio is off. The scent of her carries me to another place. We hold each other's hands, neither of us wants to let go.

The garage door opens and I return the Lexus to its proper place.

We walk to the base of her front porch and I pull her close to me. With both of my hands I draw her face close and ask, "When can I see you again?"

"Jake…" she says with a slight tilt of her head, "… tonight means so much to me. I had lost all hope that there was someone out there like you." Her head falls onto my shoulder. "I have to fly in the morning but it's only a two-day trip. I'll call you the minute I get back in, I promise!"

Her words encircle my entire body while I float without a tether in the vastness of space. I run my fingers through the golden waves of her hair and down over her soft neck. Her hands feel warm against my chest. We say goodnight with one more kiss and then I watch her climb the porch steps. The walk to my car is only steps away but I struggle to get my feet moving.

The drive to my apartment is only a blur. Back inside I stare out the window and watch the streetlights blow out like candles on a birthday cake while a new sun rises over the buildings to the east. I want to call her before she leaves on her flight because I need to hear her soothing, healing voice again.

I don't need any more helpers because my pain is gone.

34

"You're wasting your time. He's just an old guy who barely remembers ten minutes ago! I think he's at half-zeimers. Besides I've already third-degreed him and I don't think he can take much more unless you want me to rough him up a little. Man's got to be a hundred years old!" Harmon's frustration was maxed out.

Where are you, Jake?

"Bring him in," Mika ordered. "Or if you think he'd be more cooperative in his own environment we can drive over there." Mika thought it over. "Oh forget it, let's go."

She reached behind her temporary office door and grabbed her FBI stenciled windbreaker. It was always a good idea to wear one for effect. On the other hand showing your weapon when talking to a witness had a bad effect. It had a tendency to make them a bit forgetful and nervous.

As they walked out to her car Mika stated emphatically, "Like it or not, I'm driving." She could not make out what he was saying under his breath but she had a good idea. It didn't matter she had a job to do and she was determined to solve the case.

Rolling his eyes Harmon hefted his mountainous frame into the passenger seat of her car. As she drove he gave her directions with attitude and accentuated pointing.

"Left, here!" he yelled.

"Give the sarcasm a rest okay?" She was getting frustrated. "I need your help not another pain in my behind!" Mika swung the wheel and the car careened around the corner. The weight of Harmon inside caused an imbalance and the car dipped to one side.

"Where's Jake? Isn't he on this case anymore?" Harmon groaned.

"You're asking me where he is? You're his partner! You're supposed to know where he is! Did you hear from him this morning?"

Mika was being nasty because her patience was nearly gone. She was also painfully aware of what her father had said about the two of them and how she still felt about Jake. She was also unhappy even jealous about the fact that he was interested in a female witness.

Focus girl, you have a killer to find.

Harmon looked at Mika and shrugged. "I think he's still whacked about the shoot. It's been hard for him. Heavy, would have been a big load for me! I honestly don't know how he stays in the game."

She looked back at Harmon distracted for a moment from her mission while the wheels turned a little faster inside her head. "He doesn't let on it's dogging him."

"Yeah, well I thought Abrams was going to help him out of it but that came to a screeching halt. He won't go see anyone else. He doesn't believe they can help anyway," Harmon replied. "Right, turn right, next light!"

When this is over, I'll be there for him.

As she made the turn the hookers standing on the corner didn't even draw an exclamation from Harmon. The turn put them right behind a traffic jam. Her small palm smacked the steering wheel as she surveyed the situation.

"This sucks!"

Changing the subject Harmon asked, "When do you have to head back to the Feds?" He watched a group of tough young black kids outside a food store. "You would have thought they would have been more help with all of their fancy computers and experts."

"Easy, don't forget I'm one of their experts." She looked out the side window at the traffic. "And why aren't we moving?"

Harmon reached for the door handle. "Want me to go see what's up? Most of these cars are small. I could clear a path for you! I'll start with that little Honda over there." His comments elicited a small laugh and subsequently eased some of the tension.

Mika sighed. "You know, Har, maybe I'm pushing too hard."

He shifted in the seat and caustically scoffed, "Ya think?"

In the passing of a millisecond they glanced at each other. The tone of his comeback started them laughing. It quickly escalated into one of those that couldn't stop. The two of them roared until their eyes were tearing.

It continued until Harmon held up his monstrous hands to call a truce so that both of them could concentrate on taking a breath. After their empty lungs filled with precious air it started all over again until Harmon forcibly yelled, "Hey, traffic is moving again!"

Mika recovered and shifted into drive. Both dried their eyes and were back on the job. As she drove slowly down the street Harmon pointed out the old man's house. Mika continued past Abrams' residence while she tried to visualize the killer's escape route.

Profiling was what she was trained to do. She had studied every word in Dr. Brussel's texts, the man who originated the concept. Her instructors at Quantico gave her everything they had learned from years on the job. Mika was there representing all of them. She was good at it, very good at it. Since she had been with the FBI she had tracked down some of the most prolific serial killers.

But the "Who's Your Daddy" maniac was by far her most challenging case. She could feel the burn in her stomach knowing that he had not been apprehended. It was taking too long and it was affecting her confidence level.

The flower bed in front of the windows had captured his complete concentration so the old man did not notice the car pulling into his driveway. As Mika and Harmon exited the car they heard him lament, "Too little fertilizer I guess."

"Mr. Dickens?" Harmon shouted. He startled the old guy causing him to turn so fast they feared he would lose his balance or worse yet suffer a stroke. Harmon even started dialing 9-1-1 but stopped when he saw the old man wave. Squinting Mr. Dickens held his hand over his eyes to see them approach.

"Hey, you're the policeman, aren't you? Back again?" Dickens asked.

"Yes sir, Detective Harmon Blackwell, I spoke with you early this morning. And this is Special Agent Mika Scott with the F-B-I." He said it slowly making sure he got through.

Mika held out her identification. The picture of her and the printing were far too small for him to read so he reached into his shirt pocket to retrieve his reinforced reading lenses. Harmon shot Mika an "I told you so" look.

Batting her pretty eyes at him Mika said, "Mr. Dickens, I'd like to ask you some more questions about what you saw the other night."

"I already told…" he pointed directly at Harmon, "…the colored boy all that I know."

Harmon rotated to look at Mika with his eyes scrunched together. "Why don't I give Roberts a call and find out where he is. I'll leave you here with the…with Mr. Dickens."

Not waiting for her permission Harmon walked toward the car and pulled out his cell phone. It was always difficult for his big fingers to hit the tiny keys so he used the eraser side of a pencil to punch them. Roberts's phone rang once. Surprise covered Harmon's face when Jake actually answered. He didn't know Jake was hoping it was Lori calling.

"Would you rather we stand in the shade, Mr. Dickens?" Mika led him by the arm as they moved beneath an oak tree.

"About that night you said you were leaving I understand to visit relatives?"

Dickens nodded. "That's what I told him."

"Which direction sir, were you going when you saw -"

Harmon was angry. "Where the hell are you, man? You're supposed to be out here doing your detective thing. I can't do all of this by myself. Mika's running my butt all over town!"

I want him off balance so I answer, "I love you, man." I can picture him shaking that big head of his.

The phone drops to Harmon's side while his other two fingers pinch the skin between his eyes. After the phone came back up he says, "That's funny...'I love you, man!' Please, please, don't go there!"

"So, where are you?" I ask.

"Well if you had been to the briefing you would know that Harmon Blackwell, "colored boy", broke the case wide open." It was his turn to yank my chain.

"You broke the case? Now who's the funny guy?" I make light of what he said but I realize how far out of the loop I am. While I was out trying to recover my heart and soul I apparently lost my focus. Harmon chides me.

147

"I'm here with Mika right now. We're in the middle of interrogating him. She's already slapped him a couple of times. He's bleeding from the cut at the corner of his mouth. I get a crack at him next."

"Really, so Sherlock where are you?"

"Abrams' neighborhood where a neighbor, a real old, frail, tiny white man is telling us everything he knows. He's our only lead. And I'm tired of covering for you so get over here. Heal already, you hear me! I feel your pain, but heal already!" He let it sink in.

"I'm on my way." I disconnect but wonder if she'll call.

"Was that Jake?" Mika asked as she approached Harmon.

"The very same Jake we all know and love."

"Where's he been?" she asked.

"Don't know, I guess we'll find out when he gets here. Get anything from the old man?"

"Not much, a little." She looked across the street at the deserted Abrams residence. "Mrs. Abrams is staying with relatives while she grieves. We're right here might as well go in and take another look around." As she crossed the street Mika was lost in her thoughts.

What am I missing?

35

"STOP – F-B-I!"

Mika shouted and bolted toward the rear of Abrams' residence just after opening the front door. The intruder didn't heed her command. He moved gracefully and fast. If she didn't know she was chasing a human she would have thought that the intruder had wings as he flew over furniture and out the rear entrance.

Harmon took off behind her simultaneously drawing his service revolver. He had no idea what she saw or whom they were in pursuit of. He just did his best to keep up. The sound of her voice trailed off as more distance separated them but he still had her in sight.

"GRAY SHIRT, BLUE JEANS, BLOND HAIR!"

Taking all of the necessary precautions before bursting through arched doorways and rushing around corners, Mika ran as hard as she could. She lost sight of the runner several times but caught enough glimpses to continue the pursuit. She heard Harmon's labored breathing behind her and prayed he could keep up.

The man appeared to be in his late twenties maybe early thirties but she wasn't gaining enough to be sure.

Come on Harmon!

Somehow Harmon was able to call for backup in between the wheezing. As he ran thoughts about chasing down running backs in college flashed through his head. His determination kicked up the adrenaline. Besides, he couldn't let it get out that a woman had beaten him to the goal.

Fences, trees, shrubs and homes blurred by them during the

chase. More distance opened up between the pursued and the pursuers. Mika's breathing was becoming painful. She prayed for enough wind to bring him down. Rather than shouting again she conserved her wind for the chase. Harmon shouted.

"SHOOT HIM!"

He thought the suggestion might give the runner something to consider but like the wind the runner flew ahead. Sirens wailed from at least three other directions but none of those entering into the race were close enough to assist. Harmon shouted directions and progress into his handheld radio.

Where's that damn chopper!

As she stretched her stride Mika saw reflections of the blues in windows and against buildings. Backup was near but her lungs were giving out. She slowed to a stop and finally succumbed. She bent over struggling to catch her breath. Harmon came up fast and passed her. She didn't see the grin on his face.

A patrol car pulled up alongside Mika. She quickly jerked back the door and lunged inside. In a desperate effort to continue the pursuit she shouted and pointed in the direction she thought the runner had gone.

The quiet neighborhood of Dr. and Mrs. Abrams was quickly disrupted by a small army of law enforcement officers as the search took on major proportions. K-9 arrived to track the fresh scent. The chopper began a circular search pattern overhead.

The runner knew that he couldn't out run a radio. There had to be some place to hide. Although he possessed strong lungs, swift moves and great cunning even the runner knew how badly a break in the action was needed.

As he turned the corner shelter from the ongoing pursuit came in the form of a small Presbyterian church. Frantically searching the exterior of the church he found an unlocked door and went inside.

Harmon had to give up. He had lost sight of the runner shortly after Mika did and staggered to a stop. Still straining for breath he managed to radio that he had lost the prey.

The entire area for several miles in all directions was cordoned off and a perimeter established. Buildings, residences, vehicles and foliage were searched. A command center was established and Mika began broadcasting details as she knew them. As I drove up Fairchild was getting out of a black and white.

Mika's tone was cold. "Nice to see you could make it!"

"What do you want from me?" I ask politely.

While Mika glares back I think about a sign I saw while racing there. It had a black background with white letters that simply said "Will the road you're on get you to my place?" It was signed, "God."

How clever was that?

Mika turned to Ed and started rambling. "All I saw was the gray shirt over jeans and the blond hair. He had a muscular build like he's spent a lot of time on a weight bench." Her eyebrows rose with an apparent respect for the perp's athletic abilities.

"And he's fast, real fast, he's got cheetah in his blood!" Her breathing is regular now. "He was in the house, didn't say a word – just bolted. The guy ran for a reason. He may just be some sick curious type but I want to hear that from him!"

The radios were alive with call-ins. We could hear K-9 boasting about their animals. Fairchild let everyone else fill in the blanks. I felt a hand on my shoulder and turned to see Harmon. Immobilized by fatigue he crouched over with hands on his knees.

"Are you going to make it?" I considerately inquire.

Harmon gave me a disappointed look because the guy wasn't in custody. He was also concerned that too many donuts over the years had slowed him down. "I should have had him man, I should've had him. That white boy was fast. We could have used him in that game against the Gators!"

Football was Harmon's life before he signed on with the department. He had scholarships to all of the Big Ten schools right up until his ankle got blown out.

Fairchild finally chimed in. "He's still in the area. He couldn't have gotten too far. You two ran him to death and I'm sure he's hiding out until he can get his second wind." Fairchild surveyed the surroundings and personnel present.

More calls came in. Everyone was convinced the runner was still inside the net. The guys in the chopper reported that there was no movement outside the perimeter. Patrol officers canvassed for witnesses and continued searching all vehicles in the area. We knew that if enough rocks were turned over he would turn up.

The church was empty. The side door was usually left open whenever the pastor was nearby attending to church business. The runner proceeded into the vestibule but didn't see anyone. He marveled at the beauty of the stained glass.

Religion was the opiate of the people - Karl Marx.

Standing beneath a statue of Jesus Christ who died to save all of mankind runner thought that his own efforts to save humanity would be heralded in heaven. But he had no misgivings that those who didn't understand would surely send him there with the lethal needle.

I'm just a gurney ride away!

His laughter was subdued, cold as his hand slid down over the inverted bleeding cross tattooed on his forearm. The inverted crucifixion implied a harder way for the crucified to die. The heart would palpitate while the victim choked on their own blood.

Evil has never disappointed me.

He heard a door creak open and dropped down low. The singing and humming emanating from the pastor grew louder. Scanning over the pews the runner watched as the minister placed a large vase with a huge bouquet of wildflowers on the altar. The man of the cloth took several steps back to observe the ambiance of the scene.

He fell forward as the blow struck the back of his head and lost consciousness immediately. Only the grace of God kept him alive.

"I could kill you!" the runner said. After contemplating, he added coldly, "And I could violate you!" The words, backed by the smug look on his face spoke volumes about the runner's disdain for the clergy. He believed they allowed evil to go unpunished. They were the real sinners.

But aware of the time constraints and his need to escape he decided against both actions. Instead he took the pastor's white collar and black cassock. The fit was close enough for him to pass.

"I'll be waiting for you in hell!" he said looking back at the pastor who was lying on the floor still unconscious.

36

The man wearing the white collar was driving Pastor McMichaels' year-old Lincoln Town Car. He smiled and tried to present an accommodating attitude to the officer. He knew he had to play the cop to effect his escape.

An officer signaled for the vehicle to come to a complete stop. "Where are you coming from, sir?" He stooped down to look inside.

"Antioch Presbyterian, officer." He waved in the direction of the church and said, "It's a few blocks that way."

"Yes Father, I know where it is," the officer answered impatiently.

"Pastor Powers my son, 'Fathers' are in the Catholic faith," runner explained.

"What happened to Father McMichaels?" the officer asked ignoring the statement of secular fact.

"Vacation officer, he's finally taken a well-deserved vacation. We've been encouraging him for years to take one but you know how stubborn he can be. I'm going to keep an eye on the flock while he's away." He smiled to reinforce the charade and quizzed the officer. "What's going on?"

The officer's partner indicated he thought the pastor was okay to leave. Before he released him the first officer said, "We're looking for a man wearing blue jeans and a gray shirt. He has blond hair like you."

"This person you're looking for is he dangerous?" runner inquired with a fearful tone. Runner put the car in drive and held the brake. "You must want to talk to him pretty bad judging from all of the commotion.

"We just want to talk to him that's all," the officer waved for him to move on.

"Good luck officer I hope you find your man. God be with you!"

With his escape assured the runner tossed the white collar out of the driver's side window a little over a mile down the road.

37

It had been days and still no sign of the runner. The only report filed was from a Presbyterian minister who had been assaulted and stripped inside a church in the area of the search. We did not know if there was a connection. We have not been able to find or even accidentally stumble onto anything tangible that could end the "Who's Your Daddy" killing spree.

Everyone except Ed was cranky. Mika didn't say much anymore. Harmon grumbled all the time. What we all needed was sleep. At least with Lori I had someone to lean on.

But seeing Lori over the past week had become difficult because of her flights and my work on the case. While the quantity of time that we spent together was meager the quality was helpful. We talked forever on the phone to try and make up for the separation.

Most times a significant other couldn't deal with police work but Lori remained intensely interested in mine. She listened, inquired about any progress in the investigation and cared deeply about my well-being out on the streets.

And while she was there for me I was there for her. She had been through a lot with her ex-husband after years of physically abusing her and running out on them. And her daughter's suicide was a heavy cross for her to bear. She really loved being a flight attendant a job a lot tougher than I or the traveling public realized.

"How's it going?" I ask as I walk past the cubicles on my way to Fairchild's office. A few familiar faces pop up. Wendy, our CID secretary, always asks about my arm.

The faces inside Ed's office aren't smiling. A hydraulic lift could not have raised the mood. I'm the last one to arrive as usual and close the door behind me.

"Now that we're all here why don't you get started?" Ed gestures toward Mika who is leaning against the wall. She looks at each of us with a somber face and takes a moment before speaking.

"As you know it has been quiet around here. Outside of the 'runner' there has not been any more information forthcoming from the Abrams investigation. Like all of the others whoever is behind these killings has covered their tracks well." Her sad facial expression deepens.

"The runner whoever he is or what he has to do with Abrams' murder remains a mystery. He could still be just some curious, weird guy that gets off on murder scenes." She looks at Ed then to Harmon and finally at me.

"Hey sometimes it just doesn't go the way we want."

Harmon takes a turn at consoling her. "We covered all the bases, turned over the rocks and nothing."

Ed, the forever optimist, interjects with, "It's not over. We're going to hear from the 'Who's Your Daddy' killer again. Sooner or later Judgment Day will come."

Harmon asks, "What about the Vidocq Society? You know up in Philadelphia. Do you know about them?"

Mika nods. "They're forensic professionals who donate their deductive and scientific talents in order to thaw "cold" cases. They're named after Eugene Francois Vidocq a brilliant criminal mind turned detective. Their credo is *Veritas Veritatum* – The Truth of Truths."

"They don't just do 'cold' cases. They also take on open homicides and disappearances." He looks at her and insists, "Hey, it's worth a try."

Mika shrugs. "When I get back to Quantico I'll give them a call. I guess it can't hurt. I'm willing to try anything at this point maybe even a clairvoyant."

She looks defeated. I have never seen her like this before. It is my turn to throw a lifeline in her direction. "Mika, maybe we ? "

With a wave of her hand Mika stops me. "Sometimes, it just isn't going to happen. I can deal with that. It's very frustrating though not being able to complete the puzzle."

Maybe dad's right, take the job and fall in love with you again.

"Anyway, the Feds aren't going to let me hang around with you guys forever as much as I would like to so I'm heading back to Quantico this afternoon. Maybe Wellington..." She drops her head and gives it a small shake. "He's such a jerk."

The "jerk" part relieves the tension and we all chuckle until Ed speaks up.

"Why don't you tell the FBI to stick it? Come back here and stay with us." He walks over, gives Mika a hug and because he gets away with it the rest of us line up.

"That sounds real good right now and I'm going to think real hard about it all the way back." She adds, "Who knows because I can't break this case they may find someone more talented to take it on." She held up her chin like dad said to.

"There isn't anyone more talented, they know it and we know it!" Ed smiles encouragingly.

"Thanks, Ed." She gives back a half-smile.

She looks at me and it feels as if we are breaking up all over again. I still have strong feelings for her in spite of my feelings for Lori.

I should have been there for her.

Everyone begins shuffling uncomfortably around the room. Ed is the first to say goodbye and again the rest of us follow.

Finally, to end the misery, Mika says, "I've got to get going. I'll call if anything comes up particularly if anyone turns up flat-lined." Her half-hearted laugh fades. "Bye, thanks everyone!" She gives a small wave before leaving Ed's office.

As I watch her walk toward the doors of CID I want to say something to stop her from going but the double doors close and I don't say a word. I turn and look at everyone in Ed's office.

The uneasy silence is a signal for us to return to the desks we're rarely at. We failed this time. The murderer is free to kill again. All we can do is hope that if there is a next victim some clue will put us hot on the trail. My partner leans over to me while I stare out of the window lost in thought about Mika and better times.

"Hungry?"

"No thirsty, I believe this one calls for an alcohol sedative."

38

Leaving CID I feel like a dead man walking – empty, hopeless. Harmon drags alongside. Everyone knows to leave us alone. The two front doors of the precinct swing open and we make our escape just like kids bailing out of school. Outside in the natural light of the sun, I squint.

"Where now?" is all that I hear him say the rest is indiscernible. We keep walking until we reach his car.

My inner detective is harping on me. I go over the Abrams crime scene again.

What was supposed to be there - was there. What had we missed?

There was also the possibility that there wasn't anything to miss. The killer could just be that good. The only witness if he could be called that was an eighty-year-old man with poor eyesight and a bad memory who thought he saw a silver foreign car leave the driveway about the time of Abrams' murder. I wasn't convinced he was sure it was the same day.

Harmon drives in silence until he utters one word that has nothing to do with the case – "sprites". He asks if I know what they are.

"They're bright red flashes with blue tendrils that blast out of the tops of thunderstorm cells for a few thousandths of a second for up to sixty miles." I had just read about them actually. "T-G-F's are terrestrially-generated flashes or upward lightning." I struggle trying to remember what else was in the article.

Philosophically Harmon adds, "There is some real cool stuff going on in this world all around us that we don't pay attention to."

He means Mika and my lament slips out before I can stop it.

"I wish she had stayed."

"Hey man, you going to be okay?" Harmon glances several times at me while driving.

"Yeah fine, there's no show here keep moving." I play it down and quickly assert, "It was just good to be around her again, that's all."

"I thought you were all hooked up with that Powers woman?" Harmon asks.

"I am, it's just that Mika and I go back a long way."

To prevent another sad Jake story he changes the subject with, "Too bad we couldn't find 'runner.' He's dirty, I can feel it. Why else did he take off? If he was just a fan he would have grabbed a souvenir! He was fast, Jake - fast!"

"Maybe he didn't have time to grab a souvenir." That's all I can think of to say. Actually I don't want to think about it anymore. I'm burned out about it. I need some Lori-time. My demons aren't around when she is. Maybe it's time to reevaluate my career.

"When are we going to stop for a few cold ones?" I ask.

"We're in the middle of the hood, Jake! A white boy, sorry, a red boy like you can get whacked out here for no reason! I'm looking for a safe place to ? "

"STOP THE CAR!"

"WHY?"

"STOP THE FRIGGING CAR!"

162

The tires screech and the car skids into the curb. I brace with my wounded arm because I'm not wearing my seatbelt. To my right between the crack house hotel and the Korean market is a dilapidated bar with a hand-painted sign over the entrance that says "Chipper's". I look back at Harmon with a raised eyebrow and the devil on my face.

Clint "Dirty Harry" Eastwood could not have played my exit from the car better. Standing on the sidewalk I smoothly look left and then right. Sizing up the territory and in plain view I slowly undo the strap securing my holstered Glock.

Harmon walks around the car and comes up behind me contemplating my apparent death wish as I confidently strut toward the door and stop to read the sign. The two brothers on either side of the door are in shock. As I step between them to enter the bar Harmon's hand grasps my shoulder.

"Are you sure about this, Geronimo?"

I stop and turn toward my backup. "A brave man once told me that if you are afraid to enter you may never know the friend that awaits you inside."

"He's dead now, right?" Harmon asks nervously.

I smirk but continue into hostile territory. It is the kind of place where they check you for weapons at the door. If you don't have one ? they give you one. When they see me the loud base tones stop, the casual conversations stop and the balls on the pool table roll to a stop.

The bartender cannot believe his eyes and asks, "What the hell do you want?"

I can't see Harmon behind me holding up his badge over my head. Nobody moves. I think I'm doing great so I head for the bar and take a seat. Harmon puts his badge back into his pocket and slowly sits down next to me. His head twists in all directions while

I order.

"I would like a cold beer." I watch for movement in the mirror behind the bar and see a few cue sticks come down off the rack. "Harmon, what are you going to have?"

The bartender has an impressive vocabulary but it is his heightened curiosity expressed in the form of a question that stands out. "Are you freaking crazy? Ain't nobody going to let you walk in here for a beer! I suggest you get the hell out before they bust up my place while throwing you two out!"

He spoke directly to Harmon but by the end of his sentence he is looking straight at me. "Why don't you do both of us a favor and get your black and white cop asses the hell out of here!"

"THAT'S RED ASS, MISTER!"

The startled bartender leans back aghast at my outburst.

"NATIVE AMERICAN..."

I pretend to recapture control through some mystical anger management technique.

"...and buy the house a round on me."

The silence is like that after a new fallen snow. I think I hear Harmon contacting God. He is either cussing me out or damning me for all of eternity. I hope everyone in the bar heard the part about the next round but all I hear is a single, powerful voice from a table toward the back and to my left.

"Give the *red* man one beer."

As I turn to acknowledge the man into my field of vision comes the largest black man I have ever seen – twice the size of Harmon. He sits beneath a shaved head. On either side of him sits an ugly whore. He has gold teeth from one corner of his mouth to the other with a diamond stud in both front teeth. His Armani suit must have cost at least a year's salary.

Two sawed-off shotguns are on the table in front of him along with one pink umbrella drink. With the snap of two fingers the size of legs the music starts and another bank shot is made on the pool table. The bartender pours our beer. Speaking with trepidation Harmon quietly gives me the man's history.

"His name is 'Chipper' as in wood chipper. He's the man here, proprietor of the establishment. Rep is that he cuts his victim allowing the soon to be deceased the opportunity to bleed to death slowly then it's through the machinery!"

Harmon accentuates the story with, "You think whoever killed Abrams is a bad ass? There's a bad ass. He knows it, too. And, he knows ain't nobody going to do anything about it." The urgency in Harmon's voice intensifies.

"The man spent a dime, ten long, hard years in deep solitary confinement. He killed several of his cell mates while in the general population. The Warden wanted him gone so bad that they just quietly let him go. 'Silent parole,' they called it."

My initial arrogance and demonstration of fearlessness dissipates in light of Harmon's revelations. Reality torpedoes my testosterone level.

"And listen to this red man, you can't kill this guy! He's been shot twenty-eight times, stabbed sixteen, strangled once ? they even tried to blow him up! He keeps coming back."

Trying to remain composed I ask, "Let me get this straight, you're saying there's a pretty good chance that our partnership could end right here?"

"Oh and I thought you were just plain ignorant but you're stupid, too?" He shakes his head in mock ridicule.

165

I drink my beer but try to be cool about it. I figure if it is my last I might as well enjoy it. I thank the bartender who returns a derogatory social comment as I toss a handful of cash on the bar.

Standing slowly I turn with my hands visible to everyone in the place. My partner leaves half a mug of ale behind. Harmon scratches at the back of his head while I look directly at "the man" and nod a thank you.

"Don't come back here!" is his terse warning. He points at the door. I walk backwards but facing Chipper. Harmon's back stays against mine as he takes the lead toward the door.

As we step outside we are surprised by the new gang-tagged paint on Harmon's unmarked. He drives me home. I really don't have much to say mostly because the last thing I want is for some girly whimper to squeak out from my mouth. I can sense Harmon isn't in the mood for clever banter anyway. He mostly grumbles about the inconvenience of having to get the car repainted.

Climbing out of the car in front of my apartment I wisecrack, "Good night honey, call me later?"

Harmon finally loses it. "You are one crazy bastard - DON'T EVER do that to me again!"

After watching him drive away I go inside. My answer machine light is blinking and there is a message from Lori. She is back but she was going to see Emily early and would catch up with me after that. She also said she missed me.

I think about calling her. I think about Mika. I think about "Chipper" and how I could have been recycled mulch.

39

The face in the mirror refuses to tell me where that young, energetic guy is now. I feel weak and have no doubt that a steady wind could easily blow me down. My partner called and offered a ride but I told him I was going to "work out" by walking in. It isn't that far and I need the exercise. And since Mika left there's no rush to get there. I decide to secure my tie later as I slide my holstered Glock into the back of my pants.

It wasn't possible to tell just how glorious a morning it was from inside the apartment with the shades pulled down. Burly, cotton-textured clouds float over my head and mares' tails drift through the alto-altitudes. The sun is already starting to singe the cobalt hue out of the sky. By noon all that would be left would be a faded, pale blue haze. The foliage is painted in deep shades of southern green. As I walk a gentle breeze pushes past my face.

Chipper didn't kill me yesterday.

I wonder who will. Maybe it would be a deranged suspect or the revenge-filled prison escapee or maybe it would be one of the militia girl's compatriots. The butt of my Glock digs into the small of my back.

The house is still blocks away and for some reason the walk feels farther then I remember it. My body is aching and in sad physical shape. As I pass the newsstand I toss a few quarters at Sylvester the newspaper guy for a morning paper. He looks like he has lived two lifetimes and yet he keeps going.

What's wrong with you, Jake?

Tucking the newspaper under my arm I pass by the parking lot and scrutinize it to see who is already in. Harmon's car is taking up two spaces. "Pig" was still splattered across the hood along with several other unsavory social comments from the night before. Fairchild's car isn't in his space, that was a good thing because now I won't get the "Where've you been, Roberts?" interrogation.

After climbing "Cop Mountain," all three floors in the only cop shop in the country without an elevator I head for my desk. A pencil ascends into the air above the cubicle next to mine. It does several ascending rotations like it's in the Pencil Olympics. On its descent I snatch it in flight. A head pokes up above the cubicle wall.

"Hey, that's my pencil."

As I toss it back the number two quickly gets snatched out of the air like a frog tonguing a buzzing fly.

I think about Harmon Blackwell. He's not only my partner, he's my best friend. He never loaned me money or donated a kidney for me but I love him like a brother. I never found much value in material possessions. I have Harmon. He keeps me going in this crazy, screwed-up world.

"You beat the man in, you're so lucky, Roberts!" Harmon chuckles. It is a boisterous, sneaky kind of laugh. "It's a good thing too because I'm not covering for your sorry butt anymore!"

That's what he says but isn't what he means. Partners understand all of the intricacies of mood swings and personality dysfunctions.

"Are there any new corpses lying around? I want something to do, I'm bored." My feet find a place between some reports on my desk. The usual anthill activity prevalent in the office any other day of the week is nonexistent today.

"No bodies," one detective interjects.

"How are we going to justify our very existence? We're investigators, we need something to investigate," I complain while my sore arm pinches just to remind me about the real world I operate in.

"Chipper called looking for you." Harmon says across the desk. His grin is priceless.

40

Ed flipped open the cover of his notepad and said, "What have you got, I haven't got all day and I need a name for the reward money." He wanted the guy to know that he was an impatient man. The guy was weird, jittery - nervous.

"Not here, it's not safe," the man insisted.

Fairchild took the call early. He got to the office before anyone else hoping to review the Abrams case file and find that hidden clue. Sometimes the mind will eventually see something it saw a hundred times. All he wanted to do was help Mika. She was family, special and that meant a lot to Ed. He didn't want to let her down. He wanted his protégé to make it in the big time.

The call came in asking for him personally. There was no one else around for backup. He had been there before forced to deal with an obscure nobody with some hot information. The news had broadcast little progress on the case but mentioned that the reward ante was upped. The male voice on the phone gave instructions on the meeting place. He sounded sincere.

So there was Ed standing in a parking lot with a guy who claimed to have important information and the guy was terrified of something or someone. The man in his late twenties maybe blond hair was concerned about his safety. Ed surveyed the deserted lot and didn't feel the same sense of urgency.

What's with all of the drama?

"Let's go inside. I don't want to be out here where we can be seen!" the mystery man said. He walked away leaving Ed to ponder the intrigue. Reluctantly Ed followed him. He wasn't at all concerned about his safety but as an avowed homophobic Ed had other distracting concerns.

The man walked ahead of him and opened the door to a rundown, deserted warehouse leaving the door to slam in Ed's face. That made him mad.

What's with this guy?

Ed jerked the door open and went inside. It was pitch black except for the blinding sunlight stream through a large window directly across the way.

He felt the painful, numbing voltage from the stun gun and it took him down. That was the last thing he remembered. It had been too many years since Ed had worked the streets. He wasn't as sharp as he used to be. The skills of the once lightning-fast, young detective had diminished during his service behind a desk.

When he started to come around he had a severe headache and his vision was blurred. He was surprised to find himself tied to a bed and naked.

"What the -"

He tugged at the bindings that secured his wrists and ankles. Some of what Fairchild called the devils music was playing in the background. He could barely make out any of it. The song ended and instantly went into repeat. The music irritated Ed but it was the guy's voice and words that held his attention.

It was clear that the lawman was no longer in charge. Ed watched the guy read from the identification card inside his wallet while sitting on the bed next to him.

"Edward Fairchild, Chief Inspector, Homicide."
In days past Ed had seen some pretty scary sights. He lived through Vietnam and saw the vicious horrors of war. He had been in more than his share of fire fights on the job. He investigated senseless, violent and gruesome murder scenes over the years but the fear and revulsion he was experiencing now far surpassed all

of those.

His assailant used isolation and control, the same tactics that Ed used against suspects during interrogations. On the wrong side of it now Ed was vulnerable. He needed to stay calm and think.

While he struggled to find a way out he believed in all probably it was going to be his last day on earth. He would never again see his wife of all those years, the children he raised or his grandchildren. He couldn't help it a man his age, he wet the bed. Embarrassed he closed his eyes.

"Ed!" The perp shook his head and scolded. "Look what you've done!" Then with mock compassion he said, "Aw don't worry I won't tell anyone but really you should be ashamed of yourself." He contemplated while he looked at Ed. "Actually the blood will mix with it and your secret will be ours forever."

The man was visible now. Ed's eyes and head had cleared. His dignity damaged beyond repair he tried desperately to exhibit strength. He used the nickname given the man after the chase.

"Are you him ? the 'runner'?"

"Runner? I don't...oh wait I get it that's what you call me, from the other day! Oh, I like that ? *runner!*"

The look of satisfaction on his face was more than telling. He was enjoying the attention. While the perp mulled over his infamous nickname Ed took the opportunity to try and establish some kind of rapport with his captor.

"Do you have another name?"

"I do have another name. And you know what? I'm going to give it to you, Chief Inspector Fairchild; it is Michael, like the archangel and Gates, like the rich guy."

He got up and circled around to the foot of the bed while he spoke.

Fairchild's hunter eyes followed his every move. If there was any possible chance to get out of this Fairchild was ready to take it.

"In fact because I'm going to kill you Chief Inspector I owe it to you to tell you all about me." Gates stopped and thought for a moment. "I watched Thaddeus Abrams die."

Fairchild's eyes grew wide.

"From a closet I watched Abrams get whacked and I mean whacked! She cut off his dick and stabbed him to death!" Gates grimaced pretending to be sickened and produced a fake shudder to highlight his supposed revulsion.

"That crazy woman was ruthless. In the beginning I was frightened but then I got hard you know, hard. Can you believe that? It was amazing!"

The excitement in Gates' voice sent a cold spike up Fairchild's back. The perp was illuminated and appeared to be otherworldly. There was nothing in the training manuals on how to deal with this kind of psychopath. Fairchild listened, studied him and prayed silently.

As if some calming force had just fallen over him Gates' demented demeanor shifted to a more conservative one.

"I should probably back up a little." He smiled. "I was a patient of Dr. Abrams." Gates' tone dropped to an almost apologetic whisper. "We were lovers."

Fairchild's wrists began to bleed as the bindings cut into them but he welcomed the pain as a sign that he was still alive.

There is always a chance!

"You were lovers?" Ed's voice rose.

"Yes Ed, lovers. Thad hated his old lady and her domineering ways. Anna was the one with the money. She dangled it over his head and made him dance like a marionette for it so he wanted her dead. He knew that I had previous experience in that area when I came to him for counseling."

"He was bound by law to tell us. Why didn't -? He worked closely with the department!"

"Ed, stop - please!" Gates said pressing his cold index finger against Ed's lips. "Don't try to figure it all out. Thad was a very complicated man. He wasn't the man you thought he was – end of conversation."

The fact that Gates had touched him was sickening enough and Fairchild wanted to throw up. From his lips Gates' finger traced up Ed's face to his forehead. He began stroking Ed's white hair. Fairchild tried to turn away causing Gates to stop.

"What's wrong Ed, afraid of the other side? Don't be so upset, I don't want you in that way."

Ed's lips pressed tight together. All he needed was a weapon, any kind of weapon and Gates' miserable life would be over.

Dammit, let me take him down!

"I don't like that look in your eyes, Chief Inspector. Here I am spilling my heart and soul out to you and all you want to do is kill me."

Gates stood up and began pacing rapidly. He would stop, think, start pacing again, stop and glance at Ed again. He became agitated and appeared to be debating what to do next.
Fairchild tried to sound consoling. "Michael listen to me, this can stop right here, right now. I will do everything in my power to get help for you!"

Gates' outburst came like a verbal tsunami.

"I'M NOT FINISHED TELLING THE STORY, ED!"

He took a breath. "Let me finish the story." Gates held his tirade for a beat then shook off his anger during a brief private conversation he had within his mind. When he felt he had regained his composure he spoke again.

"He wanted his wife dead, you see. I offered but Thad said no way that he wanted to keep me out of it. We talked about it every time we were together. Then she entered the picture and Thad got a major heterosexual hard-on, and guess who got pushed aside!"

Gates became more agitated. Turning toward Fairchild he stiffened his body language. He sat back down next to him.

"About the time he realized that she was a very bad girl well, I think that's when he lost interest in her...at least sexually. And that's when he came up with the idea to get her to kill his old lady. He said that he really loved me and after the wife was gone and the money was his we would go away together."

A detective to the very end Fairchild needed another piece of the puzzle.

"Who is she?"

"Lori Powers. Thad invited her over to his house that night for what he referred to as 'additional, required therapy'. It was nothing more than a scam. He pretended to be concerned for her and she fell for it. After she arrived he spewed the plan about whacking his old lady." Gates shrugged it off as if it was an everyday occurrence.

"She was stunned that he knew about her but she stayed pretty mellow, cool. She played him like I had never seen before. I was in awe as I watched. I was supposed to stop her if she got out of control but then as I said, it was such a rush!"

The blade glistened from the light in the room. Gates stroked it with a white cloth alternating between wiping it clean and buffing it. Fairchild squirmed and tugged at the ropes while Gates got up and started pacing again. He watched Ed struggle and read his eyes.

"Don't fight it Ed, it's like being in space - no one can hear you scream."

Stalling for time and advantage Ed queried his captor with, "So why this? Why me? What do you gain by killing me?"

Gates froze in mid-step and nonchalantly looked at his victim. "That is a very good question, Ed." With that said, he pointed the knife directly at Fairchild and made a motion as if cutting from ear to ear. He smirked. "You see Ed, oh I'm sorry I never asked you if I can call you Ed. May I call you Ed, Ed? Oh never mind it's not going to matter in a minute or so."

Fairchild tried to pull hard enough to rip his hands from his wrists so he could slip out. He would kill Michael Gates with the stumps that remained. His pulse rate spiked.

"The reason you are going to be sacrificed if you will is because of my enormous respect for her. As I said I'm in awe of her. She's the Mistress of Murder – so beautiful, so flawless!"

His hopes of escaping faded as he listened to Gates' continued ranting. Having burned up every once of energy he had left while struggling to get free Ed lay back on the bed breathing heavily.

"I watched her, Ed. I knew I had to emulate her. Is that the right word? I knew that I needed to if I was ever going to take her place. So I'm going to do to you what she did to all of them only I'm going to get caught. And then I'm going to confess to all of her murderous sins!"

Ed had to force out "Why".

"Why what, Chief," Gates asked.

"Why get caught, what does that do for you?"

"Fame Inspector, it gives me a special place in criminal history." Gates took a seat at the foot of the bed. "I lost the one I loved, she killed him. I have nowhere to go, no one to love and nothing left. I am nothing. The only way I can punish her for what she took from me is to take away her glory and fame. I'm going to steal her thunder."

Ed knew it was over and became sullen.

"But, because I understand her and because I understand the act and crave it like she does I must defer to the high priestess so that she can continue."

"But if you are caught and she kills again doesn't that take away your fame?"

Gates stood up and walked around the bed to Fairchild's side. He started to stroke Fairchild's hair again making him squirm.

"Once I confess she will have to go underground. Oh, she will kill again and the cycle will start all over but no one will connect her to any of the previous murders."

Fairchild started to object but Gates interrupted. "And now, and this is going to make you very sad I'm afraid, it's time, Ed."

Fairchild pleaded, "No, no, wait! I've got children and grandchildren! I have a wife who loves me!"

"If you scream I'll only like it more, Ed!" A demonic look appeared on Gates' face. He raised the hand with the knife high over his head then brought it down hard and fast.

Fairchild thrashed with everything he had left. His eyes squeezed tight and his flush face crunched. His scream was deafening but he didn't feel the penetration or the pain. A shuddering, shaking Fairchild opened his eyes to see a telephone in his face. Gates' other hand held the knife an inch above his heart.

"Ed, now that you know how serious I am about this, I've got something for you to do." He waited for Fairchild's deep breathing to slow and wiped his forehead with the white polishing cloth. "Here, drink some water."

Gates held out a plastic bottle of water for Fairchild to drink from. At first Fairchild pulled away but thinking it might buy some time he leaned forward to drink. The parched feeling in his mouth and throat dissipated. His breathing was shallower but still pronounced. He watched his assailant and his executioner closely.

"I'm going to call your office. I want you to tell them where you are and what is going to happen to you. Also, I want you to tell them who I am - tell them I am the killer. Can you do that?"

Ed nodded and trembled while Gates dialed the telephone. After the second ring Fairchild's secretary answered.

"Chief Inspector Fairchild's office, Wendy speaking, can I help you?"

"I need to speak directly to someone in authority regarding Ed Fairchild's murder," Gates said calmly.

"Excuse me, could you repeat that, sir?"

"Yes, I'm about to murder your boss Ed Fairchild and I would like to talk to someone in charge before I do. I'll hold but not for very long."

Gates heard Wendy cover the receiver and mumble directions. He fully expected the phone line to be traced but he didn't care. He smiled mockingly at Fairchild as any one would when they were put on hold.

41

"SIR, SIR?"

Wendy frantically asked if the caller was still on the line. The answer came slowly as if it was taking every bit of his patience.

"I'm here."

"Sir, Detective Blackwell will be taking your call. He's on his way to the telephone now." She was frightened and shaking so severely she didn't know if the words that she said came out correctly.

"Thank you." Michael Gates waited and watched Ed struggling against the bindings.

Harmon was gruff and not at all amused when he picked up the phone. "This is Detective Blackwell. Who am I speaking with?"

"Harmon, Harmon Blackwell?"

"And you are?" Harmon snapped back.

"Just can't run like you used to huh, Blackwell?"

"What's that supposed to mean?"

"This is 'runner'! According to Ed here that's what you call me."

Harmon was staggered momentarily but quickly recovered and dropped into his professional mode. "Can you prove you're the 'runner'?"

"Hum, well let's see how many people know that nickname or better yet how many runners does it take to assault a pastor, or how slow is a big, dumb homicide dick? I could go on but what's the point? Listen, he may ramble a bit - I'm about to "Daddy" him if you get my meaning. Listen closely Harmon because the next sounds you hear will be Ed's last." Gates smirked while holding the receiver next to Ed.

Harmon's hands waved in every direction for quiet. He shared the phone with Jake. They waited. A weak and exhausted voice came on the line.

"Harmon?"

"Ed?" Harmon timidly asked.

"It's true Harmon, the runner has got me!"

"Ed, what the ?"

"HARMON, LISTEN TO ME!"

Ed stared hard into Gates' face. "The corner of Twenty-third and Delaney, brown warehouse, I don't know any more than that."

"You hold on Ed, we're on our way!" There was movement and a voice in the background.

"LISTEN Harmon, I'll be dead before you get here! The perp's name is Gates, Michael Gates." The phone was jerked away from Fairchild but they could hear him shout in the background. "Tell Lucille I love her!"

Gates started to speak but Harmon cut him off.

"You touch him and I'll kill you with my bare hands."

Calmly, dispassionately Gates replied, "I've been waiting for someone to complete my suicide detective for a very long time." He placed the telephone back on the receiver. There was no mistaking the look of resignation on Ed's face. Gates simply shook his head.

"I'm afraid it's time, Inspector."

His heart pounding out of control Ed focused on the eyes of the man who was about to end his life. He said goodbye to his wife again and followed that with a brief prayer for the salvation of his soul. Gates allowed him to finish the litany before he leaned over and whispered.

"Ed, I promise I won't rape you."

Ed Fairchild's last thought was the contemplation of that final statement. His mouth opened, his face contorted, his eyes froze and his last breath escaped.

As he had witnessed with Abrams, Gates replicated every detail of Lori's heinous acts although the thrusting and stabbing was far more vigorous. He cherished each penetration of the blade until he felt the rush of an orgasm.

Gates slowly backed away from the bed. The victim's genitals lay on the dead man's abdomen. The knife protruded upward from the center of the chest. He ruthlessly proved that the blood would mix with the urine forever obscuring their secret. He kept his promise and did not rape Edward Fairchild. The haunting song repeated.

He felt strong again. Gates knew he missed the hunt and the kill. Since he had hooked up with Abrams he had gone dormant. Now, he was alive again. It truly was unfortunate he thought that it would all be over soon.

The white cloth was dipped into Fairchild's blood and the word "Daddy" was written in blood on the wall. He left the CD playing. He had to leave some things behind for the "stupid cops" to tie it all together.

Michael Gates, the sick, demented serial killer that he was calmly walked away from the warehouse and listened for the footsteps of fame to catch up with him.

42

There are times when you cannot move fast enough. You desperately claw at space and time but the harder you fight, the harder it fights back. Obstacles that would otherwise not have hindered your progress find their way into your path. I can't get to Ed fast enough to save him.

I'm driving because I have to. I don't care about Harmon's complaints or who is in the way. We narrowly miss pedestrians and other vehicles as I swerve. The tires screech, sirens wail and blue lights flash. Harmon is alternately screaming, and crying.

I want Gates. I want him bad! I want to jam my Glock into his mouth and kill him. I want to save Ed. The second hand of the clock inside my mind sweeps faster. The seconds Ed has left are counting down. Ed had found me and believed in me. He taught me how to survive.

One more street and we're there. I can see the warehouse. SWAT teams leap out of their vans into the parking lot and surround the building. Black and whites cordon off the dirty street. Unmarked cars arrive from every direction. We all want to save him. Ed is the only father most of us ever had.

We're almost there Ed, hang on!

I slam on the brakes and the car stops abruptly in front of the doorway. Two uniforms are already there with their weapons drawn. A vice detective from the house comes out of the warehouse with a nine-millimeter Berretta in his hand, crying.

Kicking my door open I jump out of the car. Harmon grabs the detective, Williams I think his name is. He is sobbing and can barely answer.

"We're too late," he finally forces out.

"Where?" Harmon shouts. "Where?"

"Second floor…back -"

The detective's voice fades as we sprint inside and up the back stairs. As "We're too late" reverberates inside my head I know there is no need to use precautionary entry tactics. My whole body is tense and my hands are trembling. I don't want to go in.

I can't…

"Oh my God, no!"

I'm riveted by what I see, can hardly breathe or look away. Collapsing inside, I fall back against a wall. My Glock is gripped tightly in my fist. Any justification I had for mankind evaporates instantly. I reach out for Harmon but he is lost in his own horror.

Ed is lying in a river of blood like a sacrificial lamb with his arms outstretched. He looks as if he is waiting for an embrace from God. My hand slowly rises to cover the open space of my mouth. Tears burn and sting my face on their way to the floor. After all of the years on the job I thought I could take it, was prepared, desensitized…

Harmon is weeping, everyone in the death chamber weeps - the room awash in heartbreak. The paramedics push through us. They are the only ones at the scene still holding onto a glimmer of hope that Ed might still be faintly lingering. They are wrong.

I don't know how but I make it to his bedside. His vacant eyes stare upwards as if he was searching for his Maker. His body is mutilated. Blood is still foaming out of his mouth, nostrils and each wound. I reach out slowly to touch his still warm face.

"I'm sorry." He cannot hear me or see my tears. "I'm sorry, Ed!"

Harmon comes up behind me and we lock in a hug. All of those who have raced to protect Ed Fairchild begin to slowly file out of the building. Nothing is right anymore, nothing makes sense. Evil is still one step ahead of the good.

But right now, after the evil, it is up to Harmon and me to find Ed's executioner. It's our case. The impersonal detachment necessary of one human being to investigate the death of another is now required of us. We will have to bury our pain and wait to mourn another day.

We have to find the "Who's Your Daddy" killer or "runner" – Michael Gates. Now, it's personal. I make a silent promise to Ed.

I'll find him, I swear – he'll pay for this!

Harmon quietly asks, "You want me to call Mika?"

I nod because I know I can't do it. I know that I will lose it for good. There is only one mind-set now, just one. I don't care about anything else.

Harmon turns away from me and heads for a corner of the room. His hand draws out his cell phone and the number is dialed. I watch him wipe away tears thinking about how it is going to devastate her. I can barely hear him say it.

"Mika…Har, I'm afraid…you won't believe…"

That's all I can take. I close my eyes and picture what his words are doing to her. I never could take it when she cried. My fingers press against my temples.

His head shakes as he gives Mika the details. He stops talking and turns to look at me. Again, he shakes his head and stares at the floor while giving her time to absorb it all.

There is work to do. My grieving will have to wait. I draw two latex gloves out of my pocket to begin the process of evidence collection. The others have already put in a call for the crime lab along with every other resource that the department has to offer. I already know the victim, the where, and the how. When I find Gates I will find out the why – right before I put a bullet in his brain.

The process is simple and we can do it in our sleep. The cardinal rule is to not touch anything and contaminate the crime scene. Even in the initial dark moments when each of us burst into the room we were careful not to contaminate it.

I shout orders. The paramedics leave knowing their attempts to revive him are futile. They did their job and know when to leave so we can do ours. Other homicide detectives search inside. Uniforms roam near and around the outside of the warehouse searching for any possible clues no matter how minute or obscure. A few uniforms canvass for witnesses.

SWAT, whose primary function is to take down violent offenders on-site, is not needed here. They offer to help in any way but I tell them to pack it up.

The crime lab truck arrives and the technicians assail the area with brushes, tape and the other tools of their trade. The department's photographer knows her craft and captures the scene properly on film. The flash goes off repeatedly. Because the latest victim is one of us everyone works harder.

Someone has to call Lucille. Notification of next of kin is difficult enough when you don't know the victim. It's impossible when you do. Again, Harmon does the dirty job. I can't face Lucille or the kids either.

"I'll extend the departments condolences," Harmon says quietly.

Outside, members of the media are swarming. I hate them almost as much as I hate Gates. They are demanding to come inside with "It's the public's right to know" as their litany. I try my best to protect Captain Edward Fairchild's dignity despite the fact that I was unable to protect his life. I look over at him. A little over an hour has passed.

Out of my pocket comes my cassette recorder. I start recording the gruesome details. The initial significant notable difference between Ed's murder and Abrams' is that this crime scene is ripe with clues.

The postmortem changes begin with Rigor mortis decomposition succeeded by the liver mortis skin discoloration. Ed's body is cooling down, I can feel it. The techs finish with the body and make room for the coroner's people. The M.E., affectionately nicknamed "Quincy" by all of us, officially declares my captain and friend deceased. Even hearing the word sucks.

The body bag is lying open on the gurney. With all due care and respect they lift Ed's body and place his remains inside. The sound of the closing zipper is like fingernails on a blackboard. The process is cold and clinical. It has to be even for Ed; otherwise we would all lose our minds.

Officers and investigators stop what they were doing and watch as he is taken away. Sobbing is heard everywhere. I watch scenes flash through my head of the good and bad times with Ed.

He always had that quirky smile that said he thought life was really a bucket of crap wrapped in wishful thinking. Not long ago over a cold one, during a discussion of human mortality, he said we were actually dying every day of our lives from the time we were born. "There is no escape." He proved that theory today.

I had learned a lot about life from the perspective of a man who had seen more than his share of it. Sometimes, I didn't get what he was talking about and sometimes I did.

Harmon broke into my memories. "Mika is on her way."

I never wanted her to leave. I thought of a million excuses to get her to come back but not for this reason. Still, I was glad she was on her way.

43

The rage was there along with the control and domination. The body position and the killing technique were the same ? multiple stab wounds and castration. Ed had struggled for freedom as evidenced by the wrist and ankle marks. Similar restraints were used. There didn't appear to be any sexual assault. Painted on the wall was "Daddy." It was the same but not the same.

As I talk into my cassette recorder Harmon walks over with a CD hanging on a pencil.

"It was playing when Williams first busted in. He turned it off just before we got here. The CD player is set to repeat song number three. Maybe Mika will be able to shed some light as to its significance."

"We'll listen to it when we get back to the house. Did they get your conversation with him on tape?"

"I got it all. I swear, I swear on my mother's eyes!"

"I know." My hand finds his huge shoulder and I grab tight. I want to make Gates suffer, too. "Any witnesses?"

"The guys are still out there looking. It's a bright, sunny morning and it's not even nine yet. Someone had to be around, somebody must have seen something."

We keep our own anger and rage harnessed in as best as we can. We need to stay focused and check the emotional baggage. As I look to see how much tape I have left on my cassette recorder my cell phone rings.

"Tell me it isn't true! You tell me Ed Fairchild is alive!" Mika forces out, "This is madness, absolute madness! The world has gone insane! I was just with him!"

It's difficult enough without hearing her cry. There's nothing I can say to make it any easier.

"Har and I are still at the scene. We have enough right now to hang this guy! We'll have more by the time you get here," I tell her quietly.

She struggles to say it. "I'll be there soon."

"GOT A CLEAN PRINT!" The tech is ecstatic. "I'll take it to the lab and get started. I should have something for you by this afternoon."

The CD player and the CD have clean prints that appear to be the same. I have an uneasy feeling that in his enthusiastic state of mind the technician might very well lose them both. A vision of O. J. Simpson's botched investigation passes through my mind. I watch the tech carry them as if they were a human heart being transported for transplant.

With a heavy sigh Harmon asks, "Fingerprints, CD, various fibers and blond hair strands? What's up with this guy? He's never been this careless before!"

"Game's over? Time ran out? He wants to get caught? If he is as intelligent as we think he is he probably has another plan, an out, you know like insanity. Who the hell knows? Who can figure out what's in their heads."

Harmon tosses out "Mika?" at me.

That one is easy to acknowledge. She would know. I really don't care why he wants to get caught. I just want to stop him and I'm willing to do that any way I can.

A uniform bursts in shouting, "We've got a witness!" He can hardly breathe from the hundred-yard dash he has just run. We give him time to stop hyperventilating but anxiously prompt him. Swallowing hard, the officer provides the information.

"A guy down the street was walking his Doberman. He saw a male in his late twenties to early thirties, blond hair, ponytail, casually driving a late-model silver Lexus out of the parking lot right here!" His hand points to the floor.

"Do you think it was Gates?" Harmon looks at me then turns to the officer and asks, "Did he get a plate?"

"Yes sir, Alpha-Nine-Three-Lima-Golf-Tango. He wrote it down, no mistake! He said it was as if the guy didn't care if he saw it." The excited officer beams proudly. "I found him across the street, waiting. Said he didn't want to interfere until we finished up. He said he didn't want any of us beating him to death by mistake.

"What a jerk!" Harmon exclaims.

Sometimes the public's mentality is dumbfounding. You can only blame so much on the gene pool. Harmon shoves the officer in the direction that he wants him to go.

"Call in and tell them what you've got. Get me an address, telephone number – anything!" he orders. Turning to me Harmon says, "He's making this too easy."

"Who cares? We'll follow the trail he's leaving and take him down."

From downstairs I hear another officer scream out my name. We converge halfway. I can tell he is seasoned because the information he carries is presented with urgency but with far less drama.

"Anything on the plate?"

"Better, a black and white's tailing him as we speak."

44

"Alive!"

Harmon shouts into his radio. "Do you hear me? Stop the vehicle but do not take him! Advise that we're on our way!"

We vault into my filthy, unmarked car. We can't have some angry, overzealous officer taking him out before his time, unless it's me.

As usual, Harmon protests about not driving but it doesn't matter. All that really matters is that Gates is taken alive.

"Damn Jake, this is too good to be true! What's up with this guy? Clever enough to elude capture through multiple murders and then suddenly he's brain dead? I don't get it!"

"Let's just get there. We can analyze him after."

I stop talking and concentrate on driving, on Ed and on a psychopath. Harmon's hands wave in all directions trying to keep me from killing us or someone else before we get there. My adrenaline is maxed out.

"I can't wait!" Harmon squeezes out. He is the first to see where they have Gates boxed in and his hands flail around blocking my view. "That's it, that's it, stop the car!"

Sure as taxes, it is a late-model silver Lexus. Sure as death, the plate numbers match. And sure as hell, inside waiting patiently is Michael Gates.

The Lexus is surrounded on all sides by officers braced behind their cars with weapons drawn down on him. Both of his hands are locked on the steering wheel. My braking technique almost costs Harmon some teeth as my car screeches to a stop.

"WHAT'S WRONG WITH YOU, MAN?"

The senior officer on the scene approaches us as we exit my car. I study Gates from a distance of about thirty feet.

"Plate, car and perp's description are dead on," the sergeant says.

The sergeant takes us aside and looks around to see if anyone is listening. With an emotional plea on Ed's behalf he suggests something barely above a whisper that would invite criminal charges against us. "I think we should finish it right here. I'd hate to see some lawyer, judge or jury let him walk, you know what I mean?"

There is no doubt we all had the same thought. We have all seen the bad guys walk when they should have fried. Not an hour ago I would have shot Gates myself, still might, but Harmon gets in the sergeant's face and gives him a stinging reply.

"I want him by the book!"

"Just a thought," he mutters, "he's all yours."

They all loved Ed. I hope that my reassuring nod is enough. It's hard to keep a cool head at a time like this when everyone's emotions are peaked. It's never easy but that was where all of the training had to come in. I have to drop the personal side of it at least for now.

Surveying the area I see the media hounds sniffing at the scene. Gates sits patiently knowing if he moves he is a dead man. It's not his time, yet.

"I'm taking command of the scene, Sergeant," Harmon commands. "Order him out, and I don't want to hear a single gunshot! I hear shots and I'll personally shoot whoever fired them ? clear?"

"Yes, sir!"

The officer turns rapidly and shouts the order into his radio. We watch as the officers holding a perimeter around the Lexus execute their duties professionally as they are trained to do.

Within seconds it's over. Gates is cuffed and in custody. They are reading him his rights as we approach. He stares at me the entire time as if he knows something I don't. I can't wait to get him to the station and start tearing him a new one.

For Harmon this is the man who outran him during the chase and the man responsible for multiple homicides, but more importantly this is the man who murdered Ed. Harmon's lower lip quivers. I squeeze his arm as he points an accusatory finger and shouts at Gates.

"You have the right to an ass-kicking! Anything you say or do to prevent one can and will be used against you! Do you understand what I'm saying, punk?"

This is what they call a white-heat moment. Harmon is blinded by rage. I bristle and take up a position between them after I see Harmon's hand twitch toward his service revolver during his terse reprimand.

"Put the pin back in!" is the best I can come up with to settle him down. I can only hope Harmon is listening to me. Then I hear the sound of Gates' dispassionate voice. He is clear and calm as he watches Harmon.

"I hate monkeys in monkey suits."

The statement alone could hasten his demise but when he follows it by blowing Harmon a perverted kiss I have to step in.

"Easy son, I want you back at the station in one piece."

It was obvious he was fearless, daring, unapologetic and

intractable. With mock seriousness he sings a chorus from a song I'm not yet familiar with.

> It's the way that I feel,
> It's the truth in my eyes,
> I've got wings upon my back
> and I can fly!

His little rendition is followed by a contemptuous sneer. I want to smack the sneer off his face. In my mind I picture a nine-millimeter bullet whistling and twisting through the air and penetrating his smooth forehead. The cop killer is baiting us. Maybe he's hoping for a "suicide by cop." That is what some of these crazy bastards really want. They're afraid to pull the trigger on themselves.

"Good, you can sing. I can't wait to get you downtown so you can sing about how bad you are!" Harmon asks point blank, "Are you responsible for the murder of Edward Fairchild?" Harmon's inquiry is met with the opening act of the Michael Gates show.

"The white man has been subverted by indulgent liberals, political prostitutes, corporate cannibals and the mongrelized media!" he says with a heavy southern accent.

Harmon and Gates exchange "I'll get you later" glares as he is marched off to be transported. As he is escorted away Gates speaks to the media vultures. Every beady look and ridiculous sound bite is captured on videotape. It freaks me out that Gates' remarks are the same ones the militia girl used.

The last remark he makes, a reference to the death penalty, barely makes it out of the squad car as he is placed, okay forced into the back seat.

All I have to do now is get him to the precinct alive and get Harmon sedated. We walk back to the car, climb in and follow close behind the transporting black and white. I tell Harmon that I will do the interrogation because he is way too wired. He doesn't argue with me.

We make a pact along the way that assuming Gates is convicted and whatever sentence he is given after the trial be it the drip or the jolt, we swear to be there. If he does manage to be freed by some insane judge we swear that we will personally hold court and carry out our own execution of his sentence.

Driving off we snake our way through the ever-present disgruntled onlookers who jeer at us because they have issues with law enforcement. Reporters are running alongside my car screaming asinine questions. It's amazing. The job isn't worth it.

Maybe Lori and I will disappear...

Harmon, still full of his personal convictions and rectitude, can't stop himself from voicing opinions all the way to the house.

"That's one villainous, arrogant and cold-blooded, sadistic scumbag!" But his skepticism gnaws at him. "Why didn't he run?"

As I contemplate Harmon's question about Gates' lack of interest in eluding us any longer another silver Lexus pulls up alongside. I'm surprised to see Lori. Her window slides down and she calls to me. "Jake, hey, where are you going?"

I point ahead at the black and white and shout, "We just captured the serial killer!" I'm pumped.

Lori is visibly stunned by my statement. Her reaction is a contradiction. Maybe the thought of being so near a serial killer scares her.

"Call me," she says and drives off.

45

I never had sympathy for the devil, assuming there is one. As the story goes a fallen angel had a seat at the right hand of God. He knew the rules and yet he still gave it all up. Either he had a huge set of cojones or he was really stupid.

Interrogation room three is located on the third floor behind the secure doors of CID. Inside the small room roughly eight feet by ten feet there are three wooden chairs and a metal table. The paint is olive-drab. There are no windows except for the one wall with the mirrored glass.

I walk inside drop a file on the table and look at the pathetic Michael Gates. He smiles back politely at me looking completely blameless. He is seated as far from the door as possible because I want him to feel isolated and alone, disconnected from the world. I want him to feel vulnerable and exposed – like Ed felt on his death bed. I want him to know that I control him.

The runner in ankle-shackles, how appropriate.

Gates will do everything in his power to try and control me whether by the inflection of his voice, his movements or by what he is willing to reveal. We will play a game of introjections. I will feign an adoption of his sick values to gain his confidence and he will either buy it or deny it.

In any case I plan to go through all the motions. After I get him rolling I will become a sympathetic listener. They all love to talk about themselves and their sad childhoods. But before we even begin he makes a startling statement with a straight face.

"I want to confess," he says quietly.

"Don't you want to hear the charges first?"

I haven't even hit him yet!

"No sir."

"You're waiving your right to counsel?"

"Yes sir."

"Hang on, let me get the equipment and we can get started."

There is no outward sign of hostility from me. As I get up to leave Gates asks for some water. I can't wait to hear what I'm going to get out of him for a glass of water.

God help him if he's jerking me around!

Cracking the door open I direct the officer outside to get the video technician and his equipment, and a glass of water. It doesn't take long before the equipment is set up and the technician signals ready. Again he is read his rights for the tape and I take a seat. I listen while Gates, for some unknown reason, starts confessing.

"...while dad was off on some aircraft carrier chasing international terrorist bad guys, mom was perfectly at home beating me. When dad came home he took out his drunken rages on me. I hated them both. I hated my brothers and sisters who never felt the pain of abuse!"

A note is made on my legal pad to check with the Department of the Navy.

"I killed both my parents - used a shotgun and blew their heads right off! I made my siblings watch and then I killed them one by one."

Grabbing my pen I make another note to contact the National Crime Database to see if that case file exists.

Quite frankly I'm surprised by his candor. He doesn't hold back and gives all of the gory details telling each story as if he's being interviewed by one of those whack-job, talk show hosts giving him his fifteen minutes of fame.

The way he is just sitting there without a care in the world makes the process even more unnerving. While he talks I can't help but think about the fact that he looks like a good kid. Walking past him on the street you would never have had a clue how close to the edge he was or how much rage was inside of him.

Was he from a dysfunctional family, yes. Was he more than a predatory street punk, yes. Is he evil? I have no doubt about it.

Because he appears to want to tell the entire Michael Gates' story I do nothing to push him into running silent and deep. Instead I encourage him with a few understanding nods.

After two hours he is still going strong with no sign of letting up. The last mental count I made he had already confessed to fourteen murders. I will press him for details of each murder later but I right now I have to know one thing.

"So Michael, my question is why?"

"Why did I kill? I told you ? "

Before he goes off again about his screwed-up family life I cut him off.

"Actually the lawyers and psychiatrists will deal with those issues. I want to know why you decided to reveal this information at this time. We had no idea who you were, didn't have a clue that you were involved. Why do you want to confess, why now?" My eyes narrow and my jaw tenses.

"I want to release the demons inside, Jake."

Until now Gates' eyes haven't left mine but now he looks past me and simply sits up straight in his chair with both hands resting in his lap. His facial expressions and body language reveal nothing and for all I know he has been lying since he started talking. Time will tell if he is as brutal and evil as he claims to be.

All I need for him to do now is to say on tape that he murdered Ed.

Gates looks back hard at me and points his index finger to the side of his head. "There are all kinds of things that aren't right in here."

The man is articulate, well-read and probably knows all the ins and outs of modern psychiatry and criminal law. I assume he is setting up his insanity defense. The next few answers will determine what Michael Gates is up to, whether or not he will continue to cooperate and whether or not he is looking for a deal.

Gates searches the Spartan interrogation room. My guess is he is looking for a hole to crawl out of.

Nauseatingly he says, "I interrogated Ed before I did him. I'm familiar with all of your interrogation techniques." He watches closely for my reaction and continues with, "I have been previously incarcerated."

"You said something about that earlier." I make fictitious notes on my legal pad. Glancing inside a folder for effect I add, "But that was for some small-time crime. How and when did you graduate to the big time?"

"There are things you learn in prison that you couldn't possibly learn in a university."

"But from a misdemeanor to murder?" I query.

"You're trying too hard, Jake. You don't know me. You will never know me. I've had to make choices you are incapable of understanding."

There is a noticeable change in his mood. I sense restlessness, uneasiness. He starts fidgeting. "I knew my day would come. This is my day, Jake."

Since the beginning of our talk I have been using the relaxed "nothing you say is too big" persona. But Gates is making me more irritable now than when I first walked in. I oscillate between wanting to figure him out and wanting to beat him to death.

One thing I know for sure is that I have been in this chair too long. It's no more made for my comfort than his so I stand. Gates makes a shallow inquiry about my comfort level.

"Are you getting cranky, Jake? I didn't rape him you know. I killed Ed but I never touched him sexually. I want you to know that."

Got him!

I try to count to ten but that never works for me, a deep breath helps. I have to let that sick, perverted psychopath ramble on no matter how abhorrent the story is.

"Did you enjoy killing, Michael?"

"I would have to ask you the same question, Jake. You killed that young girl, did you like it?"

His facial expression displays honest and sincere interest in my answer yet I know he is testing me. Depending on how I react will now determine how much more I will get from him. I have seen it before, he's just like all the other wise guys trying to spar with their keeper. They think it empowers them. Gates studies himself in the mirrored glass.

"I had no choice Michael; I'm sworn to protect society. I didn't seek her death, unlike you I don't seek out victims." I give him time to digest.

Out of nowhere he says, "I don't like guns." He turns impish and slips into a childlike rhyme. "A gun...is no fun!" He looks at me with a stupid grin. "No, I'd rather watch a face contort from my blade than hide behind a tree and fire a gun."

He looks upward for no reason, certainly not because he is seeking divine guidance. "I'm completely amoral and malevolent, Jake. You can look up both words later. I don't just like to kill. I love to perpetrate evil – especially death! I embrace death, I don't fear it. I experience the eroticism of death through each of my victims." He pauses. "But I don't understand why they didn't love me."

"Why who didn't love you?"

He becomes animated and impatient. His hands clench. "What are we talking about here, Jake? My victims, of course. I mean why didn't I matter to them? Take Thad, for instance, we were fine until she came along!"

46

Because of seniority Ed's death had elevated Harmon to the lofty position of Chief Inspector. The new position was a blow to Harmon's entire outlook. No longer was he able to shirk certain disagreeable rules. Now, he had to enforce them with impartiality.

From behind mirrored glass Harmon grumbled to himself, "There are real consequences for your actions!"

Junior grade Detective Melissa Collins joined him. She had been out doing follow-up at the crime scene.

"What do you have for me?" he asked sternly.

Collins told Harmon that the coroner was about to start Ed's autopsy if he wanted to be present. Harmon told her to call the man and tell him he would not be able to.

She added, "News is out in the hall screaming for answers, sir." She counted a beat. "And the rest of us are collecting a fund for Lucille and the kids."

Harmon just nodded. She watched him reach into his pocket. All the while he never stopped staring at Gates through the glass.

Outside of the observation room the air was thick with anger, frustration and sadness. The usual banter and excess volume between all ranks was noticeably absent. Instead they spoke in muted whispers. As Collins left the observation room Harmon heard her apologize.

"Sorry ma'am," she said after almost bumping into Mika.

As Mika turned the corner into the room it was obvious she had been crying since leaving Quantico. Her eyes were swollen and her lips were drawn in tight. She grasped Harmon. Her voice trembled as she talked through the tears.

"I just can't believe it!"

Harmon threw his two big arms around her as if protecting her from an imaginary assailant. He searched above her head for God. A single tear trailed down his cheek.

"He got in early before any of us, took the call. All of the files were on his desk. He was trying to find something we all missed. He wanted so much to find it, for you."

Harmon released Mika, nudged away another tear and pointed an outstretched finger at Gates. "That's him, that's the man. We have him now. He won't do any more harm. And he will pay Mika, he will pay!"

Mika focused on Gates. Her mind whirled through all of the dismal, grisly murder scenes as she tried to put his face to each. She tried to pull together all of the interlocking pieces of the puzzle in her mind. The last piece she placed was Ed's.

She also watched Jake inside the barren interrogation room. He was only inches away from the suspect. She instinctively knew what he was thinking.

Harmon withdrew from her and said, "I'll be back. I have to brief the vultures. Can you believe it? Ed's passing left me in charge!" The big man looked to her for sympathy.

"You're a wonderful successor to a great man," she said proudly because she understood how heavy the pressure was on him. "He'll be watching!"

Harmon forced a smile. He turned and quietly left the cramped observation room without saying another word.

Mika stepped as close to the glass as was humanly possible. She placed a hand against it. She resumed her professional demeanor because there was work to do. She had to concentrate on the words of the man inside the next room. There could not be any shadow of a doubt.

47

"Who is *she*?" I ask patiently although I'm tired of his mind games. He's arrogant.

You're busted Gates, give it up!

"Lori Powers."

His answer staggers me. He could not have blindsided me better if he had used a Louisville slugger. I can't believe he said her name!

How did he know Lori - my Lori?

"She was a patient of my late, great lover Dr. Thaddeus Abrams just like you. Small world isn't it?" Gates presses a finger to his lips. "Thad told me all of the intimate details of your two pathetic lives. It almost brought tears to my eyes - Ms. Powers' troubled past and you all broken-hearted over murdering that girl. I'm sorry, did I say *murdering*?"

He is pushing all of my buttons but I can't react. I need to stay in the game so I can make absolutely sure that he pays for every syllable. I need to hear all of it.

Focus Jake!

"So anyway, like I told Ed, Thaddeus got a hard-on over her and ?"

"You lost him to a woman? You killed Abrams over jealousy? Couldn't do it for him anymore?"

"THAD LOVED ME!" he fires back.

Gates finally loses it. Another place and time, and it would have been me tied to the bed but I control the room while Gates feels the pain.

This boy's got a temper!

"I never said they were lovers!" he says firmly. "Thad saw her professionally. He did, for a while he told me, feel sexually attracted to her but he got over it!"

That brings an inward sigh of relief to my psyche. I focus on cool, impartial and all business. "So why did you kill him?"

"Because Thad thought he was better than me just like all of the others. They were controlling, dominating, misguided fools that deserved to die! The world is far better off now because of what I have done!" Gates cools to a hardened, cold-blooded predator. "I'd do them all again. Let me out of here and I'll clean up the rest!"

My heart is breaking, my soul is crying and my head pounds like never before. I see Ed lying on the blood-soaked mattress. I see the girl's frozen death face. I see Lori's face with a look of bewilderment. I desperately need to walk away.

Michael Gates is a biting, edgy character in a sick, perverted play. Standing, I march toward the door. He expresses surprise that I'm leaving because he wants to continue blustering about his evil career and philosophies.

"Michael, you're done cleaning up. Keep in mind that those evil people you murdered are going to be sitting right next to you in hell for all of eternity."

Slamming the door behind me I know would have lost control if I had stayed another second. The officer guarding the door asks if I'm okay. I can't answer. Gates finally got to me. I need to decompress. If I'm ever going to collapse under pressure from the job this is the time.

I have a pain that requires medication so I reach into my pocket for what I have left of my pain killers. As I start down the hall toward observation I'm surprised to see Mika come out. She sees the prescription bottle in my hand.

"No Jake, that's not going to help. We all need to pull together, as difficult as it is. I need you're help on this!"

My only other alternative is punching my fist through the wall. I don't want to disappoint her or break her heart, not now and not ever again. I look down at the pills in my hand. She is just what I need to get back to normal, and she's right.

With a dour look on his face Harmon approaches the two of us in the hallway. His eyes are wet and red. His words are quiet but deliberate.

"That was one of the hardest things I have ever had to do ? announce to the world the death of someone I love."

Mika and I exchange looks. We know what has to be done. We have to finish it.

Just then, there is a commotion down the hall.

48

A bright orange and yellow flash is followed by a clap of thunder that reverberates inside CID. The spent shell ejected from the officer's stolen weapon bounces and spins to a stop on the floor.

Everyone scatters for cover, most drop to the floor while others find refuge behind walls or under desks. Each of us tries desperately to control our panic. Weapons are drawn and the smell of cordite is strong.

"Shots fired ? officer down!" is shouted out so everyone knows what to deal with.

After the struggle with Gates I see the officer fall back into the hallway. Crimson bubbles rise up out of a hole in his chest. A river of blood flows from his chest to the floor. His body quivers several times before he expels his final breath.

I'm unarmed. My weapon is inside a lock-box just outside of the door to the interrogation room. It's department policy to secure it there during the interrogation of suspects.

Caught between the dead officer to my right, Mika to my left, the ceiling, floor and walls – I have no where to go. Gates steps out into the hallway and draws down on me. I fall hard to the floor. Curled up I wait to feel the burning sensation of the entry wounds. A double-tap rings out. The sound of two thuds as if a hammer pounds on meat follows.

Sometimes shock prevents the pain, I don't feel a thing. I see Gates go down. He lets out a high-pitched wail during the fall. Blood spouts out of the two holes in his chest. A trickle of blood drips from the corner of his mouth.

When she first saw Gates with the weapon Mika shoved Harmon

back into the observation room. She targeted Gates in an instant and fired twice. Harmon recovered quickly with his service revolver drawn and took a position in front of her. There was no way he was going to let her take a bullet.

Had I not hit the floor when I did I'd have been joining Gates on the other side. That wouldn't have been so bad because it would have given me more time in eternity to torment and punish the worthless scumbag. Mika's expertise and precision with her service weapon however prevents my early departure.

I get up off the floor and race to Gates and the officer. Harmon checks the officer's pulse – he's gone. Gates is still breathing slightly. The stolen weapon is taken away. Mika comes up and stands over Gates with her hands locked around her Beretta pointing it in his face.

He slowly opens his glassy eyes and coughs up more blood. He blinks several times until he can see her. Two words pass through his lips but there is no sound to accompany them. There is no mistake about what they are.

"Thank you."

A millisecond later Gates is dead. The only regret any of us has except for Mika is that he didn't suffer. A detective checks for a throat pulse near the hemorrhaging wound and nods. The division shifts into overdrive.

Mika turns to me and asks if I'm okay. Grasping her forearm with one hand I force a smile and brace myself while my other hand searches my body for any sign of physical trauma. I hope everyone is too distracted to see my hands shaking.

"Fine, I think!" My hand stops searching but Harmon starts pawing me for injuries.

"You okay, Jake?"

My hands are still shaking but not as bad. Harmon notices. I check to see if Mika is okay.

"Are you okay, Agent Scott?"

What it feels like to take a life cannot be defined or described. Everyone reacts differently. There is no book that tells you how and what you should feel or say. The reaction is very personal.

Mika stares at Gates. She knows what he was and what he has perpetrated on society. Like all of us she wanted him to pay for his sins but none of us wants to be the hand of God, to affect the final judgment.

As I take her service weapon for ballistics her hand is trembling but she is amazingly strong-willed and takes command instantly.

Individual officers respond and go about the job of securing the scene. The paramedics and techs arrive. Harmon commands the rest of the troops to stand down.

"It's all over, people!"

I swear I hear Ed in Harmon's voice.

49

It's six P.M. and dusk is approaching from the east. This morning our friend was murdered. By late morning we had captured his killer. Through the hours since we learned the details of his miserable life. By early evening the perp was dead.

It's a time of conflicting emotions. Mika and I walk outside and look for a place to hide. A dimly lit booth will serve the purpose. A bar is always a great place to hide in. Everyone in there is hiding from something so they understand.

The place is small and nondescript but nearby. Mika's head turns constantly as if she is expecting someone to notice her as the person who killed the psychopath. The media vultures are still circling over the precinct. They don't have a clue who shot Gates. When they find out the circus will begin.

"Is the world a failure or are some of us just failures?" she asks.

There's no real answer. Her mind is just wading through the morass, part of the post-traumatic thing.

"Does a guy like Gates plead insanity before God?"

She needs to get it out; someone to listen and I understand what she is going through.

"The shield says Fidelity, Bravery, and Integrity - not assassin!"

"Don't even go there; sometimes a situation requires necessary violence. You saved my life!"

She just became a member of the club. Few of us join by desire. The militia girl paid for my membership.

Her facial expression changes rapidly from angry to uncertain. She alternately dominates the conversation and then goes stone silent. Mika is analyzing, rationalizing. It comes with the territory. For her the color of truth has changed to a darker shade. The nightmares will come later.

"Back in 1999 I arrested a skinny, drug-infested, white-trash biker girl who was responsible for numerous robberies, rapes, abductions and murders. She flirted with me as I drove her in. Said she wanted to have hard-core sex with me in the backseat. Didn't faze me at all, I just did my job."

"Two years ago I took down a male suspect - a Latin Kings enforcer named Bobby 'Bang-Bang' Benitez. He had just 'hot-shot' a drug-dealing competitor with a syringe full of battery acid. The remains of the victim grossed out all of the guys but I took it without a problem."

"Last year, I bagged another female suspect with so many rough edges a sandblaster couldn't smooth her out. She had bleached blond hair, crooked teeth and a miniskirt that covered her by a hair. Single-handedly that goddess had bludgeoned and stabbed four people. I hauled her ass in and never once had the slightest urge to vomit."

Mika's stories are nauseating me. I put my beer down on the table. I know what's coming next.

"But Gates...Michael goddamn Gates bothers me!"

After a few heartbeats pass I tell her, "I don't think you heard most of what he said in there. It might make it a little easier."

"No I didn't, I got there a few minutes before you came out."

As I speak, I see Gates sitting in that interrogation room with a demonic look in his dark eyes. "He professed bizarre, fanatic religious views and anti-government rhetoric, his preference for castration. He said if he was horny he'd get it on with the corpse!"

"At times he was perfectly calm and then he'd flip into a rage. Not once did he show any indication of remorse. God only knows how many corpses he actually left decomposing. He was up to twenty plus when you ?" I catch myself and apologize.

She moves right past my apology. "There was a guy in Russia - Rostov, who dismembered and disemboweled his victims. He ate their testicles after boiling them."

"As far as Gates' bragging about the quantity of victims he has a long way to go to pass up at least two others, one from Peru and one from Italy. And then there's Dr. Harold Shipman from Britain," she says with a shrug.

The waitress drops off two more cold ones but neither of us is interested in getting wasted.

It's my turn. "Strangely enough he was a very religious guy, full of God, penance, right and wrong ? confessing. Obviously, he didn't get it, the right and wrong part."

"Religion has always been a breeding ground for terror," Mika says.

After a half-smile and a nod I continue about Gates' sick mental state, how he believed in what he was doing and how he even enjoyed murdering.

"Of course he enjoyed it." Not surprised she asks whether or not Gates mentioned anything about his sleeping habits or pattern.

"Nocturnal insomniac."

"Makes sense."

She looks casually around the room and notices that the televised National League baseball game is interrupted with a news report about the shooting. No one else in the bar pays attention.

We can see the report but miss most of what is being said. The report cuts to Harmon briefing the reporters, followed by a photo of Gate, followed by an old precinct photo of Mika.

"Well, it didn't take them long did it?" she asks as she turns away.

"It never does. Get ready for the second-guessing. They come at you from all sides dissecting your every move. The problem is they weren't there. They just know the outcome, the end result."

"Anything about his childhood, siblings, parents?" she asks.

My head bobs with every one of those. "He gave me the standard abusive, unstable, dysfunctional family speech. Swore he didn't do drugs. He also said and I don't if it's relevant that he abstained from killing when he and Abrams were together."

Mika's internal hard drive downloads and processes the information. "And he returned to the scene, that's the first time I've come across that in all of these cases. I should have put surveillance on the victim's funerals. He might have attended one or even possibly all of them." She looks past me.

I want to give her as much background information as I can but I can't help tossing out my opinion. "He gave me a story about why he finally led us to his front door but it didn't make sense."

Mika scornfully says, "Gates was a serial killer. He doesn't have to make sense." She contemplates before continuing.

"Premeditative and spontaneous, targets familiar victims and strangers, antiseptic yet he leaves enough evidence to hang himself at the last one. I think he's created a profile category all his own."

"He needed to die," is my answer to that.

"I don't think he was afraid of dying, I think he was more afraid of living," she philosophizes. "Maybe he finally realized that he was a monster. He didn't say 'thank you' to be sarcastic, he said it because he meant it. Self-destruction for some reason was impossible for him. He needed someone else to finish it."

"Like I said, he needed to die."

50

An ominous shadow covers our table. Harmon's tracked us down. His face is changed, he's different now. Being thrust into the loneliness of command and the circumstances surrounding it is taking an early toll on him. He isn't smiling but then again there really isn't much to smile about.

"It wasn't hard finding you two. You can bet the reporters will figure it out soon enough so I wouldn't hang around here too much longer unless you want to be in the spotlight." He talks just above a whisper and looks cautiously around the bar.

"Jake, maybe you should take Mika ? "

"Are you crazy? I'm a federal officer!" Mika tries to throttle down the remark but she draws some unwanted attention from the other patrons anyway. "I can handle it," she huffs.

"Jake, explain it to her, I'm not in any mood to argue."

"Har's right, you're going to need some room to recover, decompress maybe not right this minute but it will start to dog you soon." My best head tilt follows.

Mika takes a hard look at both of us. "I know you both mean well but I can't, I need to finish this."

Her lips firm up and that look in her eyes clearly says the discussion is over. I've known Mika long enough to know she isn't going to change her mind. It's time to swing the conversation in another direction. Harmon looks like he needs a boost to take the edge off.

"So Har, do I call you Chief Blackwell now?"

"Depends on what you mean by 'Chief'!" He glares. "Do you mean a respectful Chief Inspector Blackwell or do you mean like an Indian wisecrack thing?"

"I'm going with the wisecrack thing."

"Funny Roberts, there isn't enough on my plate right now so I need some of your adolescent behavior?"

Ouch. The day has changed everything. The old Harmon is gone, replaced by one that's all business. I'll have to find a new way to cope because the jokes aren't going to smooth out the rough spots anymore. No jokes and no more helpers, I need Lori.

"Any new information since we've been gone?" I inquire of my new boss.

Harmon leans forward on his two large elbows. "Butzer and Rabinowitz found course materials from the university's Criminal Justice Department that describe how various crimes are committed, crime scene investigation - the whole enchilada. There were also books on psychology and profiling." He glances at Mika and then looks for a waitress.

"They were in a closet in his room at his parents' home along with a file full of obituaries. The guys are comparing names to the victims he claims." He waves at the bartender to get his attention.

"In the apartment he was living in, paid for I might add by Abrams, they found gray flesh trophies – skulls, hands, various anatomy parts ? all packaged, catalogued and labeled by Gates."

I air an opinion with, "Bet mom and dad are proud."

Both Harmon and Mika deliver disapproving looks at me. Apparently my level of compassion exists at a point somewhat lower than theirs. But I just can't understand how two parents can fail to notice that junior's just a little different than the rest of the kids.

"The parents Detective Roberts, are understandably traumatized as any parent would be after finding out such horrific things about their son!" Harmon is stern.

I shrug while running a mental list of the evidence. I tell Mika about the CD and ask her if it has any significance.

"I'm certain that it must have had some deep meaning to Gates."

Harmon says, "Course we won't find out why now."

His subtle reference brings an unfortunate spike of reality to Mika but she immediately dismisses the remark. "Everything suggests he's our man."

"Why do you think he gave up?" I ask for argument's sake.

Harmon tosses in his supposition. "In early Rome the soldiers used to swear an oath by holding their testicles. They didn't place their hands over their hearts or on a bible. That's where the word 'testify' comes from, the root word is 'testes.' Maybe Gates thought someone was sooner or later going to cut his off!"

"Maybe he just wanted to be somebody," Mika conjectures.

It's painfully obvious we're pretty much brain dead by now. The emotional reserves are depleted as well. All I can think about is getting some sleep. I look at Mika.

"Want me to ?"

"No, I'm going back with Har. There are some things I need to look at before I'm going to be able to shut down for the night. I'm way too wired right now."

I give her my "are you sure?" look.

"Yes, I'm sure. I want to look into them while it's all still fresh in here." She points to the side of her head and gives me one of her reassuring smiles. "Thanks Jake, but I'll be fine."

"Okay, then just call me 'Hibernate Jake'! I'm going home and try to get some sleep. It's been a long day."

Harmon gives a hard look in my direction. He reaches out and places a hand on my shoulder for emphasis.

"Jake, I'm serious about this. I don't want you taking any more of those pills do you hear me?"

Harmon isn't speaking as my friend and partner now, he is "the man" giving me a strict warning but he's right. I reach into my pocket, grab the small prescription bottle and hand it to him.

"Now I'll sleep better tonight," he says.

51

The very moment dusk turns to night the streetlights illuminate. The city transforms into silhouettes and heavy hues. The residents of my city bathe in the shadows and morph into people they weren't only an hour before.

The nature of the job requires constant evaluation and reevaluation. So I'm stuck in this cerebral vortex about my ferocious craving for Lori versus my career.

Maybe I need to throw the big cosmic switch and take a chance on a life outside of the badge. Maybe I'm just too tired and hallucinating. Everything revolves around my job. It has always been my reason for living.

I wonder if it's too late to call.

In my righteous opinion Lori has saved me. I was faltering, struggling and drowning in despair when she came along. She has the capacity to wipe away my pain with a simple word or a single look. She understands and knows exactly what I mean without a need for a long dissertation. When she's with me I don't feel lost.

I'm going to take a hot, steamy shower, wash the job off then give her a call. I'd use my cell phone but I want to hear her smoky, sensuous voice through a clear fibre-optic line.

Standing at my front door with my key in hand I think about spending the rest of my life with her. I could be happy just watching a burning sunset with her. Peace, I need peace in my life and I believe Lori my answer and my salvation, amen.

52

The kitchen had always been a place of refuge for her. She found it easier to push away the troublesome thoughts there. Food preparation particularly the cutting motion of a knife against meat or poultry replaced other more grisly recollections.

Lori was dining alone again that night. She missed having someone, a companion to be with. As she sliced through the tomatoes for her dinner salad she watched the memories pass through her mind.

Her husband had been an angry, vicious man mostly marinated in alcohol. The beatings she had endured and the sexual abuses of Emily were both mentally and physically devastating. And yet there were times when she felt so loved that the horror disappeared in a mist.

The knife she was using was the very same one that ended his miserable life.

She claimed that Mr. Powers had abandoned them and even had the presence of mind to file a missing person's report with the police. The search went on for years but he never turned up.

Friends and neighbors believed her when she said he ran off. There was no extended family of his to contest the accusation. It was suggested that he couldn't handle the responsibilities of married life and a child. Some thought he left with another woman. Whatever the reason they believed it because no one liked him anyway.

Whenever asked about it Lori cried real tears and everyone sympathized with her. They never knew the tears were for what she couldn't confess. And as more time passed they understood when Lori and Emily Powers became distant and estranged from them.

Emily never knew what her mother had done. Instead, she struggled silently with her own demons. She couldn't bring herself to talk about dad's secret, late-night, drunken sexual assaults on her young mind and body. She was certain mom knew. The hard part for Emily was trying to understand why her mother let it continue to happen.

As an adolescent girl growing into womanhood Emily found it impossible to have any normal loving relationships because of him. She oscillated between the extremes of the religious sisterhood and being a whore. She chose the later and the reputation she carried on her shoulders during her high school years was unbearable.

It all became too much for her and Emily decided to opt out. She left a letter describing how she felt about her mother's reluctance to stop "daddy" before she overdosed on her sixteenth birthday.

Emily's death crushed Lori. To recover she developed a ruthless determination to avenge her daughter's death. She decided to take the life of any man she encountered that played the same controlling, sexual games. Each execution was carried out with the same justification.

She found the process easy after she had murdered her husband but after multiple homicides she knew she couldn't get them all. It had to stop. Told that Abrams was the consummate professional and a trustworthy practitioner Lori sought his advice and counsel. In her wildest dreams she never thought he would disappoint her like he did.

She now arranged the carrots around the meat and sprinkled salt and pepper over the entire tray. With one hand she opened the oven door. With the other she placed the tray inside. After closing the oven she set the timer and smiled when the thought of Jake Roberts surfaced.

He seemed different from all of the others. He was sincere, considerate and caring. She had no doubt that his affections were genuine. She didn't believe such a man existed anymore but there stood Jake. Lori was willing to try one more time to find love, to be loved. She had to know that someone could love her without inflicting pain and suffering.

Jake, please be that person.

Just as she finished that thought the telephone rang and startled her. Is would have been a perfect time for Jake to call but the airline was looking for Lori to cover another crew member's flight the following morning. Crew schedulers were considered the enemy by flight crew members. They turned your life upside down more than any microburst. Disappointment spread across her face. She needed time alone with him.

"No, I'm sorry I just got in from another trip and unfortunately brought a sinus infection home with me, my head's all stuffed up. You know I would otherwise, sorry." She sniffled a few times to bolster her story.

They weren't all cold-blooded. The crew scheduler assured her that he understood completely and recommended some cold medications that worked for him. He added that he hoped she would be feeling better soon and said goodbye.

As soon as she replaced the receiver in the cradle it rang again. She prepared to sniffle some more but the voice on the other end was a pleasant surprise, a sweet sound to hear. Lori felt the butterfly fluttering in her stomach and noticed how quickly her mood was transformed into a blissful state. Her breathing rate increased. There was no doubt she had strong feelings for him.

"Hi, Jake, I saw you on the news!"

"I wish there was some other reason for me to be in the news." I want her to know that I'm more than just a cop but I'm just happy to know she's thinking about me.

"I'm sorry."

"For what?" she asks her inflection rising.

"For not calling sooner, for being preoccupied with ? "

Cutting me off in mid-sentence she says, "I'm just glad to hear from you! I understand, I really do understand." Lori has a way of staying ahead of me.

"Really?"

"Yes, I do." She hesitates. "I hope you understand when I have to fly. It's not easy being in a relationship with a flight attendant. I leave town for several days, travel all around the country and fly back at odd times to get home. I hope that's not too hard on you."

"Waiting for you is like waiting for Christmas! Any chance I can see you tonight?" I can't see her smile, the small bite of her lip or the tilt of her head.

"I'm in the kitchen right now preparing dinner and there's enough for a quiet dinner at home for two!"

"Half an hour?"

"Give me an hour because I want to look my best for you!"

The thought of a quiet, romantic evening alone with Lori races through my head. I'm reenergized and disregard my need for sleep. I renegotiate.

"Forty-five minutes."

"I'll be ready!" she says and lightly drops the phone down.

Mine stays in my hand longer while the daydream passes through, then it hits me. I start searching for a better shirt and check my face in the mirror for a possible quick shave. My pulse noticeably elevates. Tonight is the night.

My passion kicks in. I want to be primal and free, I want to be a man. I don't want to think about the scum I deal with, about the girl or Gates. I just want to be with her and not ruminate about the consequences.

If I flash the blues I can run all the lights.

53

Harmon grew up on the meanest streets and was considered a traitor to his race when he joined the police department. He knew who the bad guys from the neighborhood were and they believed he would use that information to persecute them.

But while he was capably street smart Harmon Blackwell was also a book smart man who played his intellect down. Ed once told me, "Brilliant is born; educated is grown." Harmon was brilliant.

As he walked back into his new office Harmon was exhausted after giving what felt like his thousandth briefing to the news people. They could drain your blood faster than an open carotid artery. All he wanted was a peaceful break in the action.

The door to his office closed loudly enough to signal to everyone that it was break time – Do Not Disturb. He dragged his chair out and collapsed into it. Opening the top drawer of his desk he retrieved a Scientific American magazine he had stored there. After adjusting his glasses Harmon began reading hoping to finish the article he started days earlier.

The article described how the silicon chip currently used in computers performed its magic at two billion times per second by using fifty-five million transistors. However, in the span of a few years mankind could reasonably expect computers to be developed that used single-molecule, DNA strands or quantum-effect chips to perform god-zillions of computations at light speed.

After the first five paragraphs and after being significantly impressed he began to read out loud. "Biomed implants, microscopic nano-computers that are injected into the body, will seek out disease and eliminate it effectively bringing an end to all invasive surgical procedures." Harmon dropped back in his chair.

Incredible.

But it was going to be Harmon's last chance to take a break. His head jerked up when he heard a knock on the door. He couldn't believe someone was dumb enough to interrupt him. To his surprise the door opened and Mika walked in.

Since leaving the bar she had found time to walk and think. It happened. Trauma made your feet move. You couldn't sit still. You thought movement alone would somehow help you to lose the sunken ship feeling.

Harmon noticed the distant look on her face and the enormous amount of compassion he had inside of his massive body rose quickly to the surface. If it was anyone else besides Mika who had interrupted his off time they would be pulling their head out of their behind with both hands. He asked if she was okay.

"Yeah, yeah...just been walking, thinking."

"It was justified. You're not still debating the shoot are you?" He waited.

Without raising her eyes to look at him she nodded an "I know." She started to pace with her hands locked on her hips.

"What's wrong?" Again he hesitated. "Come on Mika, we've been friends for a long time let it out." Assuming he knew why she was there he added, "Sometimes we have to make choices and ?"

"That's not it, Har. It's what Jake said tonight. It doesn't add up but I can't seem to figure out why." She collapsed into a chair and stared off into space. "It all points to Gates, he confessed but for some strange reason it bites at me that he wasn't the one I was looking for!"

"Mika, Gates is dead, the case is closed. The public hysteria is over. You did a great job! We should be rejoicing and not analyzing!" He walked over and placed a hand on her narrow shoulder.

"Personally, I hope I never hear the name Michael Gates again."

She looked up with her two beautiful Asian eyes and a pouting face. "I guess you're right, maybe because of the shoot I'm…" She became resolute. "I probably should get some sleep."

"I'll drive you. Where's that hotel you're staying at?"

"I don't want to sit in that awful hotel room alone." Mika glanced up at him like a child seeking a parent's approval.

"Would you drop me off at Jake's?"

54

As she hustled around her bedroom Lori recalled her early morning visit with her daughter. The visit was different from all the others because she wanted to reveal to Emily her thoughts and feelings about a relationship with Jake.

Where have you been, mommy? You know how I look forward to your visits.

"I know sweetheart and I'm sorry. Time seems to be moving much faster these days."

Emily's tone turned accusatory, angry.

It's because of him, isn't it?

Lori looked away from her daughter's headstone where the girl's voice always emanated from. She pondered the question for a moment and sighed.

"Emily, I really like him." Waiting for Emily's answer and approval she fidgeted with the leaves that had fallen on the grave. "He's different, gentle and thoughtful. He makes me feel happy again!"

She looked back at the headstone but her daughter's reply never came. The silence ended when the taunting voice spoke.

One mistake after another with you. Didn't you learn anything from all the others? Men are not to be trusted, or loved! What don't you get? What's the hard part?

She didn't want to hear it again and her daydream came to an abrupt halt. She looked around the bedroom to regain her bearings. Sitting on the edge of the bed she decided to make it work with Jake.

55

What a rush! I feel like a teenager on a first date. As I walk up the front steps I also have the feeling that I'm home. I try to imagine what it would be like to come here every night, to Lori's house in this quaint, picket-fenced neighborhood. The muted exterior colors against the lush foliage suggest peace and happiness. What a gift it would be to fall into her arms after a hard day.

I hope her old man takes it easy on me.

As I reach the front door I'm amazed at how pumped I am. Life seems to be starting all over again. After pressing the doorbell the front door opens and Lori appears in a clinging, black, mid-thigh dress. Neither of us speak, we embrace and kiss. My hands roam over her shoulders and lower back. Her hands lock behind my neck.

The kiss lasts for more than the measure of a minute signaling that the evening will be memorable. Pleasurable thoughts start to swirl around inside my head. As our lips separate she gently caresses my face.

"I've missed you but I didn't know how much until now," she whispers. She grasps my hands and pulls me inside. Any hesitation I may have had about falling in love with her ends here. All I have to do is keep my animal instincts in check. I need a distraction.

One step at a time, Jake.

During my official visit to her home I noticed that the interior of the house was a complete reflection of Lori Powers. If it was millennium chick then it was in here. But while Lori watches me pulling surveillance I notice something is missing.

"No television?"

"Jake Roberts! You came here to watch television?" she asks astounded with mock disappointment.

"No, I'm just curious. That's a great stereo system over there, an incredible CD collection, real paintings and expensive furnishings. I just don't see a television." I throw my arms around her waist and pull her close. "Which makes sense the more I think about it. Who needs television when you're in the room?"

The second kiss is followed by several more. The chemistry is powerful, pure peace and serenity. Lori stares deep into my eyes and I return the favor. She is breathtaking in the soft glow of the living room lights.

"Got in late last night?"

"Yes, didn't you get my message? I left one on your machine. I did an all-nighter from San Francisco, a red eye. I'm actually glad you didn't see me. I looked a mess!"

You are the one.

"Somehow, I can't imagine you ever being a mess." I don't want to let go of her. After the past few days I desperately need to hold on to something or someone that I can believe in, someone who is real.

"Could we just stay this way for awhile?" I ask. "It's been a real bad day!" Her scent draws me in. My heart is exposed and I want her love to embrace it.

"Roger, you're cleared for the approach, over!" she says teasing provocatively. Another lengthy kiss follows. She leans back and studies my eyes with concern.

"A bad day?"

Her interest in my life always surprises me. Most people hate cops but she is at ease with me, supportive. I feel my facial muscles tense as I look up at the ceiling.

My job revolves around murder. I can't discuss that abyss with her!

"It's all right, Jake, I can take it. I want you to know that I'm here for you. If you're hurting then so am I." she insists.

Her offer of support props me up and her eyes say it will be alright. This case is more spectacular than most so maybe I can. I decide to take the chance, this time.

"Captain Edward Fairchild, my friend, was the last victim of the killer we've been searching for. He was lured out by this guy, Michael Gates."

While she listens I let go of her and move loosely around the room. Pacing helps me. Lori slowly sits down on her sofa and leans forward with her hands clasped together.

"We didn't get there in time to save him, the whole precinct is devastated. Ed was family. We can't grieve because the investigation is ongoing. The funeral is delayed because of the autopsy." That statement hurts. The lump in my throat grows larger.

"Ed was a father figure to all of us, someone the whole precinct looked to for guidance, encouragement. He taught me everything about how to be a good cop. When I fell down, he picked me up, brushed me off and sent me out again!"

Michael Gates' face bursts into my thoughts. "And that cold-blooded, psychopath murdered him! I didn't get to Ed in time…couldn't save him."

56

"The key should be under the…" Har said as Mika got out of the car.

"I still have one thank you," she interrupted and smiled sheepishly. She didn't feel it was necessary to explain why. Maybe she would on some other day, an easier day.

In her heart she knew that she kept it as a reminder of happier times. She also felt it had some good luck attached to it because whenever she was with Jake she always felt safe and protected.

"Are you going to be all right, Har?"

He thought about it for a moment. "Yeah, I'm a big boy. And I've got more things to keep me distracted now that I'm 'the man'." He slumped down in the car seat.

"But keep next week open, okay? It will hit me hard then and I'm going to need a lot of special care."

Mika blew Harmon a small kiss and waved goodbye.

Since Ed had been so hastily taken away it seemed more important than ever to see someone you loved as long as you could. You almost felt that the longer you kept looking their way the safer they would be. Ed's murder proved that no one was safe any more. Mika watched until Harmon made the turn at the end of Jake's street.

There were plenty of people out walking and traffic moved briskly along the street. Mika decided to stay out on the sidewalk for a while and take it all in. She studied the faces and the surroundings out of habit.

All she really wanted the rest of the night was to find comfort in Jake's arms. She wondered what his reaction would be at finding her at his front door.

She knocked and waited but there was no answer. Jake she knew was a light sleeper. She rang the bell and waited for a light to illuminate. She peeked through the curtain to see if his shadow was approaching. Finally, she found the key in her purse and slid it into the lock. The tumblers tumbled and Mika walked in.

"Jake?"

She reached in the dark for the light switch on the wall. It was warm inside the apartment but not uncomfortable. The air conditioning was set on high meaning Jake wasn't home. She noted that the apartment hadn't changed much since she moved out.

While she contemplated what her dad had said about settling down with Jake she also wondered if her career had been the correct path. At the time she was convinced that her career came first and that there would always be time for a relationship. Now, standing in Jake's apartment she doubted it had been the best path to choose.

Then it hit her with full force. The morbid thoughts consumed her and she started to cry, couldn't stop. Her strong, toned legs weakened and collapsed beneath her. Lying on the floor she cradled her arms around herself overwhelmed with feelings of exposure, vulnerability and guilt.

57

"Gates managed to kill an officer while he was trying to escape. Then he drew down on me, I was in his sights."

While speaking I drift back into the distressing scene. "I wasn't armed so there was nothing I could do, there wasn't any place in the corridor to hide. An FBI agent, a friend of mine, shot Gates. She fired twice across my shoulder as I dropped to the floor. I could hear the bullets hiss as they passed by my ear. It was all of two seconds…and it was over."

"Oh my God, I didn't know that!" Lori says as she reaches for me. She grasps my hands and draws them to her lips giving them a gentle, loving kiss. Her dire expression turns to one of relief. She holds me close.

Good, Gates is dead mommy. Now they won't know about you!

The aggressive, demanding voice follows Emily's.

Kill Roberts before it's too late!

A strange, twisted look appears on her face and it's obvious I've said too much. "Lori, are you okay?"

Dammit Jake, why didn't you leave it alone!

She looks lost, probably contemplating whether or not she needs to hear any more of it. She quickly recovers and looks up at me with her beautiful cyan eyes.

"I'm just so glad that you weren't hurt! I don't know what I would do if you were. It frightens me to think that you could have been."

Our embrace is strong and suggests that together we can do anything at all in the world. She is an extraordinary woman and I'm a lucky guy.

"I lost my friend today but we got that sick sonofabitch!"

Although I try to be reassuring I know that it is a difficult conversation for a civilian to take and I regret talking about it. "I won't bring the job home again, I'm sorry."

At the same time in the same room we both realize what just slipped out of my mouth. I can't deny it, we both heard it. I'm speechless. A grin appears on both of our faces.

"Jake, did you just say 'bring the job *home*'?"

I'm actually glad it slipped out. It's just as well because I want her to know how I really feel. She pivots toward the kitchen.

"Why don't I get us both a drink?" she says.

"Is it all right if I put on some music?" I shout toward the kitchen.

"Music's good."

Wandering over to the bookshelf I can't believe my Freudian slip about being home. As my index finger runs across her extensive music collection one CD stands out among the others. I stop there, index finger pointing and remove it from shelf.

What are the chances?

Inside the kitchen Lori finds the appropriate glasses inside a cabinet. She holds out a bottle of Canadian Club for me to see. "With Seven?"

"Perfect."

Lori places the drinks on a serving tray. Tucked away behind the knife holder and concealed in a vial inside a sugar canister are the tranquilizers she uses to disable her victims. Emily's voice beckons her.

Kill him mommy, so it's just you and me again.

As Emily's voice fades, the other insists.

What are you waiting for? All men are evil! Kill him now!

Lori stands rigid and terrified waiting for the voices to stop.

No, I can't, don't you see?

As my hand touches her shoulder she jumps. She looks traumatized and stressed. I've never seen her like this.

"What's wrong?"

"Nothing Jake." Scrutinizing the look on my face she knows that I'm going to need more information.

"Sometimes the flashbacks of the days with my ex-husband come when I least expect them. One minute everything is fine and a split second later, this. I'm sorry, Jake you shouldn't have to deal with this." She blinks rapidly and exhales.

"Lori, I'm sure you know by now that I care a great deal about you, I mean I used the H-word tonight!" My small grin fades. "I shouldn't have been talking about my work. I'm a homicide detective and that's an extremely upsetting subject. I shouldn't have done that, I'm sorry for upsetting you. Please forgive me."

As I wait for forgiveness she surprises me with a question as she points at the CD I still have in my hand.

"What are you doing with that?"

Holding it up I rotate the CD and study it. After what I had just said about not bringing home the job I'm not sure I want to tell her why.

"Again I apologize, while looking through your collection I found it. Gates played the same one at every crime scene, Ed's...it played over and over on song number three. I'm not familiar with the group."

Lori asks slowly, "Do you think it means anything?"

Kill him mommy, he knows!

"Must, but I don't know why. I was surprised to see it on your shelf, haven't had a chance to listen to it. Do you mind if I do?" I'm distracted and fascinated by it as I walk over to the stereo.

"Gates was one sick puppy!" I say setting it in the tray and looking for the Play button. "You should have heard the things he said. What kind of sick mind has someone got to have to do such cold-blooded things?"

"Why do you consider him a sick puppy?"

That question hits me oddly so I stop with the CD and look at her.

"The mind is a crazy place, Jake." She says sounding strangely defensive. "It's hard to tell why someone would do such things. It's difficult to say this because of your friend but sometimes I suppose some people are led, destined, even directed to do such things. They don't have a choice."

To say I'm astounded by her defense of Gates is grossly understating. You can only carry liberalism and the "Ban Capital Punishment" banner just so far. A lot of people because of their circumstances and what life handed them could give up and become bad, but they don't.

"Are you saying Gates may have had an excuse for what he did? He was driven to kill?"

Shrugging her shoulders Lori replies, "I'm just saying that circumstances have the power to change us be it for good or bad. Not everyone has the capacity to handle what happens to us in this life, that's all I'm saying, Jake."

My answer to her philosophy of understanding is brief, pointed, aggressive and sarcastic.

"So let me get this straight, I need to understand that Michael Gates was abused or spanked or whatever so it was okay for him to kill my friend! Oh, I get it, my God what was I thinking?"

The temperature in the living room plunges from pleasantly warm to bitterly cold.

See mommy, I told you!

The fight inside overpowers her and she decides to stop it there before it gets ugly.

I don't want to hurt you!

She looks torn and bewildered. "Jake, I'm sorry. I don't know what to say. Maybe I'm just not ready, I don't know. I think I'm going to need more time..."

I'm crushed. I have been suffocating her with my life and my job. It's too much for me so it must be way too much for her. I don't know what to say or if I should say anything at all.

What's wrong with you, man?

As I turn to leave I stop and look back hoping she will invite me back into her arms. The moment seems to last for an eternity but her eyes plead with me.

I gently close the door behind me. Standing outside I have no sense of body position. I'm numb. Reluctantly, I make my way back to my car.

Walk away man, just walk away.

58

"Daddy, it's you're little girl. I need you, daddy, I did a bad thing!"

He listened over the telephone line while his little girl collapsed under a mountain of anguish. He was a powerful man yet he knew that he was powerless at that moment to rescue her.

All he could provide was compassion, understanding and the familiar voice that dispensed the logic of life. His grip tightened on the telephone. "Mika, where are you, baby? I can be there ? "

"No daddy!" Mika forced out the words through her sobbing. She knew she was stronger but this time her raging emotions took complete control.

There wasn't a chapter in the parent manual that Robert could refer to in order to help his daughter. It wasn't a subject parents normally faced. During his early years in Special Ops he had killed but never close up. He never saw the victims. "Death by detonation" his comrades called it.

All he could do now was to listen to his little girl who was hurting that was what she needed most. So Robert Scott, captain of industry, who was highly regarded as an effective communicator and hard-nosed negotiator by heads of state, struggled to hold back his own tears.

Mika finally settled down and told her story. The fact that he was there for her meant everything. The words came out slowly and deliberately as if she were writing her FBI report. "I just needed to talk to you."

"Where are you, honey?" he said in a soothing tone.

"I'm at Jake's."

"Good, is he there with you?"

"No, I don't know where he is right now but I'm sure he'll be home soon." Her intuition told her differently when she first arrived. She took a shallow breath.

"We were at a standstill in the case – no leads, no clues. I had gone back to Quantico to regroup. Harmon called and told me Ed was murdered. I flew back immediately." She stopped to wipe away tears.

"When I got back to the precinct I met Harmon and we watched through the one-way mirror while Jake interrogated the suspect." She took another halting breath.

"Jake left the room for a minute. What he had been listening to during the confession turned his stomach." Her head slowly shook from side to side. "Daddy, after what he said, after what he has done…God could not have created such a monster!"

Robert sat down slowly in his chair. He was careful not to miss even one word. Mika continued as more tears fell.

"Jake walked out into the hallway and saw me. He started walking toward me when there was a shot fired behind him. Gates had taken an officer's gun…shot and killed him. After the officer went down. Gates turned and aimed at Jake!"

She choked. "He…he was going to shoot! Jake wasn't armed…once, twice, reflex…" She pushed hard to get the words out.

"Mika," Robert said and tried to reach out to her through the telephone line.

"Jake dropped to the floor just as I fired! I thought I hit him…but Gates went down instead."

She stopped speaking as every detail of the shooting replayed in her mind from the sound of the discharging weapon, to the spurting of blood, up until the last breath she saw him take. Her confession was over and she waited for forgiveness.

"I can't do this anymore. I, I can't do this anymore…"

"Stay there until Jake gets home, be with him - he understands. I will do whatever you want, get whatever you need, sweetheart. You are not alone, Mika! Jake, I, we're all there for you!" His voice cracked with concern and hurt.

"I love you Mika, so very much!"

"I love you too, daddy!"

Robert heard the line go dead. He stood for a long time staring out at the city lights through his office windows. He thought about life, the world, people, why, why not, and about the human struggle with good and evil.

Across town those same thoughts passed through Mika right before she crashed into a deep, coma-like sleep. It was the mind's way to sooth the pain.

59

A brilliant astrophysicist said that chronology particularly the past is protected. He said that even if you had a time machine and traveled backward the past would remain intact. Yet we always try to alter it. We try to paint it over in different colors of perception-red, reason-blue and excuse-yellow. What we simply should do is learn to live with it.

So far the bad in my life is running far ahead of the good. I thought my relationship with Lori would change that. I was wrong. Falling in love happens all of the time in the movies, why can't it happen for me?

What were you thinking, Roberts?

It occurs to me that I'm driving in circles. Harmon is right I didn't belong behind the wheel of a three-thousand-pound lethal weapon. I figure it's time to hose down the fire inside.

For some strange, mystical, illogical reason I pull up in front of Chipper's place. It's way too late for me to be here, alone. I've forgotten about Chipper's warning. I must be completely out of my mind. I guess that happens when you just don't care anymore.

My feet completely disregard the warnings from my brain and I resolutely march toward the front door. Beneath Chipper's sign I come face to face with several of the brothers who are understandably irritated and in shock.

"You got a death wish or something'?" one asks coldly.

I must have because I'm outnumbered and outgunned. An Uzi is brought up under my chin and I'm forced into a stare down with the brother holding the weapon until I hear a familiar voice.

"YOU MUS' BE ONE DUMB MUTHA!"

The words provide a temporary reprieve from an early demise because the trigger man looks at Chipper. The big man prevents my impending death not out of respect for the badge or love for me but because of his curiosity. He wants the answer before I'm executed.

I look at the muzzle first and then at the man behind the weapon. "You have the right to remain silent!" I declare.

Roaring with laughter Chipper rolls back rotating his three-hundred-pound-plus frame three hundred and sixty degrees around in his pinstriped Armani suit. He starts banging the wall hard with his meaty fist as he gasps for air to replace the laughter.

"You...you are one crazy sonabitch!" He waves at me. "Come here, come here!"

My right hand rises up and nudges the Uzi away. The scornful, disappointed look on the brother's face says that in another place and at another time I can plan on a rematch. Like Moses parting the Red Sea I make my way to Chipper who throws an arm around me and leads all of us in a procession inside.

At his table he kicks out a chair indicating I should sit. I graciously and politely accept his invitation and do exactly as I'm told. As he wipes tears of laughter from his eyes Chipper gets back to business.

"Whatchu doin' back here, man? I told you the last time not to come back!" He sizes me up. "Either you are deaf or jus' stupid, I don't know which!"

He shifts his massive frame back in his chair and raises his empty glass. It is instantly replaced by a full one. The woman who sits to his right wipes his brow and strokes his bald head. It strangely occurs to me at this particularly odd time that I would pay money to see Chipper and Harmon in a wrestling match.

"But I jus' gots to know, crazy man, what the hell are you doin' here?"

My head bobs, I smirk. After a few shakes of my apparently empty cranium I respond, "A woman."

"Getouttahere, I knew it!" He roars again only stopping to ask, "You ain't jivin' me are you?"

"No jive."

"Damn, how many times that story been told!" he says with a knowing look.

I force a grin. I don't understand why I'm speaking to him like we're best friends. Then again, he is the only one interested in my sad story.

"I need to fall into a deep, deep hole…and drown." The intensity in my eyes backs me up.

"I know dat's right!" he says assuredly.

He looks around the interior of the bar at his contemporaries who are stunned by his taking me under his wing. The look is enough to convince them to go back to what they were doing which they do with complete disregard for the fact that I'm an officer of the law.

Illicit business transactions take place. The jukebox cranks back up and booms base lines against the interior walls as some nasty rap lyrics talk about killing white folks. The air is heavy with smoke.

Chipper signals and a stiffer drink arrives in front of me. I can tell it's strong by the smell. A few of these and I'll be stiff which is what I'm there for. It also happens to be the best money could buy. To my surprise, it is also on the house.

I knock it back and as the alcohol slithers into my blood stream I go into a form of temporary cardiac arrest. It feels as if my eyes are rolling back. I try to stay sitting up and not embarrass myself.

"So, what is your story, crazy man? I like sad, sentimental stories, they make me cry!" he says. Chipper is on a roll. He laughs so loud I can't hear the music any longer. Then he settles back into his chair, hands tented and waits patiently for my answer.

My glass has been replaced with a full one. I don't even notice how or when it arrived.

Some detective you are, Roberts!

Just as I open my mouth to answer Chipper has a major revelation.

"Hey! You're the pig I saw on the news! You...and that serial killer guy!" he exclaims while snapping his fingers. He also says it as if he doesn't have a list of his own victims to claim. I don't understand why I'm friendly with Chipper the serial killer and not with Gates, probably because Chipper didn't murder my friend.

"Blew the mutha away and you've got lady problems, too? Hey bro, your life really does suck!"

The man said a mouthful. After telling the amused Chipper the highlights or rather the lowlights of my life, my day ends face down on the table in an alcohol-induced, deep sleep.

60

She held the frame with the picture of her beautiful Emily smiling back at her frozen in her sixteenth year. The photograph was taken the day before the suicide. It was the last happy moment they had together. It was the last happy memory Lori had. She hoped that would have changed with Jake.

I'm glad you made him leave, mommy.

Lori shrugged but then the other voice broke into their conversation and scolded her.

He's trouble, just like all of the rest. They hurt and beat, and you suffer. They all have to die!

She answered out loud because there was no one left to hear. "But I really think he's different than the others. He's caring, gentle – passionate. He would be good for me. He would take care of me."

He'll abuse you. He doesn't care about your pain. He wants filthy sex and to control you.

Emily spoke from the photo.

It's just us, mommy, if it wasn't for daddy I'd still be with you. He hurt me, mommy!

Tears welled up in Lori's eyes. The scene of Emily's suicide, the note she left and the funeral all played in her mind. Watching the mourners throw the dirt on the casket was too much to bear. Maybe the voices were right. But he was different and right for her. She wanted him.

But what if he discovers my dark secret?

She needed time to think. She had to find a way to make it work
and a way to silence the voices.

"I love you Emily, but I still need to live my life!"

Lori picked up the phone and dialed. She waited. The voice at the
other end of the line said, "Crew scheduling, Monica."

"Hi, this is Lori Powers, employee number zero-zero-three-zero-
one. I thought you might have a trip that you needed covered, I'm
available."

"You must be psychic because I was just trying to fill an overnight
to Boston, interested? It leaves at eleven in the morning and will
be back by midmorning the next day. Oh wait, I show you in the
computer as out sick."

"That was earlier, something I ate but I'm okay now. I can take
that overnight."

"Great, I'll show you on the trip!" The crew scheduler was ecstatic.

"I'll be there, thanks," Lori said replacing the phone on the
receiver.

She listened. The voices were gone. She wandered out into the living room and listened closely but she didn't hear them anymore.
After repositioning the flowers on the table she saw the CD Jake
had found. She picked it up and replaced it on the shelf.

In her bedroom where she thought she would be sharing the night
with Jake she instead gathered her things for the flight. She had
just enough time to pack and get a little sleep.

Boston was a favorite layover of hers. She loved walking around
the city and knew exactly what to pack for. She could go to the
real "Cheers" bar regardless of the fact that it didn't resemble in
the least the set of the famous television show. Another option if

the temperature was right would be to get some sun in the park with the swan boats.

She also thought she might stop by one of the many palm readers to have her fortune told. Maybe her future still included Jake.

61

Man deserves to get wasted!" With a wave of his hand Chipper gave specific orders like a commander out in the field to the brother who arrived.

"Call up his partner," he says sternly. "You tell the man where he is and to come get him now! I cain't have no white...red...or whatever the hell trash he is lying 'round here!" He leans over and pretends to take my pulse.

"Should have gone into a life of crime, dawg - it's so much easier!" he whispers into my ear. "I mean it this time - don't come back here again!"

After he pats my head two more brothers hoist me up and carry me outside. An irreverent toss of my limp body lands me on the hood of my car. My carcass remains there until Harmon arrives. Everything stays mostly blurred until I hear Harmon's voice which startles me halfway back to reality.

"JAKE!"

There is no mistaking the disappointment on his face, in his eyes or flying out of his mouth. Before, he would have taken it in stride. Now, as Chief Inspector he has a very different viewpoint.

Harmon's voice sounds as if it is coming from somewhere inside a very long tunnel. He tells the detective he brought with him, "Help me get him in my car. You drive his. We'll drop him back at his apartment."

His arms wave in several directions stopping long enough to look at Chipper who offers up a taunting salute. The two of them exchange a cold glare. I'm not the only one who wants to see them go at it. The next thing I hear is a car engine start.

It takes me awhile to get my coordinates. The fog isn't lifting fast. I squint and press my fingers hard into my temples. It's hard to raise my head for some reason.

"Har, is that you?"

"Yeah, it's me."

Deserving to be smacked up alongside my head I instigate him shouting, "LET ME DRIVE!"

I groan and start laughing my butt off. I can't stop. The brothers watch the pathetic scene until they can't watch any longer. Walking away they wave us off with middle fingers raised. Harmon grabs the nape of my neck and shakes me hard. There is no doubt about it, he is in one of his "I don't need this" moods.

What was in those drinks?

"Are you as out of your mind as you want me to believe?"

"HEY! Who asked you to come get me, wasn't me!" I slur out.

"No Jake, it wasn't you, it was your new friend Chipper! What the hell is wrong with you! And what in God's name are you doing there in the middle of the night ? ALONE! Dammit, Jake!"

"Investri…grating."

Harmon is livid. He had finally found a quiet moment in a quiet room to sit and decompress when he got the call from one of Chipper's homies.

"Investigating? Investigating what, how fast a bullet can travel though your thick skull?"

Too caught up in my own misery and too wasted, I don't realize how much he is hurting. I haven't been a very good partner or a very good friend. And still he's here for me. His tone softens as he props me up inside the car.

"You'll be okay," he says then patiently listens to my drunken ramblings.

"None of it worked out, man! None of it's ever going to work. My life is nothing but a waste of carbon and water!" My head falls back against the seat and then snaps upright.

"WE'RE ALONE! Do you get that? You, me, EVERYBODY! Sure, we all share the same space but inside that space we're just ALONE!" I have an urgent need I haven't had in many years.

"Stop the car!"

"What?"

"Stop the car, I'm going to hurl."

"Oh no you ain't - you hold it in! We've only got a few blocks to go!"

"I can't!" I start to reach for the door. Harmon swings into the curb and screeches to a stop. Shoving the door open I wretch the contents of my stomach on the pavement. The putrid taste is…putrid and encourages another involuntary release.

The heaving helps to reduce the side effects of the alcohol. After I toss what I pray is the last of it my head starts to slowly clear. With nothing else available I wipe my chin on my sleeve.

"Sorry."

"Yeah I know, sorry again."

"No I mean it, I'm sorry!" Guilt pervades me. "I thought maybe…it was going to work out with Lori. I thought ?"

"It didn't work out?" He sounds almost convincingly disappointed.

"No, it didn't."

"Sorry, man." He grabs my arm. "Maybe you've been looking in the wrong place, did you ever think of that?"

"I've used them all up my friend, there's no place left to look in. I'm telling you man, it's not out there for me!" I look at the passing cars.

"Sure it is! The right one has been under your nose all along. You just don't want to see it."

He is losing me, I'm having trouble with which way is up and he wants me to think harder? With a side-to-side head wave I insist he is wrong.

Harmon parks in front of my apartment. It's after three in the morning and I smell bad from my night out at Chipper's. As I climb pathetically out of the passenger side my peripheral vision sees my car pull up behind us and the headlights go out. I hear a door slam and footsteps approach.

Harmon leans out his window and shouts, "Give me a minute."

The footsteps walk away and in the shadows a cigarette is lit. Harmon looks at me from the driver's seat as I bend down to say goodnight.

"Jake, I dropped Mika off here hours ago. She's inside, and she's hurting. She needs you." He waits and stares straight out the windshield. Turning toward me he says, "And you my friend, need her."

I feel stupid, really stupid. He's right. What would I do without

Harmon?

He simply waves me on and starts the car. The shadow returns, smiles and slips past me into the passenger seat. I acknowledge his efforts to return my car. They drive off, my partner and what's-his-name. I watch the taillights disappear. It's time to go home.

The lights are off inside the apartment. She is either asleep or waiting in the dark to blind-side me with a blunt object. God knows I deserve it.

I go with asleep so I try to be as quiet as I can. As I close and lock the front door I know that I need to clean up my body, and my act. As I walk through the apartment I see a trail of clothing ? blouse, bra, pants, panties, socks and shoes. At the end of the trail and in my bed is Mika, out cold.

Who's been sleeping in my bed?

I know what that is like. It was the same for me after shooting the girl.

62

It happens in steps. The first was staring at the bottle of barbiturates. Step two required a decision. The third step involved ingesting them followed by a down wash of a fifth of alcohol. Of course it should be one's preferred alcohol as it would be the last thing you would enjoy before step four.

The last step, also known as the final step, was falling asleep and not coming back to this life, not ever.

Lori had all of the ingredients. She even rationalized that Emily's choice years earlier didn't seem as harsh or misguided as she had once thought it was. She also considered the fact that nobody would care if she died. Lori was after all the last of her family line, there was no one left to grieve for her.

What was the point of going on? Her job had lost its luster years ago. There were just so many times she could go to Paris, Rome – Omaha. The hotels sucked. All of the restaurant food tasted the same and most were borderline outbreaks of salmonella. And the crew members gossiped faster than light speed.

The worst part was there was nobody left to fall in love with. Jake was never coming back she was certain of that. The others were never right for her. Even if Jake and she had made a go of it how could her life ever return to normal? Sooner or later her secret would surface and how would that be? Jake arresting her for murder? And then there were the voices, they would never go away.

Decision time approached and Lori was stuck at step two. She looked up at the clock on the kitchen wall. She watched as the second hand circled for a complete minute while counting each second along the way.

Maybe she should go to see Emily one last time. With the right words and the right coaxing perhaps Emily would see that Jake was right for her. If not, Emily might have some encouraging words to say about the philosophy of suicide. For some inexplicable reason it was so much easier to end someone else's life than your own.

Lori pushed the bottle of pills away and got up from the kitchen table. She wiped down the counter top and placed the dishes inside the dishwasher. All the while she thought about Jake.

A quick glance at the clock again and she decided to get some sleep. If in the morning she still wanted to end her life, she would. She turned out the kitchen light and walked through the dark to the solitude of her bedroom.

63

Why should anyone care about me?

It is the question I ask the ragged face I find in the mirror after toweling off the steam from the shower. The image says the same words back to me in reverse at exactly the same time.

A shower feels good like starting over - a new beginning. The dirt of life that you accumulate and drag around on you everyday gets washed down the drain. The problem is the dirt always comes back tomorrow.

Feeling much better than even ten minutes ago my head is clearer. The only remnant left of my social outing with Chipper is my churning stomach. That weird, burning sensation would have to find its destined path all by itself.

Now what? Do I go out into the bedroom naked, climb into bed and press up against Mika as if all were fine with the world? Or, do I retreat and wait for my tired and worn body to be discovered beneath the covers on the couch?

I retreat. As I make my way out of the steamy bathroom I head for the bedroom door in the dark. I know the way, have been there and done that. As my hand drags the door closed I hear her voice.

"Jake?" she asks softly. Her head rises above the pillow and I see her squinting into the darkness. Her hand tosses back the covers and exposes her naked body in the moonlight.

"What are you doing? Where are you going?" she asks sounding groggy as if she has taken some sleep medication.

"I didn't want to wake you, sorry. You need to get some sleep. I'll take the couch. We'll talk in the morning."

Just as the door is about to close I hear, "FREEZE, F-B-I!" Her volume is startling. I don't know which way to go – in or out. I leave it up to her. In a pouting voice she gives me the answer I had hoped for. "Don't go, stay, I want you to hold me."

We had been there before. We didn't make it then, why would we make it now? Why be crushed all over again? I didn't think my heart could take another solid hit right now.

"Are you sure?"

I have to give her every opportunity to avoid the heartbreak and pain. I won't push, insist or take advantage of her.

"I'm sure."

She holds her arms out for me. I want to lie next to her and be held by her. I want everything to be right in the world. I don't want to make any more mistakes.

How could Mika be a mistake?

64

I love to read. In particular I am intimately familiar with all of the great philosophers from the ancients and the Greeks to the Romans, on through the Renaissance to modern. I have a good deal of accumulated philosophies of my own gathered from my years on the streets. But who would have thought that Forrest's mom had it right?

With Mika's head lying on my chest I listen while she talks about her life and the questions we all carry around silently in our heads.

"I've decided to leave the FBI."

That one falls hard. I'm not sure I heard her right; maybe it was the after effects of my foray into Chipper's hazy world.

"Say that again."

"I said I'm leaving the FBI, quitting ? resigning." She repositions herself on the pillows against the headboard. She says it so casually that it is obvious she has already weighed the pros and cons.

Tough call, I don't know if I should encourage or discourage her it is after all coming on the heels of yesterday. I had the same debate inside my head about my job after the shooting, still do. One minute my job is devastating and the next it's everything I am.

We listen as a night shower begins to pelt against the windows. The storm intensifies rapidly and cleans the dirty world outside. We watch as lightning flashes illuminate the bedroom. Simple rules governed our lives inside. The hard lessons of life were outside that window, just like the storm.

A great friend of mine used to watch out for me a long time ago. He saw to it that I had a smile on my face when things weren't going my way. It devastated me when he was killed in a small plane crash.

Although I don't believe in much anymore, the usual things like religion, politics and people I do believe he's still watching over me. I can't explain feeling his presence, like an angel. I decide to try and be an angel for Mika.

"What are you going to do instead?"

"Private practice I think, security – a private eye! That way I can control my life."

That same thought has banged through my head on more than one occasion. The private sector is always looking for talented, well-trained professionals to protect them. The pay is good and the hours aren't any worse. One has to play the game, maybe kiss some behind but that's normal.

"I'm in!" I tell her with confidence.

Mika rises quickly off the pillows. "Do you mean that?"

"Yeah absolutely, I need a change!"

Revelations, they come in many different shapes and sizes even out loud sometimes. I look at her. We don't speak but the thoughts gush between us as if they were being shot out of a fire hose. It's funny how the world looks the same from her small dark eyes and my big hazel eyes.

Outside the thunder pounds against the pavement like one massive Huey helicopter or a parade of Harleys. I can't help but wonder if it is a sign from my angel waving us off.

Quietly Mika admits, "I can't stop thinking about it, him."

"Gates?"

"Yeah, I know he deserved to die. I just didn't want to be the executioner. I guess you felt the same about the girl?"

The words jam up inside my head. "Still do. You think that's why we want out...because it would be easier to hide?"

Be a good angel for her, Jake.

"Maybe," she answers grasping my hand and holding it against her breast.

No longer mesmerized by the rain pelting the window I look at her. I feel the warmth of her body against mine as we embrace. Somewhere along the way our lips press together. There is no tomorrow, there is just the two of us floating in our own private universe.

65

"Hi, I'm Benjamin and I'll be working the lead position. This is Kara, Bobby and back there sitting quietly by herself is poor Megan." They all giggled while Benjamin continued with his briefing.

"Meg's a little down right now. Apparently, her plans to become the next Mrs. Captain Nick Parker have washed out!"

Kara said, "Captain 'Slick' in the cockpit broke her heart last night but that's nothing new with him. That's why he chases the new ones!"

Lori looked down the cabin aisle and saw a distraught face that didn't just tell of a broken heart or another sad rejection. To Lori, Megan's face expressed severe inner pain. She made a mental note to ask her about it later.

"That's too bad."

After the introductions the flight attendants scurried about the cabin preparing the aircraft for boarding. Following the deadly terrorist attacks there were many more things to check before departure. The crews were more cognizant of the consequences associated with air travel.

They exchanged small talk while they went about their duties such as who was sleeping with whom, who got fired recently and there were thousands of weird passenger stories.

While she completed her duties Lori couldn't help but be drawn to Megan. The girl was young, almost too young Lori thought. She looked as if she hadn't graduated from high school yet. She also looked dazed, lost and afraid.

With ease Lori made her way to the back of the cabin until she was within a few feet of Megan who didn't seem to notice her right away.

"Hi Megan," she held out her hand but all she got was a brief nod back. "I'm Lori. Is this your regular line?" Lori watched closely to see if she was getting through before she continued. "I picked up this trip late last night."

Lori's smile, the same that touched most everyone, finally affected Megan who reluctantly acknowledged her. Megan she guessed was about the age Emily would be if she were still alive.

"I'm sorry, I'm a little distracted right now and I have a lot on my mind." She glanced at Lori. "Yes, this is my line, has been all month."

Grasping Megan's shoulder Lori asked, "If you want to talk about it, I'm here."

Megan was taken by surprise by Lori's statement and tried desperately to conceal her feelings. She backed away and turned toward the galley where she started to fidget with the drawers and doors. She didn't know what to say. Lori did her best to calm her.

"Megan I know it's none of my business but you look a little spooked to me. As a crew member I need to know if there's a problem before we get going here."

Not wanting her abilities as a flight attendant questioned Megan took a firm stand. "I'm fine thank you, there's no reason for you or anyone else to be concerned about me!"

"Really, Meg, I was just offering a shoulder if you needed one. I've been doing this a long time. I know a little about some things." A reassuring nod followed.

Megan eased off. "Thanks, I think I could use a shoulder right about now actually."

"Listen, I'll trade places with Bobby and work back here if it's all right with you. I don't think he'll mind." Lori flashed another irresistible smile.

Megan replied, "I don't want to be a bother."

Lori squeezed Megan's arm lightly and said, "Not a problem! I'll get it done and be back in a few minutes."

She turned and walked up the long center aisle to relay the change in staffing assignment. There was no objection as Bobby and Benjamin were roommates. Passengers followed behind Lori as she made her way back to the aft cabin. They started filing into the various rows of assigned seats.

Approaching Megan again Lori said, "It's just you and me, babe."

Feeling a little more at ease, Megan started to open up and confide in Lori. "I'm sorry, I've -- "

"Don't worry about it, we'll get to it later when everyone settles down." Lori smiled causing Megan to finally smile back. They went about their respective duties. Each time Lori saw the chance she tried to establish a stronger bond with her.

66

There is renewed excitement in Harmon's voice as he states, "We've uncovered some interesting information."

He definitely isn't the same Harmon. Now he is Harmon Eldrige Blackwell ? the Chief!" He is more direct, unyielding and confident.

It is apparent to even the least observant that every detective in the room has a newfound respect for him. I know I do. He addresses me directly with, "Roberts, nice to see you could make it in today."

Well, I thought I'd like the new Harmon. The jury is apparently still out.

"Good news Detective, the Grand Jury *and* Internal Affairs cleared you on the girl shoot. I believe the official term used is 'justified'. Of course some of us knew it all along but you apparently had your doubts."

His words take a mountain of grief off of my back. I wonder if anyone sees me breathe a sigh of relief. I glance at Mika who is standing by my side. She hasn't said a word about leaving the FBI to anyone yet but I feel her squeeze my forearm. Harmon shifts his attention to her.

"Agent Scott, I believe you asked about residents in our fair city who own late-model, foreign automobiles?"

"Yes I did, Chief." She is not as aggressive as she usually is and waits for Harmon to divulge what he has.

"Well as we are all aware Gates was driving a late-model silver Lexus when he was apprehended. What we didn't know until late yesterday was that he leased the car the day before the murder. A receipt for the CD also for the day before was in the center armrest."

Harmon waits for the exchange of looks to subside before continuing. Mika gives a quick look back in my direction and becomes more animated.

"Which would seem to indicate that he is a copy-cat killer and not the original!" she says.

Harmon snidely replies, "You're the expert, F-B-I Agent Scott!"

67

"Cabin service is complete and they're all snoozing," Lori said. It's as good a time as any Megan to have our conversation." To get her to open up and reveal what was distressing her Lori had spent the better part of the flight getting Megan to feel more at ease with her.

Although hesitant Megan was ready to talk about it and there wasn't going to be a better place then at thirty-five thousand feet over the eastern United States in the back of a Boeing 737.

Well, home or in a lounge would have been better but the aircraft was going to have to do. Both flight attendants sat down on the aft jump seats. Lori held on to a plastic bottle of Evian while Megan sipped at a Coke.

"Meg, I know we don't know each other well but sometimes that's better."

Megan agreed. Making a motion in the direction of the others she said, "They think I'm stupid and naïve. They laughed at me. I didn't tell them anything, they just think they know what happened." She sighed. "I mean, they think I was taken advantage of by the captain, Captain Parker."

Lori shrugged slightly and asked, "This is about a bad date?"

When Lori saw Megan's eyes well up with tears and her lower lip quiver, she knew it was far worse. She put an arm around Megan and gave her a gentle hug. Megan stared down at her Coke.

Her trembling hands rose to wipe away the tears. Lori handed her some tissues. Megan buried her face in Lori's shoulder and didn't speak as the tears fell. After several moments had passed the story unraveled in bitter pieces.

"I thought he was a good man. I mean, he's an airline captain! People look up to them! How was I to know that he was evil and sick! At first, he was so kind he helped me with my chair, he was concerned about how I felt, listened to what I had to say." Megan shook her head.

"He was so polite, so caring. Then, without warning he changed into a filthy animal!"

Lori began to realize what Megan wasn't able to bring herself to say. Captain Parker had taken Megan against her will. "Megan, are you telling me he --" But she didn't have to finish the question. The trauma on Megan's face and in her eyes told the rest of the story.

"I feel so ashamed!" Megan sobbed uncontrollably while trying to hide from the view of the passengers. Lori put her arms around Megan in an attempt to protect her although she knew it was too late.

See mommy, all men are evil!

Megan's face became Emily's. Lori felt every sting and bite that her Emily had suffered all over again. She understood Megan's trauma all too well.

He should be punished, mommy!

As Lori held Megan she suppressed her anger and outrage. She maintained a calm façade. Although it burned she was determined to keep her anger buried deep within her until she could inflict it on Nick Parker. He would pay for what he had done to that child.

"You mean this captain, the one flying this aircraft?" Lori asked struggling to hold back her astonishment.

When she was able to Megan faced Lori and said, "Please don't say anything to anybody, promise me!" The fear in her eyes was obvious.

"He said he had friends and I could lose my job...that no one would take my word against his because he's a captain!"

Lori pressed Megan's head against her. Megan's pleas became muffled and muted. "When did this happen?"

"Last night, on the layover, please don't tell anyone, I don't want anyone to know! I just needed to -- "

"I won't, I promise. Do you need any medical attention?"

Megan shook her head no. Lori knew she would keep the promise but she also knew that Captain Parker would never ever hurt anyone ever again.

68

Sometimes what we say can burn a hole. When he puts his mind to it Harmon's statements can burn down a forest. He likes to provoke a reaction. The sparring is meant to stimulate ordinary and mundane mental activity. And today isn't any different.

"All white people have black hearts!" he states as fact.

"Are you referring to ancestry or character?" I inquire politely, curiously.

"Ancestry according to noted prominent anthropologists who have determined beyond a shadow of a doubt that all of mankind started in Africa. Now if you want to talk character a case could be made."

"Harmon Blackwell, you stop it! If you think I'm going to sit here and listen to you make such a ridiculous statement then you better be prepared for a 'wuppin'!"

Mika never hesitates to speak up. It's in her nature. Besides she can usually back him down. It's okay for Harmon and me to have such discussions but Mika takes it personal.

Harmon quickly adds, "Hear that Jake, 'wuppin' ? the white woman said 'wuppin'!"

I interrupt with, "What about red men?" I keep it going for the fun of it. "Do all red men have black hearts?"

After a quick glance at a fuming Mika, Harmon answers with a nonchalant, "All men."

She still hasn't told anyone that she wants to quit the Feds and maybe she won't. Frustrated with us she exclaims, "There is something very wrong with you two!"

The three of us left the house and are headed for the Abrams residence. The possibility that Gates might have actually been a copy-cat killer gives us cause to take another look. Maybe, in light of our new perspective we will see something different now. We also plan to go back to the warehouse.

We have been to Abrams' residence so many times that even Mika knows the shortcut through the 'hood. It gives Harmon a chance to scope out the whores who overall look quite presentable today. He gives each one a friendly wave and some of the girls return a mock proposition.

"I wonder, because of my new position, if I get a discount."

"Maybe now you can afford one," Mika says as I watch her drive.

Across the street from the Abrams mansion our Mr. Dickens is outside as usual watering and tending to his flower garden. He doesn't even glance at us as we turn into the driveway. That supports my theory that he never saw anything on the night of the murder.

The Abrams house looks almost forlorn with the shreds of yellow crime scene tape still fluttering in the breeze. It is midmorning but the interior is dark. We don't speak as we wander through the premises.

The scent of death still lingers inside.

69

Captain Parker had noticed Lori from the open cockpit door. He remarked loudly enough to make his first officer jerk his head up from his paperwork to see who Parker was talking about. Both watched as she introduced herself to the other flight attendants.

There wasn't enough time for her to enter the cockpit and say hello as boarding began right after and passengers obstructed her path.

Parker confidently said to his first officer, "It's a long layover in Boston, she'll need a guide."

The first officer asked, "Didn't you bang Megan last night?"

"Of course but I have an insatiable appetite and I like to eat out." He grinned while staring down the cabin aisle at Lori. "She looks like a gourmet meal to me."

His copilot grinned at Parker's blustering. He knew that some captains' egos didn't stop in the cockpit. Some just needed the world to believe that they were desired by all women. But this captain was excruciating.

Parker finally lost sight of Lori and returned to his flight preparations. While she occupied his thoughts he also planned for a backup just in case.

Maybe I'll take another turn with sweet little Megan!

The first officer completing his paperwork asked, "Is twenty-six thousand still good on the fuel?"

With a dismissing nod Parker let him know that the fuel request was correct. Then he continued with his fantasy about Lori only this time he added Megan in on the outside chance of a threesome. Benjamin poked his head in and asked if either pilot needed anything.

Parker replied, "A shapely blonde with great legs for me!"

"A Coke for me," the first officer tossed.

Both he and Benjamin had long since learned to ignore Captain Parker's errant ramblings. After Benjamin left to retrieve the Coke the copilot chided his captain.

"Didn't you just get married?"

Parker ignored him. He didn't like to be interrupted in the middle of his fantasies. But because the question was raised he thought about his recent marriage to Susan. In his own way he wanted her especially when she wore that thong. And she was always so anxious to please him.

But to Nick, Susan was really nothing more than backup. He would have her if he failed elsewhere, she had a great body. She also had a seven-year-old daughter from a previous disastrous marriage who was what he coveted more than anything.

He had absolutely no illusions about who he was as a person, it was all about him. Although he was a good provider he only did what was necessary and required unless it accommodated his own self-serving desires and interests.

By nature he was callous, biting and crude. His lack of respect for women was surpassed only by the size of his ego. Parker believed it was his responsibility to enlighten all women in deviant sexual practices especially those never before touched. Even while he plotted a rendezvous with Lori later that evening he stored a thought in the back of his mind for when he returned home.

Little Tabitha is about ready for a lesson!

He never sought help for his sickness because he never once thought he had a deviant personality although some of his victims like Megan had suggested he had. Besides it was up to them to understand and make allowances.

After all he thought, even the good guys had bad sides too.

70

It has always been my fervent hope that someday, with the help of genetic research, scientists would be able to tighten some of the loose screws walking among us. Of course that would end my career but it would be worth it.

I get down on my knees and look under the bed beneath where the slaughter took place. And I dig through dresser drawers but only find the same stuff that was there when I last searched the residence. It has collected more dust but that is about it.

"Harmon, help me move the bed over a few feet, it's too heavy for one guy."

He walks over and places one of his huge hands on the frame while I struggle with both hands. The bed shifts toward the wall. The light from the bedroom window illuminates the carpet underneath the bed.

Harmon asks, "Did any of the techs move the bed?"

"No, I don't believe so," Mika answers while she pulls clothing out of the wash basket in the hall. "I don't think they were in here either. You know how techs are, if it isn't lying in plain sight!"

With my cheek nearly pressed against it I search the sunlit exposed carpet for hairs or fibers. The nauseating smell permeates the bedroom and is distracting even to a seasoned professional like myself. I don't see anything.

While we search Mika asks, "Where do you guys stand on high IQ versus criminally insane question?"

"I've never been accused of being either," is my casual reply. "Gates had a very high IQ. Are you asking if he was over the edge or sane?"

"Put me down for insane, there's no doubt in my mind. You can't do something like he did to Ed without having screws loose!" Harmon adds.

Mika follows with, "To commit such acts suggests insanity, right? And to be able to elude the heat as long as he supposedly did suggests above average intelligence."

Harmon and I exchange looks.

"I guess what I want to know is was Gates that good?" She stops digging through the basket and looks at the two of us. "Or just incredibly lucky?"

This time Harmon and I exchange shrugs. I offer up some background for the discussion.

"When I had him in interrogation he seemed as normal and sane as Harmon here. That was the eerie part for me. He spoke calmly, clearly and detailed. He became defensive at times but was mostly in control."

Mika interjects with, "Calm, clear and detailed right up until he grabbed the weapon and shot the officer. He had to be insane to think he could get away with that inside the station!"

"But he was sane enough to know that it would end someday and he *chose* suicide by cop." That is the total of my two cents.

Mika counters with, "I'm not talking about what method he chose to die. It's more, why did he want it to end? He was on top; it doesn't make any sense unless he really wasn't the one."

While I enjoy the challenging conversation I think we're wasting our time. "Well that's why we're here, to see if we can prove it one way or another but I don't see anything that's going to reopen the case. Theory and speculation isn't going to be enough."

Mika steps into the walk-in closet and starts pulling things apart. She apparently sees no reason to preserve the crime scene any longer and no one in their right mind is going to occupy that room again at least not in the near future.

Harmon says, "I'm going to take a walk outside and get some fresh air. I hate the smell in here." He gets as far as the door before he adds, "I need to call in to see how everything is going back at the ranch. I'll be back."

He's not the only one who wants out. This is just one more in a series of futile examinations of this crime scene. I also have to do my duty while on duty.

"I need to use the bathroom."

"I'm almost done here," Mika says "We can head over to the warehouse when you both get back."

I stop to peek around the corner at her before I hit the head. She looks back, smiles and makes a gesture that suggests we will escape for a quiet evening later.

Abrams' bathroom is overly ornate. I hate this kind of excessive décor. It's overdone, tacky and a waste of hard-earned money. If you have so much money that you do this to a bathroom then it needs to be reapportioned to those who could use it just to survive.

It warms me to know that I am about to relieve myself in this ostentatious arena. I think the gentile thing to do is to run some water to disguise my running water. As I reach over to open the faucet my eyes shift across the floor, past the shower, over to the counter and finally to the faucet.

With an easy grip I go about my business until I look back at the loose drain cover. Something rattles around in my head about it, it's odd. Finally finished, I replace my best friend. I walk over and step lightly into the shower stall enclosure of marble and glass to take a closer look at it.

There, in the middle of the shower floor it is almost centered but not completely. Stooping down I take out the pencil I carry for just such occasions. I poke at the cover and find that one of the two screws that hold the cover in place is missing. It moves easily pivoting on the other screw.

Out of my other pocket comes my mini-flashlight. One click and the drain pipe is illuminated somewhat. I look as far down as I can but I don't see much of anything. The voice of an old friend of mine from Jersey echoes in my head. The accent is heavy and says "Forgetaboutit!"

As I stand and begin to walk away something nudges me, my instincts maybe or possibly my angel telling me to probe deeper. It is probably nothing but I march back to the drain for another look.

My pencil slides the cover back and forth. Then I hear it, I think I hear it. I slide the cover back and forth, I hear it again.

With every bit of self-control that I can muster I move it one more time. It tinkles. On the back of my mini-light is a screwdriver that rotates between a Phillips and a straight edge. I use the Phillips end to unfasten the remaining screw holding the cover and gently lift it up.

In the light from the bathroom window I see what looks like a small charm from a bracelet dangling from the cover. I hold it up to the light. On the charm is an engraved name - Emily.

71

Logan International was a busy, high-traffic-density airport. International flights were in and out of there constantly. It was also the airport that one of the hijacked aircraft left from before flying into one of the World Trade Center towers. The security camera replay of the hijackers nonchalantly walking through security was burned into every American's memory.

Captain Nick Parker touched down smoothly on runway four-right and taxied to his assigned gate at the expansive terminal. He may have been a lowlife but he sure could fly.

It was the last flight of the day for the crew. They deplaned and piled into the hotel van that would take them to the Marriott. Megan sat as far from Parker as she could. They didn't exchange eye contact the entire time although Parker watched for an opening. He spent the rest of the ride clandestinely eyeing Lori.

She could feel it. Although she had originally agreed to meet with Megan for dinner Lori cancelled at the last minute claiming fatigue. In fact, she had other plans. Lori spent the time in the van from the airport to the hotel trying to come up with an excuse to meet with Parker.

By the time she walked into her hotel room she was still struggling to come up with something, anything to get to him. As she started to settle in the telephone rang. It was Parker. She was disappointed that she simply didn't rely on his predictability.

Lori knew all too well how to play the role and she sang her greeting into the phone adding the proper measure of seductiveness.

"Hello?"

"Lori Powers?"

"Yes?"

She abhorred everything about him particularly his voice but Parker absolutely loved the intoxication of hers. He quickly shifted into his persistent mode and burrowed ahead not giving her a chance to speak.

"Hi, it's Nick, the captain. I didn't get a chance to meet you on the aircraft because of the brief turnaround time and the early boarding. And of course the hotel van was so crowded so I thought I'd call and say hello!"

"Well hello, Captain Parker!"

They're all the same, mommy!

"Anyway I was wondering if you had any plans for the rest of the evening. I thought it would only be polite to offer dinner. There's a restaurant nearby called Legal Seafood. It's a great place, the best if you like seafood."

"I love seafood!" she cooed back. When she was done with him she thought he would be fish food. She laughed to herself when she pictured the fish hook and line dangling from his mouth.

"I'll take that as a yes?"

"I'd love to! Did you get anyone else from the crew to go with us?"

That was the last thing he wanted unless he had a chance to fulfill his fantasy of seducing worldly Lori and baby Megan but he knew that was a long shot. He did find it fascinating that he was forsaking the younger, tasty Megan morsel for the somewhat leftover Lori buffet.

"You're the first." he said trying to conceal his true intentions. "If you like I can make you the last!"

All she had to do was reel him in. She needed to keep Parker in his room. It would be the appropriate setting to make him pay for what he had done to Megan. It was the perfect place for Captain Nicholas Parker to go down in flames.

"That works for me, captain."

"Nick, please!"

72

Mika couldn't resist asking about Lori after we were on more solid ground. It wasn't the time or place for such a question especially when I had in my hand what I hoped was a solid lead. All three of us were jogging back to the car. We needed to find out if Thaddeus Abrams knew an Emily.

Could she have been relative? A family friend? A mistress?

Mrs. Abrams could answer those three questions. I have to answer Mika's.

"I thought I was in love but I guess I was just in lost." It isn't my best answer but it will have to do. "I don't know what I was thinking because I hate to fly, it's inherently dangerous. And then I would have had to deal with all of the security screenings, wandings and taking off my shoes. And that was just to get into her house!"

Harmon and Mika crack up and I escape further interrogation. But Harmon can't resist the opportunity to skewer me.

"I thought you told me you were starting to bend to the left so you needed a right-handed woman to straighten you out!" Sounds like he hasn't swung all the way into the dark side after all.

"I said a right-*minded* woman."

Superior rank or not he is going to pay for that some time later. Right now the charm is like a magnet. We pile into the car. Harmon insists on driving and neither I nor Mika care if he does.

Mika reaches across the front seat and asks for the charm so she can take a closer look at it. I hand it over. I can see a ray of hope in her eyes as she studies it. I have a funny feeling in my gut.

What is it about that name?

Harmon decides to go for the flashing lights and wailer as he becomes impatient about getting back to the station to see what the little jewel reveals. The excitement is growing in each of us.

It's small, platinum and hanging on to an even smaller metal ring but it is something, something after months of nothing. It may very well turn out to be insignificant but right now we are tingling with anticipation.

Mika is first out of the car. I follow Harmon. He is actually shoving uniforms out of the way. The dash isn't over until we are behind the closed doors of Harmon's office.

He grabs the phone and the file. Finding her number he punches in Mrs. Abrams' number. Each time the telephone rings the second hand on the wall clock freezes. No answer.

"Damn!" he yells. "Where is she, some charity event?

Harmon is close to exploding. I can tell because he never swears. Mika is pacing like a caged animal. The feeling that we have something intensifies. I take several deep-hold-release breaths.

73

"Why don't I meet you in your room after I get ready?"

She threw out the suggestion and he didn't hesitate to agree driven by his basic male urges. As the receiver hit the cradle Parker did a victory dance. His blood was flooding his veins so much so that he decided to pass on the Viagra. He had no idea he was being stalked like prey.

Parker never imagined it would go so perfect and it was throwing off his timing, his entire routine. He stopped dancing and began to prepare for her arrival. He unpacked the candles and the massage oil that he brought along on every flight just in case the opportunity presented itself.

He hustled around desperately trying to create an intimate atmosphere inside the otherwise conventional hotel room. He reviewed the important memory items – compliment, be spontaneous and sincere and savor the moment.

She's hot, really hot!

Two flights down Lori's choice was the mid-thigh red dress. She had awesome breasts but there was no doubt in her mind that Parker was a leg-man and her killer legs would keep him off balance.

Killer legs, how funny!

In any case she was determined to make the night one that Nick would remember for the rest of his life as brief as that was going to be. A few well-placed sprays of perfume and Lori was ready to rock.

He's a bad man, mommy, a very bad man!

As Lori cracked open her hotel room door she heard Benjamin and Bobby out in the hallway. They were just leaving their hotel room and heading out to a dance club. She watched them walk just far enough down the hall to feel safe to hold hands.

As soon as she heard the elevator doors close behind them she took another look in both directions to see if it was safe to venture out. It would be tragic for Megan to see her now. It was fortunate that Parker's room was two floors up. Still, getting there unnoticed would be a challenge.

Convinced that the coast was clear and prepared for the events of the evening Lori set out to accomplish her goal. As she quietly closed the door to her room she wondered what Jake would think when he found out that Gates wasn't, and that she was, the "Who's Your Daddy" killer.

She had to put the thought out of her mind. She was good at that. As strong as her feelings were for Jake and craving a normal existence she knew deep inside that it wasn't possible. She had to let him go.

You were the one, Jake Roberts.

As she passed the elevator the doors opened and startled her. A young couple exited quickly wrapped in a cuddling embrace. She watched them kiss their way to a room near hers. She saw Jake's face on the young man's and her own face on the girl's.

Not wanting to attract attention Lori decided to use the nearby stairs. Dressed the way she was she could easily have been mistaken for a hooker. Holding tightly on to her purse she climbed the two floors it took to get to Parker's room. Inside her purse she carried only the minimum tools necessary to accomplish her diabolical task.

Just what do you think you're doing? How many times have I told you that you have to plan? You're going to ruin everything for us!

Lori did not answer. There was no planning anything, anymore. She had to do Parker for what he had done to Megan. He deserved everything that he was going to get and more. And there just wasn't time to prepare. The avenging angel was willing to take the chance.

Don't listen to her, mommy. He hurt me!

"I know baby, mommy knows what to do." She whispered but her voice magnified and echoed in the hollow stairway.

The fire door to Parker's floor was all that stood between her and her goal. She slowly cracked the door open enough to scan the hallway. Seeing it was clear she looked for his room number, the one she saw on the sign-in sheet when they first arrived.

Fortune was with her when she found Parker's room only a few doors down from the stairway. That was going to be helpful later when she would have to flee from the scene of the savage, brutal crime.

74

Emily, who is Emily?

It seems like I just heard the name somewhere but I can't place it. The charm holds my complete attention as it dangles from the wire. It hasn't been touched by any of us. After I saw it hanging on the drain cover I had the presence of mind to preserve it for analysis.

Harmon hangs up the phone. "Mrs. Abrams said she doesn't have any relatives, friends or associates named Emily."

Mika suggests a list of possibilities beginning with, "Maybe we're on another wild goose chase. Maybe it was there since the place was built."

"That house, forget the crime scene, is spotless. There isn't as much as a toothpick out of place." Harmon hypothesizes saying, "Someone would definitely have noticed the loose drain cover if for no other reason than to get it repaired."

Full of hope I agree with him. "It had to be left there during the commission of the crime. And I don't think anyone would have seen it during the initial investigation because I only saw it by accident."

"Did Gates ever mention an Emily?" Mika asks.

I stare at the charm and answer, "Not that I recall. We can read through the transcripts though and see if he did." I look at Harmon. "What about the car? Did they sweep it like the bathroom or should we go tear it apart, too?"

"They were pretty thorough but we can always take another look. It seems to be a good day for second looks." His huge frame collapses into the high-backed leather chair behind the mahogany desk that used to be Ed's.

Something annoying is making my eye twitch and rubbing it only makes it itch more. The new detective chick knocks on Harmon's door. Five foot five, azure eyes and golden-haired Melissa walks in.

"Yeah, what did you find out?" Harmon asks.

"No Emily's mentioned in the transcript, Chief."

"Thanks Melissa, tell Williams to bring me that other item we talked about, the, you know, the--" Harmon's impatience was getting the best of him.

"The cloth?" she asks.

"Yeah, bring it in here, will you?"

She bolted out of the office and headed for the crime lab. Where she really wanted to be was headed out to the streets to catch bad guys. But like Ed before him, Harmon felt the need to protect Melissa a little longer from that.

"What did you want that for?" Mika asks Harmon.

"There were some questions earlier about the -- "

"HOLY JESUS!"

My raised volume unravels both of them. "What's wrong with you, man? You scared the --"

Harmon stops in mid-sentence. His eyebrows clench as he reads my face. "What is it, Jake?"

Mika continues patting her chest to settle down while she waits patiently for the rest of my revelation. "Jake, slowly, breathe - what?" she encourages.

"Emily! A silver Lexus! The CD! Abrams the psychiatrist! The abusive husband and the daughter's suicide!" My mouth hangs open as I put it all together.

"WHAT, WHAT" Harmon pushes.

Mika tugs at me. I reach out and take her hands. My mind is racing trying to remember, to recall and to separate the days all at the same time.

"I KNOW WHO THE KILLER IS!"

I say it but I can't accept it. I feel an eerie chill run my spine almost like I'm an accomplice somehow.

I kissed her, held her in my arms. I was falling in love with her. I wanted to spend the rest of my life...

"Say it Jake, what?" Harmon demands an answer.

I regulate my breathing and focus. I can't believe what I am about to say to them. I can't believe any of it!

"A daughter named Emily. The girl committed suicide a few years ago for reasons she never said but I think I know why now."

"Who!" Mika impatiently asks.

"The killer drives a late-model, silver, foreign car – a Lexus."

Nobody is speaking now except me.

"When I was there I found a CD, the exact same CD in her collection!" I shake my head slowly because the initial exuberance of the revelation is wearing off and the hurt is beginning.

"The ex-husband abused her and disappeared, that's supposedly the reason why she was seeing a psychiatrist, a Dr. Thaddeus Abrams." I can't say the rest.

An astonished Mika screams out, "LORI POWERS!"

"Jake, are you sure?" Harmon is dumbfounded.

"It all fits! It's as clear as glass now! She's a flight attendant!" I turn toward Mika. "I bet if you track her flights she was in every town that your victims turned up in!"

"Jesus, Jake," Mika pieces it all together. "Where is she now?"

"Home, as far as I know. I went over to her place for dinner last night and we started talking about Gates. She started defending him…defending him! She said that I needed to try and understand why he did what he did. I told her she was wrong because of Ed." I pause. "She broke it off and asked me to leave, that's how I ended up at Chipper's!"

After some of her own reevaluation Mika gently adds, "She must have really loved you, Jake."

"What?" I'm not ready for female intuition right now.

"No, I mean she really must have loved you probably more than you will ever know!" Mika says softly.

"I don't get it, what are you saying?"

Mika walks over and sits down beside me. She nods toward Harmon who moves to stand in front of me. Her hand slides across to take mine.

"Jake, if you're right about her then I think she must have really loved you because you are a law enforcement officer – a man in a position of authority." From my hand, hers slides up my arm and around my shoulder. There was a gentle, sympathetic look on her face.

"You're the perfect profile of her victims and yet she 'spared' you! She didn't want to hurt you emotionally, or physically."

But Mika's statement hurts anyway, a sucker punch I feel right below my ribs. If what Mika is saying is true I'm lucky to be alive!

Harmon shifts into overdrive. He punches a finger down into the intercom and commands, "Call them all in, now!"

Wendy on the other end of the intercom quickly dials the extension of the dispatchers downstairs. Within minutes every detective assigned to the "Who's Your Daddy" case is told to report to the house.

Mika watches me understanding the conflict of emotions going on inside of me. "I'm sorry, Jake."

75

Nick barely heard the knock on his door. Lori didn't want to draw attention from the other guests at the hotel although she was certain that after Parker was found she would be the prime suspect.

He tried to be as presentable as possible under the circumstances. The sport shirt was new and so were the khaki slacks but the navy blue blazer had some miles on it. His hair was perfectly groomed after the shower. The captain was as "G-Q" as he was going to get. Opening the door with a gratuitous, charming smile he over-enunciated.

"Hey Lori, you look great!"

His brow crunched together and his mouth formed an "O" as she twirled to provide a panoramic view. She carefully accentuated her breasts with a deep breath and pointed a toe at the end of a long, shapely leg.

"Okay?" she purred.

Although not wanting to appear overly aggressive she nevertheless stepped inside his room quickly.

"So, where is this incredible, tantalizing restaurant you're tempting me with? You said it was within walking distance? I hope it's not too far for these heels!" She watched his eyes travel down her legs.

"It's not far at all, close actually. The specialty is King Crab legs mounds of them that will make you quiver." He was still admiring hers. "I speak with authority!"

"Captain Parker, that sounds to me like you would know exactly what to do if there were great legs right in front of you!" She attached raised eyebrows and a pouting mouth to her suggestive exclamation.

Right then, Nick knew how the evening would end. While he had originally planned to be the one doing the seducing he quickly realized that he was the one being seduced. He decided to let her play it out.

"Nick, please."

"I'm sorry, Nick." She smiled.

While he saw her as just an easy flight attendant she was still an exceptionally beautiful woman with an awesome body. He didn't plan on a long affair with her anyway. He didn't know much about her and wasn't interested in her personal life. He just wanted to play.

"Are you ready to go? I have a table reserved for eight-thirty. The place is usually packed by nine," he said. As he spoke he pictured himself walking through the front doors with her on his arm. The other men would be salivating with envy. He liked that.

It was part of his modus operandi to wine, dine and be seen. It was mental foreplay for the master. But she surprised him and piqued his curiosity. He never anticipated that she would be spontaneous and unpredictable. "We could, unless…" She looked deeply into Nick's eyes.

"Well pretty lady, what did you have in mind?"

"Why don't we order up room service, something to get the evening started – say champagne? We still have plenty of time before the reservation and you said it was a short walk."

His read the playful look on her face and it intensified his expectations. If this went right he thought for the price of a bottle of champagne he might save the price of an expensive dinner, and still score. Pilots only thought about sex and money. Cheap dates were a win-win. He smiled and reached for the telephone.

"Yes, could you send up a bottle of Ballatore champagne to Suite 753? Thank you." He dropped the headset down.

"I have always believed that it is best to give the lady what she wants!" The grin on his face has a devilish twist to it.

76

Shouting orders faster than any of us can get them done Harmon believes that any further delay could cost another life.

"Call Judge Thornton, he'll write a search warrant!"

Mika is on a conference call with Wellington in Quantico. I can hear him trying to interrupt but she tells him to shut up. Wellington got spanked.

"...follow up with her airline. Call her supervisor. And find out if her schedule coincides with the murder dates and locations. Call me as soon as you have something." She slams the phone down and looks at us. "There, that'll get the ball rolling!"

Harmon asks me if Lori is still home.

"As far as I know she is. She's not supposed to fly until tomorrow afternoon. The only other place she might be is at the cemetery. She visits her daughter regularly." I try to sound as if I have a clue about her life. I wanted to spend the rest of my life with her but I'm astounded by how much I don't know about her.

The floor is filling up with detectives. They keep looking at Harmon to see what's up. They know it has something to do with the "Who's Your Daddy" killer but he was dead. Finally, Harmon addresses them.

"All right people, listen up! There has been some new information that suggests that Michael Gates was *not* - repeat *not* - our serial killer. It appears now that he may very well have been a copy cat killer. We now believe the perp to be a female named Lori Powers. We have an address and we'll head there right after this briefing!" He is interrupted by Melissa.

"Sir, the search warrant has been signed by the judge and will be transported to the residence. It will be there by the time you arrive."

"Thanks detective. Okay here's how it's going down. Jake, I want you to make it look like you're just visiting and draw her out. The rest of you will take up positions out of sight and be ready to move on Jake's signal."

He gets my reassuring nod.

"Agent Scott is still tactically in charge of this case. You will follow her commands to the letter! I will only be on site as an official observer." Turning to Mika he asks, "Will you need the services of our fine SWAT team, Agent Scott?"

"No sir, I've already requisitioned more agents from the Bureau. They should be there when we arrive."

"Be sure they wait outside the perimeter until we get there. I don't want a bunch of over-zealous Feds fouling things up!" Harmon snaps.

"I agree and they have been advised as such, Chief."

To the troops Harmon asks, "Any questions?"

After the detectives present exchange looks one asks about whether or not the use of lethal force is approved. That hits me in an odd way.

"If need be," Harmon replies looking hard at every detective in the room.

Harmon takes the lead and I'm right behind Mika. The doors to CID close behind us. The rest of the troops follow with determined looks on their faces.

Outside, in front of the precinct, car doors slam shut and the squeal of tires fills the otherwise quiet and peaceful summer evening. We are on our way to catch the real killer.

77

Parker knew she was a player. He thought about dropping the sincerity and dropping her to the floor instead. Rough, raucous sex was probably the norm for her he thought as he watched her move about the room.

Their conversation was provocative, suggestive and salacious. He decided to restrain his perverted desires until after the champagne was gone. Then it would be a free-for-all.

The expected knock on his door from room service came and Lori quickly excused herself to the bathroom. Parker opened the door and watched the waiter push the cart with the white tablecloth inside the room. Inside the ice bucket on the cart stood the chilled champagne alongside two tall stem glasses and a single red rose in a vase. He tossed the waiter a five.

"Are you all right in there?" he shouted to Lori.

From inside the bathroom Lori answered while she tugged at her skirt and straightened whatever she thought needed it. She took a quick look in the mirror to check for smudges. "Yes Nick, be there in a second!" she sang.

I'm so proud of you, mommy! You know how bad he hurt me! Don't let him hurt me again, mommy!

She whispered back at the mirror, "I won't, baby!"

Before she opened the door she checked her ring to make sure that the sedative was still hidden inside. She was ready - showtime. The door swung open and Lori stepped out. She gave Nick one of her special Lori Powers smiles.

"Sorry I took so long." She looked at the bottle of champagne.

"Oh, that looks inviting!"

Parker took the foil off and started working out the cork. After the anticipated popping sound he poured a glass and handed it to her. Lori graciously accepted and he poured another for himself. They raised their glasses high and toasted.

"To a night to remember!" he said.

She held her glass against his and said, "Nick, I want this to be a very special night -- one you won't forget for the rest of your life!"

To a nightmare to remember!

He felt his pulse rate jump and a throbbing between his thighs. He was an empty champagne bottle away from taking her. A quick glance at the clock on the nightstand revealed that their dinner reservation time had arrived.

"Uh-oh, we've got to go!" he chided.

Lori sipped at the champagne. Their eyes met and she said provocatively, "Or...we can stay right here!"

"That would be okay with you, pretty lady?"

"Nick, I really love champagne. It makes me lose my inhibitions. I feel like I'm able to experience things otherwise considered...improper?"

She was everything he had hoped for.

Thank God, I didn't waste my time with Megan!

The thoughts that were running through his mind would alone be considered illegal in many states. He reached for the bottle but Lori stepped forward and placed her hand lightly on his chest.

"You captains are always so concerned about us! Why don't you let me take care of you tonight?" Her hand dropped and lightly brushed against the front of his khakis. He missed a breath.

Oh God, she's good!

With a slight nudge she made him sit on the edge of the bed. He didn't hesitate to accommodate her. Pivoting toward the cart she refilled his glass while he focused on the back side of her dress. He followed the back of her legs down to her heels then reversed course and went up until he became lost in the flowing curls of her flaxen hair.

Opening her ring she let the contents fall into his glass and poured champagne over the drug. The bubbles provided the perfect cover as the two ingredients mixed together. It would take only a minute after the glass was empty for the drug to take effect then she would be able to subdue the rat.

But in the midst of her preparation she felt his hand touch her from behind. It slid down along her arm to her hand. She wasn't sure if Nick had seen what she had done. She tensed. His other hand started to knead her behind.

Abruptly he spun her around and took her in his arms. "I want you, you make me hard!" He started to kiss her neck and shoulders.

She wanted to smash the bottle into the side of his head but fought the strong urge instead. "Hey, mister, what about the champagne?" she prodded. "How am I supposed to get in the mood without some champagne?"

But he manhandled her groping from top to bottom. He put both hands on her hips and started grinding into her. "I don't need champagne!" Nick was on fire. "I'm already aroused and I want you right this second!"

Stop him mommy, stop him!

"Nick, Nick!" she exclaimed trying desperately to slow him down. "We've got all night and what I have planned for you can't be rushed!"

"Let's get started right now. You make me so hot I can't wait!" He tugged at her blouse. Holding her hands together over her head with one hand he pulled her skirt up with the other. He fell on top of her on the bed knocking the wind out of her lungs.

Oh my God, no! He did this to Megan!

She gasped for air and struggled with Parker trying to persuade him to stop but he was relentless. He tore her panties while pulling them down. She wanted to scream but knew she had to hold back. And then she felt him pushing violently against her thighs. Nick Parker forced himself inside of her. Her breathing became deep and irregular just as Nick liked it.

Kill him, mommy, kill him!

Lori tried to regulate her breathing so that she would not pass out. She found herself counting every thrust until he made his last.

Nick stopped moving and stayed on top of her until he recovered. He rolled over face up on the bed with his manhood exposed and said, "I'll have that drink now!"

She wanted to crush his skull with the bedside lamp or to sear his exposed flesh with a flame. She wanted to stab him with the knife in her purse.

Most of all she wanted to cry. But in order for her to finish him she knew she would have to play the game a little longer as repulsive as that thought was.

As she raised herself off the bed she exclaimed, "Nick that was incredible! The whole fantasy rape thing was such a turn-on! My God, Nicky, it was so exciting!"

Did she really think I was pretending!

He opened his eyes as she carried on. Her response confused him. "You liked it?" he asked quite surprised.

She stood up and straightened her clothes. He sat up on the edge of the bed. He wasn't sure what to do next. This was normally the time where he threatened the victim with their job but she was into it.

"I can't wait for round two!" she added quickly reaching for his glass. She held it out for him. Parker didn't know what to say. He took the glass and slugged it down. Lori watched until he held the glass out for her to refill.

"Are you going to be able to sustain that energy level again?" she asked.

"Well, I guess you're going to find out, it's still early!" he boasted.

She teased asking, "Aren't you glad we didn't make our reservation time?"

His eyes rolled. A deep yawn followed and he was surprised by it. He looked at her with an apologetic look. "Must have been a longer day than I thought it was."

He yawned again then another time. He couldn't stop and decided that he better splash some water in his face, and take a Viagra. He knew he was going to need one if she expected more. He got up and staggered into the bathroom closing the door behind him.

Lori didn't want him in there. She wanted him to pass out on the bed. It would be difficult for her to carry him to the bed if he fell in there. She knew that the sedative worked quickly. Her anxiety level rising, she prayed he would come out.

I told you not to do this! Now look what happened!

Lori hated that voice. She hated being scolded and preferred when only dear Emily spoke to her. Lori heard a glass fall into the sink and break. She started to panic until the bathroom door opened and Parker slowly shuffled out. He kept shaking his head as if he were trying to clear it. He held on to the walls as he got closer to her.

"I don't, I don't know what's wrong," he slurred.

Lori quickly reached out to support him. "Nick, what's wrong? You don't look well! Here, get over to the bed and lie down."

A complying patient he did as he was told. He finally blacked out after falling back onto the mattress.

Lori quickly removed the bindings from her purse and secured his hands and feet to the bed. She removed the glimmering, stainless steel knife from her purse.

"Goodbye, Captain Nicholas Parker."

78

There is no answer. I knock again and lean to look inside but the house is dark. Lori isn't home. All I can do is retreat and discuss our next move with Mika and Harmon. The officers who are strategically hidden throughout the neighborhood stand down on command and wait. Mika's cell phone rings.

"Scott." She listens while looking at me. "Thanks."

Disconnecting her cell phone Mika says, "Chick's flown the coop! Headquarters called her supervisor who called their crew scheduling department who informed them that she accepted a flight to Boston to cover for some other crew member."

Harmon looks around until he sees the person he is searching for running down the street toward us.

"Here it is, chief!" Melissa hands him the search warrant and Harmon proofreads it.

He turns and signals. "Take it down!"

Two large male uniformed officers approach the front door and kick it in. With weapons drawn they secure the interior and within minutes they are outside shouting.

"CLEAR!"

The three of us proceed inside and search for anything to support my theory. My gut says I'm right. Now I have to prove it.

I know the interior so I head to the back rooms. Inside her bedroom I feel strange. The last time I was inside the house I had every intention of sleeping with her. There is nothing there now so

I walk back to Mika.

Harmon is in the kitchen and grasps a small, brown prescription bottle on the counter-top that had the name of a strong sedative on it. The pills are gone. He rejoins us in the living room.

Mika's cell phone rings again. "Scott."

She glances around the room. At the stereo she drags the CD case from the stack, opens the lid and sees that the disc is gone. She holds it open to show me.

"Anything else?" she says into the phone. "Have the plane ready to go when I get there."

Harmon displays the empty prescription bottle. We take a look and Mika relays what she has learned.

"She's probably going to do it again. They've found out what hotel she's in. My people are fueling the plane and we'll be in the air in thirty minutes. You two are invited to go along."

"Let's go!" Harmon says. Outside he places Osborne in command and then forces his way into the driver's side.

"I'm driving!"

Mika looks hard at him. "You really need to get over that!"

It is funny, stupid actually but with all that is going on all I can think about is how much I hate to fly ? fancy F-B-I jet or not. As I fall into the back seat, Harmon speeds off.

Lori Powers, what are you thinking?

79

The mind is truly a remarkable creation. The way it operates. What goes on routinely inside of it is nothing less than miraculous. It can add and subtract, multiply and divide all of what life throws at us. It is responsible for basic functions of the human body and can contemplate abstract concepts. It is a fascinating thing - the human mind.

Inside Lori's mind was a ticking clock that was counting down. Although there was no reason for her to believe that we were on her trail, she sensed it. If there was one thing done wrong it was that we severely underestimated the intellect and talents of the breathtaking Lori Powers.

Standing at the foot of the bed she stared at Parker. He was a pig, a wild animal that needed to be destroyed. There was no doubt of that in her mind and she didn't even know all of the atrocious things he had done during his lifetime. All she really knew about Nick Parker was that he had hurt Megan and that he had just raped her.

Don't let him hurt me again, mommy, please!

The other voice pushed Lori.

You've gone this far, you might as well finish it.

With the concurrence of the voices she didn't waste another second. The ritual began. The third song on the CD played on the stereo beneath the television in the room. She kept the volume low enough so no one could hear.

Lori walked to the side of the bed, the gleaming knife in hand. Parker laid spread-eagled, tied and still out from the powerful sedative. She was disappointed that she wasn't going to be able to taunt him before he received his final punishment. She couldn't afford to let him scream like the others.

She stabbed him in his cold, black heart. The blood shot up in spurts. She dragged the blade across his throat severing the carotid artery. In an instant, Captain Nick Parker was dead.

After watching him take his last breath Lori reached for his manhood that had just violated her and held it firmly with her free hand. Slowly and purposefully with an almost artistic stroke she severed it and dropped it on his chest just as she had done with all of the others. She thrust the blood-soaked blade into his heart one last time and left it protruding there.

Now he won't hurt me again, mommy!

Lori placed the chair from the desk at the foot of the bed and sat down. Seconds passed and she reached into her torn panties and started to massage her private place. She quickened the pace and fell into her dream.

"Daddy, did I do it right? Was that what you wanted, daddy? Faster daddy, and don't be angry! Faster daddy, I want...you...to...love me!"

Just like all of the times before Lori awoke from the dream and felt nothing, no sensation at all. She slowly retracted her hand and stood. She straightened her blouse and adjusted her skirt.

Lori returned from the bathroom with a white wash cloth in her hand. She mounted the bed, dabbed the cloth into the puddle of freshly spilled blood and wrote one word on the wall. But unlike all of the other times she didn't wipe the room clean or take away any incriminating evidence.

Someone knocked on Parker's door and startled Lori. She froze. The last thing she could afford to do now was panic. She moved slowly toward the door to peek out through the security hole. It was Megan.

What was she doing here?

Megan had come to face Parker. She wanted to hurt him and tell him that she wasn't going to live her life in fear of him any longer. But no one answered while she stood in the hallway, arms folded.

Lori wondered if Megan would ever leave. Maybe she was having second thoughts and wanted Nick. Maybe Megan was a sick puppy playing games. But as fast as that thought entered her mind it was wiped clean. Megan was in real pain and Lori had no doubt of that.

Taking another peek out through the security hole she didn't see Megan. She heard sobbing and then the elevator doors open and close.

Before leaving Lori thought about Jake and what might have been. With a smile on her face, she looked both ways before slipping out of Parker's room.

80

The massive, powerful Gulfstream corporate jet owned and paid for by me and the rest of the taxpayers' blasts off into the night sky. The sudden acceleration forces throw me back into my seat. The FBI pilot pulls the nose up and we seem to be climbing straight up into space. Then the hotshot banks as if we were in some kind of Top Gun dogfight.

Mika smiles as she watches how uncomfortable I am. I hate to fly. Harmon isn't happy about it either. I see his massive fingers on both hands dig into the leather-covered armrests.

There aren't too many things that I am absolutely sure of anymore but I am certain beyond a shadow of a doubt that I can never be a pilot! There has to be something wrong with them. If the Creator wants us to leave the confines of gravity He would provide us a means to do so, like wings. He gave us feet, end of discussion.

As we level off at some angelic altitude I start to acclimatize. Landing of course will give me another reason to panic. I sit close to the defibrillators stored onboard. The aircraft has its own flight attendant. I can only wonder what she is costing me.

Noting the grimace on my face Mika smirks and asks, "Are you okay?"

"Yeah, better...sure." It is only the second time I have ever been in a plane. "You're probably used to this!"

"Safest way to travel," she tosses back. "So, when we get there..."

Harmon leans closer to hear.

"...one of the agency's Suburbans will meet us and take us to the hotel. We'll check the crew's rooms and track anyone who may have gone out."

"Do you think she'll be there?" Harmon asks.

"I hope so."

My turn. "Can you get some agents to the hotel before we get there?"

"Good idea, hand me that phone over there please."

After she completes the call and sets things in motion we all sit back and take some quiet time. I keep thinking about Lori and the times we had spent together. It all had such promise. The truth is still hard to swallow and I still can't believe it has gone this way.

Mika interrupts my plane of thought with, "What are you thinking about?"

"One minute I get it and the next I'm totally confused. I guess she really did me a favor!" Taking Mika's hand I smile and disappear again into my thoughts.

I hope things work out for me and Mika. I hope she leaves the FBI and comes back home and we can get out of this life. But I don't know how anyone can walk away from all of these perks. Just jetting around like this is enough for someone to suck it up.

When this case is over and Lori's in custody Mika will be a heroine. She will be offered all sorts of bonuses and perks maybe even a top cop job. It would be difficult for anyone to turn the offers down. I don't know if she can truly walk away from it...just for me.

"How about you, what's going through your head?" I ask.

"When this is over, I'm going to take some time off and do some real soul-searching," she says and gives me her best smile. She looks deep into my eyes searching for some sort of a sign but I can't give her one. She has to make the decision on her own.

81

Inside the security of her hotel room the hot water cascaded over Lori and washed away her crime. Then she heard the voice.

Lori Powers, you've been a bad girl! They will find you!

"They will find you?" She smiled as the water fell over her face. "Maybe Jake will find me and we can run away together!" She was no longer intimidated by the voices.

Lori decided not to pack. There was nothing she had to take and no looking back anymore. Even when they found Parker it wouldn't do them any good she thought. In spite of what the voice had said they were never going to find her. It was time to go.

Hurriedly, she departed the hotel.

The only light shining on the city street came through the few shaded windows of the townhouses that lined it and the bright entrance lights to the hotel. A few cars were parked along the avenue. Their owners had no plans to leave until the early morning rush hour.

The only sound outside besides those from a few passing cars were coming from her high heels. They made a clicking sound that echoed between the buildings. She picked up the pace down the sidewalk. Her breathing quickened from the brisk walk. Lori scanned for a nearby taxi and waved one down.

"Logan, please."

The driver, a recent Islamic immigrant obliged. As she sat in the back she removed a tissue from her purse and dabbed at the corner of her eyes. The driver stole looks at her in the rear view mirror at irregular intervals. He decided American women were hot.

341

It was worth it he thought to be an illegal immigrant.

At the ticket counter she bought a nonstop ticket. The flight to Portugal would be lengthy but it was the first flight out of the country and that fit her travel plans perfectly. Lori Powers would disappear before they arrived, and...after the evil she had exacted.

82

It is written in blood, his blood - a guy named Nicholas Parker. The three of us stand at the foot of the bed and stare. Harmon doesn't speak. Mika doesn't say a word. And even if I knew what to say, I can't.

Right up on the wall over Parker, written in dried blood red letters is

$$J-A-K-E.$$

The rest of the investigators present mostly FBI agents and locals go about the gruesome task of collecting evidence. The captain is going to be bagged, tagged and frozen in the morgue at least until the autopsy is completed.

The rest of his flight crew has been rounded up and is currently sitting in the lobby in deep shock. They are providing as much detail as they possibly can in between the trauma and the crying. A young flight attendant who can't be more than twenty is shaking so severely they are going to sedate her.

There is one crew member missing.

Lightning is direct current. A bolt can account for twenty to forty thousand amperes, two hundred million volts. It is calculated to be hotter than the surface of the sun. When you are struck by lightening it leaves feather burns on your skin that slowly fade after a few days. Death occurs in milliseconds.

Sometimes, I hate to be right. Sometimes, I turn the other cheek. Sometimes, I just want to run home and hide under the covers. There are times when I wish I had never been born.

I would rather have been struck by lightning than to live through this. At least it would have been over in milliseconds. What a world we live in.

All flowers look beautiful but some are poisonous, even deadly.

*Also available from your favorite bookstore
or online retailer*

Cary Allen Stone

Through A Mother's Eyes

Inside these pages, Julie will tell you why she took the life of her six-year-old son, Charley. It is a compelling, riveting, and true story.

ISBN: 0-7596-5784-X

Printed in the United States
34022LVS00001B/1-39

9 781420 855555